Bad Boys
Southern Style

Bad Boys
Southern Style

JoAnn Ross
E.C. Sheedy
Jill Shalvis

KENSINGTON PUBLISHING CORP.
http://www.kensingtonbooks.com

BRAVA BOOKS are published by

Kensington Publishing Corp.
850 Third Avenue
New York, NY 10022

All Kensington titles, imprints and distributed lines are available at special quantity discounts for bulk purchases for sales promotion, premi-
ums, fund-raising, educational or institutional use.

Special book excerpts or customized printings can also be created to fit
specific needs. For details, write or phone the office of the Kensington
Special Sales Manager: Kensington Publishing Corp., 850 Third Avenue,
New York, NY 10022. Attn. Special Sales Department. Phone: 1-800-
221-2647.

ISBN 0-7582-1478-2

First Kensington Trade Paperback Printing: July 2006
10   9   8   7   6   5   4   3   2   1

Printed in the United States of America

CONTENTS

LOVE POTION
#9

JoAnn Ross

One

A full moon rode high in the southern sky, casting an unearthly white light over the Lowcountry, illuminating the woman who moved through the marsh with the sleek grace of a swamp panther.

The thick air, pregnant with the disparate scents of salt, decaying Spartina grass, and night-blooming jasmine, dripped with moisture.

Herons glided on wide blue wings while an alligator slid silently across water the color of burgundy wine. Fireflies glowed amidst the branches of old growth cypress, which stood like silent sentinels over the watery world, silvery moss draped over their limbs like feather boas discarded by ghostly belles.

Bullfrogs croaked; cicadas whirred; somewhere in the dark a lonely owl hooted for a mate.

The familiar scents of the southern Georgia marsh reached deep into the woman's soul; the night music stirred the wildness that dwelt in her heart. It was music from an ancient time, a time when primitive man trembled with fear against the unseen denizens of the dark.

A time when her people ruled with wisdom and power.

A time of magic.

Her hooded black cape blended into the shadows as she

made her way through the swirling mists of fog. Upon reaching the sacred grove of live oak she knelt and plunged her hands into the inky water. When she brought them out again, her long, slender fingers glowed with green, phosphorescent ghostfire.

Sparks fell back into the water, like a shower of stars, as she lifted her hands—palms turned upward toward the midnight velvet sky—offering a blessing to her mother, the moon.

Her exquisite face bathed in a shimmering light, the woman began chanting the words taught to her while she was still in her cradle. Words from before time passed down from woman to woman through the generations, words that flowed warmly through her veins, along with the blood that made her who she was.

What she was.

A witch.

After completing her invocation, she untied the hooded cape and let it fall to the ground. A zephyr blowing in from the nearby Atlantic caught her freed hair, whipping it into a wild jet black froth around her face. The black bodysuit she wore beneath the cape fit like a second skin, revealing every lush curve. Black leather boots, polished to a glassy sheen, encased her legs to midthigh, while a metal breastplate shaped her breasts into two glistening cones.

A silver amulet, dating back to medieval times and suspended from a hammered silver chain, nestled between her gloriously voluptuous, magnolia white breasts.

She took a small vial from the amulet. The scented oil—which she'd blended herself on Midsummer Night's Eve—was a dark and sultry concoction of scarlet rose petals, black dahlia, belladonna, dragon's blood, and, of course, wolfsbane. Best known for its properties of protection against werewolves, few were aware that Medea had embraced the selfsame deadly plant in her many works of vengeance.

She sprinkled the pungent oil over the rowan branches

she'd gathered earlier and stacked in a circle of white angel wing seashells.

With the powers of midnight vibrating through her, the woman known as Morganna held her hands out over the wood, causing it to ignite in a sudden whoosh of wind and flame.

Closing her eyes, she concentrated on the faces of her life-sworn enemies, those who would use the darkness of the night to cloak their wicked ways.

She envisioned them melting like candle wax amidst the dancing flames. Felt the fire crackle in the very marrow of her bones. Heard their agonized, bloodcurdling screams. A lethal heat suffused her, fire flashed along her every nerve; suffering the evildoers' every torment, the witch swayed.

But she did not flinch. Nor did she cry out.

Any spellmaker who dealt in the dark side did not escape such acts unscathed, but given that her fate was both preordained and inescapable, Morganna bore her pain in silence.

And when it was finally completed, when a cooling, benevolent rain began to fall to drench the scorching flames, she lifted her pale white arms again and offered a prayer of thanksgiving to the goddess moon for having allowed her to survive.

"It is done."

Then, drained from the torturous burdens she'd willingly undertaken, Morganna, Mistress of the Night, folded to the damp ground and surrendered to the darkness.

Two

"I cannot believe you allow garbage like this comic book in your shop."

Roxi Dupree, owner of Hex Appeal, glanced up from stirring crushed lavender into a love spell potpourri at the book the older woman was holding up between two fingers, as if afraid of contamination.

"It's actually a graphic novel." She sprinkled a handful of scarlet rose petals over the mixture. "And I like Morganna."

"She works the dark arts."

Roxi shrugged and refrained from pointing out that the Morganna stories were, after all, fiction. Fiction she'd grown up devouring. Stories that had fed a young girl's imagination.

Another thing she'd only ever shared with one person—her best friend Emma—was that Morganna had been a childhood role model. Oh, Roxi hadn't grown up to turn cheating boyfriends into toads (though there had been one or two who deserved it), or burn alive wicked people who harmed children, but she had taken Morganna's independent spirit to heart.

"All of us, witch or not, have our dark and light sides." Given that patience was not her strong suit, Roxi had to work at the mild tone. "Isn't all life about striving for balance between the two?"

"That may be," the older woman reluctantly allowed, even as her narrow face remained as pinched as a prune that had been left to dry too long in the sun. She tossed the book back onto the shelf.

"But Morganna, Mistress of the Night, certainly doesn't spend a great deal of time on the light side," she sniffed. "She's an angry, vengeful creature who embarks on a crusade of blood and brimstone in every book."

Roxi found it interesting that a woman who'd proclaim the popular Morganna stories garbage seemed to be so familiar with the stories.

"Not exactly brimstone," she murmured, thinking how that very word played into detractors' misguided view of pagans as devil worshipers. "And that particular crusade, by the way, is against undead spirits of the underworld who have infiltrated the bodies of humans."

Wiry wisps of steel gray hair surrounded the woman's frowning face. Her thin lips firmed as she skimmed a finger around the rim of a hammered silver chalice. "That couldn't possibly happen."

Closed-minded old biddy. "There are those who don't believe it's possible to draw down the moon, either."

The mention of the ancient rite brought to mind last night's x-rated dream where she'd been in the sacred grove drawing down the moon when a stranger, clad all in black, had appeared from the shadows and fiercely ravished her beneath the midnight sky. Just remembering the way his teeth had tormented her nipples was enough to have heat pooling between her thighs.

"She gives witches a bad name."

Martha Corey's grim accusation had Roxi reluctantly dragging her mind from her dream of a wild, midnight sexual tryst back to their conversation.

"I believe witches had a PR problem long before Morganna

came on the scene." The Spanish Inquisition and the Salem hangings were two that came immediately to mind.

The woman abandoned the chalice, moving on to the iron cauldron Roxi had filled with fragrant purple and white lilacs for Beltane. "Did you hear that some Hollywood hotshot director is going to make a movie based on the comic books?"

"Graphic novels," Roxi repeated. Her frustrated sigh ruffled her dark bangs. "And yes, I believe I heard something about that."

Not only had she heard, Emma's husband, Gabriel Broussard—a former hometown bad boy who'd been named Sexiest Man Alive—was going to costar in the movie as Damien, a rival witch who just also happened to be Morganna's lover.

Actually, the dark and dangerous male witch was the reason she'd begun reading the Morganna stories. He'd certainly fueled fantasies of an entirely different sort. Ones she hadn't even understood at the time. Now that she thought about it, the man in her dream resembled Damien with his ebony hair and piercing blue eyes.

"I also read in *People* magazine that it's going to be filmed right here in Savannah."

"Imagine that." Having not seen Emma and Gabriel since their wedding six months earlier, Roxi had been looking forward to them coming to Savannah while Gabe was on location.

"Naturally, the coven is planning demonstrations."

Oh, hell. This was all she needed. Hex Appeal had only been open a few months. She'd established the original shop in Louisiana, but after Katrina blew the building away, Roxi had decided that as tragic as Katrina turned out to be, in her case the ill wind had offered an opportunity to spread her wings beyond Blue Bayou, the provincial Cajun community in which she'd spent the first twenty-five years of her life. Savannah, with its haunted and magical undercurrents, had seemed the logical choice.

"Well, that should certainly liven things up."

Practically biting her tongue in half, Roxi took a pink candle she'd made last night down from the shelf, infusing the wax with essential oils of lavender and ginger. Both powerful love forces by themselves, recent studies had shown that the combined scent of lavender and pumpkin pie increased blood flow to the penis by forty percent.

The spell she was packaging for her customer might technically be a love spell, but any woman, witch or not, knew that lust was the fast way to get any male's attention.

That idea had her unruly mind flashing back to the way her dream lover had feasted on her hot and needy body.

"Of course you'll be there."

"Be where?" In her mind his roving mouth had clamped hungrily over her breast and his wicked hand was creating havoc between her legs.

"At the demonstration."

"The demonstration?" Roxi repeated absently, trying to keep her mind in the here and now while her body, which was on the verge of melting into a hot puddle of need, desperately kept returning to last night.

She placed the small linen bag containing the potpourri into the opening of a conch shell she'd picked up on the beach just last week.

"We're creating our schedule now." Martha radiated impatience; a dark, muddied red aura of seething anger surrounded her. "The plan is to disrupt shooting so if those damn movie people insist on making their anti-witch propoganda, they'll at least have to move to another city."

"Perhaps Salem."

"That would be more suitable."

Given that the irony had flown right over the older woman's head, Roxi tried again. "Why don't you just cast some go away spells?"

Although he was now a married man, Roxi suspected that once the local witches got a look at Gabriel Broussard up close and in person, they wouldn't be in such a hurry to send him away.

"We plan to." Martha had moved onto a group of unicorns, lifting up a crystal one to check the price sticker underneath. "The demonstrations are merely our backup plan."

"Don't you think you're jumping the gun just a bit?" Once again, Roxi tried to remind herself that patience was a virtue. "Perhaps if you were to read the script—"

A sharp chin shot up. Faded blue eyes turned as stormy as her aura. "I don't need to read any script to know that we'd hate it. As any *true* witch would."

Ah. Here it was. What she'd been waiting for. The challenging of her credentials, which somehow managed to come up in the conversation whenever the old witch visited the shop. Just because Roxi chose to be a solitary witch, rather than join Martha's illustrious coven, she was considered suspect.

Fortunately, not every Lowcountry witch was as closed minded as their high priestess, or Hex Appeal would have had to close its doors after the first week.

"We're having a planning meeting tomorrow evening at my home," the elderly witch said. "I know the others will be pleased to have you join us."

With that, she left the shop like a schooner at full sail. Without buying anything. She never did. Which was just as well, because she'd undoubtedly declare anything from Hex Appeal faulty since it wasn't sold by a "real" witch.

Sighing, Roxi rearranged the remaining unicorns to make up for the one that had walked out of the shop in Martha's oversized straw bag.

The old woman wasn't really a thief. At least not if her niece, who routinely paid her kleptomaniac aunt's monthly bills from shopkeepers all over town, could be believed. But she was definitely a trial.

Three

Sloan Hawthorne dreamed of her again. The sultry witch slipped into his sleep, into his mind, like a soft and sultry mist.

They'd been in the forest, where she'd been standing in the sacred circle, waiting for him.

Overhead the midnight sky was a vast sea of black velvet scattered with diamonds. Ice crystals sparkled in the frosty air.

Neither spoke. Words were not necessary when hearts—and souls—were in unison.

Rather than her usual black, she was clad from head to toe in white, the color of the season. But there was nothing wintry about the heat shimmering in her thickly lashed eyes as she looked up at him. Offering everything she was. Everything she would ever be.

With hands that were not as steady as he would have liked, Sloan pushed her white fur hood back. A slight gasp escaped her rosy lips, hovering like a ghost on the chilly air between them as he gathered up a fistful of midnight black hair.

She trembled, but not from the winter's cold as his free hand unfastened the silver fastener of her cape and pushed it off her shoulders. From anticipation? Or, perhaps, fear?

It's all right, he soothed as he kissed her temple, her eyes, which drifted closed. *You need to trust me.* Her cheek. *I wouldn't ever hurt you.*

Although he did not say the words out loud, he knew she understood. As his mouth covered hers in a deep, claiming kiss, he felt her body relax in soft, oh so sweet surrender.

She stood before him, gloriously naked, clad only in skin as pale and smooth as freshly churned cream. A silver amulet, carved with mysterious Celtic symbols from another time, nestled between her breasts.

Although he'd lived in sun-drenched southern California for a dozen years, had worked in the movie industry for eight, Sloan had not known it was possible for any woman to be so beautiful.

He drank in the sight of her, his gaze moving over her face, taking in her eyes with their sexy, feline slant, her nose, which tipped up ever so slightly. Having always found perfection boring, Sloan approved of the faint flaw.

Her slightly parted lips were a soft and dusky pink against her milkmaid's complexion, reminding him of late summer roses on a field of snow.

She swallowed ever so slightly as he continued his slow, judicious study. When he bent his head and touched his mouth to that soft, fragrant hollow in her throat, he felt her pulse hitch. Imagined he could taste her low, deep hum of pleasure.

Her long hair draped her breasts in a jet black curtain. He smoothed it back over her shoulders. As her nipples tightened beneath his hot and hungry gaze, it took every vestige of self-control Sloan possessed to keep from taking those pert berry tips between his teeth.

He managed, just barely, to keep a tight rein on his rampant need to ravish as his roving eyes moved lower, down her torso, over her taut stomach to the nest of curls between her smooth, firm thighs. Beads of moisture glistened in the silvery moonlight like morning dew.

No longer able to resist touching, he trailed a sensual path through those thistledown silk ringlets with a fingertip and slid a finger into her moist, hidden sheath.

The body clenching around the gently invading touch was hot and tight. And, he thought, with a burst of primal male satisfaction as he flicked a thumb over her clitoris and brought her that first, sharp release, *mine*.

She was clearly staggered. Her gleaming gold eyes were blurred. Color rode high on her cheekbones and her lush lips trembled on an unsteady breath.

Just as he was worrying that he might have rushed things— rushed her—she smiled.

A slow, sexy, siren's smile.

And the spell was upon him.

Sloan had planned, while following her to this secret witch's place, to have her. To ease the woman hunger that had been bedeviling both his mind and body for too long. But, as he'd also always prided himself on being a tender, thorough lover, he'd also intended to take his time.

As lightning-hot need jolted straight to his loins, a ravaging madness flashed through Sloan. Patience broke, intentions scattered. With a violent heat raging in his blood, he muttered a half oath, half prayer, and crushed his mouth to hers.

No less hungry, she kissed him back, her avid mouth moving beneath his, murmuring words in some mysterious, magical language Sloan couldn't understand.

His clothes disappeared, thrown to the four winds swirling wildly around them. Her nails dug into the bared flesh of his shoulders as she arched her fluid body against him. Her heart was pounding a fast, primitive beat through her blood, against her ribs, so hard he could feel it against his own chest.

Primal need clawed. At her. At him.

As the animal inside Sloan snarled and snapped its steel link chain, he dragged her to the ground, shoved her knees up, and mounted her.

"Mine." He needed to say the word out loud. Needed to hear her response.

She didn't hesitate. "Yours," she agreed on a harsh, ragged breath.

For all time.

He pistoned his hips forward, surging into her, claiming her innocence in one deep thrust.

Her cry, born not of pain, but pleasure, tangled with feminine triumph, echoed over the winter bare treetops.

Clinging to him, her body bowed, her slender hands racing up and down his back while she chanted those musical words from an ancient time, the witch opened completely. Utterly.

It began to snow, soft white flakes drifting down like feathers shaken from some pagan god's goose-down pillow. Moving together in an age-old rhythm, steeped in the magic of the night and of each other, neither Sloan nor his witch felt the cold as the snow covered them like a pristine white blanket.

"Okay. That's it."

Damn. He'd done it again. Fallen asleep at his computer. Sloan lifted his head, relieved he hadn't drooled and shorted out the keyboard.

His head pounded, his mouth was as dry as when he'd filmed that adventure flick last year in the Sahara, his body ached like the devil, and he didn't need to look down to know that it was still reacting to his hot and horny dream. He had, after all, been suffering from a damn near perpetual hard-on since he'd begun this frigging Morganna project. He was also getting sick and tired of icy morning showers.

It was time for action.

Time to take charge.

"Time to get laid."

He reached out and snagged the phone from beneath a pile of comic books. *Make that graphic novels*, he reminded himself.

Though, personally, having grown up devouring superhero comic books, Sloan couldn't understand why there'd be a stigma to the term, but after all the years and trouble he'd gone to convincing Morganna's creator Gavin Thomas to sell him the film rights to the sexy, crime-fighting witch, the last thing he needed to do was accidentally slip up one of these days and insult the writer's work in public.

Especially given that, having already managed to incite the ultraconservative right with that pirate movie he'd made with Gabriel Broussard, he suspected the zealots would be heating up the tar and dragging out the feathers when Morganna hit the silver screen.

He was idly flipping through the pages while the phone rang and he paused on a scene where Brianna, Morganna's virginal good witch twin—who represented the white magic side of the duo—made love to a mortal male in a sacred circle of stones.

The black and white frame depicting the snow falling on the naked lovers caused the dream to come crashing back in vivid detail, which in turn had the muscles in his belly knotting painfully.

"Hello," the familiar voice on the other end of the line answered. At least that's what he thought she'd said. It was difficult to tell with all that hot blood roaring in his ears.

"Hey, Emma, darlin'." His southern drawl, a legacy from those halcyon days growing up in Savannah, rasped with unsatisfied lust as he struggled to drag his testosterone-crazed mind back to reality. "I've got a favor to ask."

Five minutes later, Sloan was online, booking a flight to Savannah.

Then went into the bathroom for yet another cold shower. One he damn well hoped would be his last.

Four

Seven months after her grand opening, thanks, in part, to Savannah's tourism trade, business was booming. Enough so that Roxi had even been able to hire a part-time employee, a descendent of a long line of voodoo practitioners who moonlighted as the lead singer in the Papa Legba Voodoo Priestesses.

Named for the most powerful of all the voodoo spirits, who, along with all his other responsibilities was in charge of all things erotic and sexual, the pop group was starting to generate crossover appeal, which Roxi attributed in large part to Jaira Guidnard's mile-long legs, poreless dark chocolate skin, and a body that caused males from eight to eighty to trip over their tongues.

"Do you believe this?" Jaira asked ten minutes after a busload of Swedish tourists had descended on the shop, located on the city's colorful Riverwalk. "It's like a damn Viking invasion."

"They're also paying our rent for the next three months," Roxi said. "Not to mention your salary."

"Well, there is that," Jaira agreed. "And some of them are actually kind of cute if you go for the hunky blond Scandinavian type."

She flashed a blindingly bright smile at one of the Vikings, who immediately walked into a display of pewter wind chimes hanging from the ceiling.

The temperature and humidity outside the shop was approaching the nineties; the constant opening and closing of the door, as customers left with their packages to make room for others to enter, was putting a strain on the hundred-year-old building's air conditioner, making it nearly as hot inside. Her hot pink Hex Appeal tank top was beginning to stick to Roxi's body and her hair felt like a thick dark curtain hanging down her back.

While Jaira went over to model jewelry and flirt with a trio of bedazzled males ostensibly shopping for their mothers back home—if, in fact, Swedish mothers actually wore chandelier garnet and seashell earrings—Roxi wrapped up a voodoo doll for a tall, stunningly voluptuous woman her own age who easily could've been a member of the Swedish Bikini Team.

Interestingly, none of the Vikings who were swarming around Jaira seemed to be paying any attention to her, which Roxi took as validation that blondes didn't always have all the fun.

As the blonde left the store with two more members of the team, all sporting fuchsia Hex Appeal baseball caps with its signature witch logo, the phone rang.

"*Bonjour*, Hex Appeal," she answered, tossing in a bit of her native Cajun French, which customers seemed to enjoy. "Love spells for the sexy sorceress."

The laugh on the other end of the phone was rich and familiar. "It's me," Emma Broussard said.

"I know. I recognized the number on the caller I.D., but wanted to try out my new branding line. You're the first person to hear it. So, *chère*, what do you think?"

"I like it better than the one you've been using."

"I do, too," Roxi agreed. "I decided this morning that more people would rather be sexy than sassy."

The revelation had come from last night's hot, hot dream. The one that had her waking up with her hands between her legs. And still, dammit, unsatisfied.

"How's the creature from the deep lagoon?"

"Should I be offended that you insist on calling my unborn child a creature?"

"Hey." Roxi shrugged and grinned. "You should've known you were taking a risk when you sent me that sonogram." Her voice, and her mood, turned suddenly serious. "You and the baby are okay, aren't you?"

"Of course. I've never been better. After I started drinking that ginger peach tea you sent me, my morning sickness disappeared."

"That's what it's supposed to do." Ha! She might not be a card-carrying member of a coven, but thanks to growing up with a Cajun *traiteur* for a grandmother, Roxi definitely knew her herbal remedies. "So, what's up?"

"I have a favor to ask."

"Anything."

While they now lived a continent apart, there wasn't anything Roxi wouldn't do for her best friend. And she knew the feeling worked both ways. Plus, she figured she owed Emma for having let her choose her own maid of honor dress instead of sticking her in pink taffeta. Or worse yet, the southern belle, *Gone with the Wind* fantasy that continued to be a popular wedding theme south of the Mason-Dixon line.

"Well, actually, it's more a favor for Gabriel."

"Better yet. Tell me you've grown tired of the sexiest man alive and want me to take him off your hands."

"Thanks for the offer, but I believe I'll keep him a while longer," Emma said, proving her talent for understatement.

Roxi figured Michelle Kwan would be doing triple toe loops in hell before Emma wanted out of the marriage she'd been dreaming about since seventh grade, when she'd taken to writing Mrs. Gabriel Broussard all over her notebook.

"Funny how you can grow up with someone and not realize what a selfish bitch she is," Roxi teased. "So if you're not ready to recycle the drop-dead sexy father of the lagoon creature, what do you need?"

"It's about the Morganna, Mistress of the Night movie."

"Coincidentally, I was just talking with a local witch about that yesterday afternoon."

"Given your tone, can I deduce it wasn't a very flattering conversation?"

Emma might not be a witch, but her intuition was usually right on the mark. Including when she'd tried to break off her engagement to the dickhead. Unfortunately, her mother had laid the guilt trip of all time on her, so Emma had caved.

Bygones, Roxi reminded herself. Besides, not only had Emma overcome the collapse of a marriage that should have been de-clared dead at the altar, she'd emerged from the rubble a strong, bold, kick-butt heroine who could hold her own with Xena the Warrior Princess or Lara Croft, or even Morganna, any day. And in doing so, had won herself a sexy, caring man who openly adored her.

"Let's just say there's a bit of local concern about Morganna's Wiccan legitimacy."

"Would you be surprised to hear that Gabriel agrees with those detractors?"

"Really?" A faint sound, like that made when Clarence, the angel, finally earned his wings in *It's a Wonderful Life,* chimed in the back of Roxi's mind.

"Really. He just finished reading the most recent script and is concerned the movie could come off looking like a comic book."

"Which isn't all that surprising, since it *is* a comic book," Roxi said, conveniently forgetting her earlier correction when Martha had called it that.

"True. But what a lot of people don't know is that *The Last Pirate* began as a superhero comic book type version of Jean Lafitte's life. It was only when Gabriel insisted that Sloan Hawthorne expand the concept that it became the movie every-one saw."

Everyone being the definitive word. Earnings for the film

depiction of the Louisiana pirate's life had topped even Depp's *Pirates of the Caribbean*.

"Good for Gabe. So, what's the favor?"

"Gabriel thought it might be a good idea to get a witch's input on the script. And you just happen to be the only witch we know. Which is handy, because I remember you enjoying those Morganna comics."

"Actually, they're graphic novels, but yeah, I did enjoy them." And, as Emma well knew, she'd devoured them like chocolate pralines. "So, what do you want me to do? Read the script—"

"Oh, absolutely, we'd appreciate that! But rather than have Gabriel pass your opinions secondhand to Sloan, which can always result in miscommunication problems, we felt perhaps you should meet with him directly."

That niggling little chime sounded again. Louder, and a bit more insistent this time.

"I'd love to help you out, *chère*. Right now's a busy tourist season and I only just hired a part-timer helper, so it may take me a couple days to arrange things, but I'll check the flights and—"

"Oh, we wouldn't want you to have to go to all the trouble of coming here," Emma said quickly. Too quickly. The chime was now an alarm bell. "As it happens, he's coming to you."

Make that a damn siren. Like the civil defense one Paul Rigaud kept insisting on testing once a month back home in Blue Bayou.

"You're kidding. Some wunderkind movie screenwriter is flying all the way to Savannah just to get the opinion of a woman he's never met?"

"Sloan's directing the film along with writing the screenplay. He's also very hands on, which is why he's insisted scouting out shooting locations himself. He'd originally planned to shoot in New Orleans and out in the bayou, but then he lost a lot of the sites to Katrina."

"I can identify with that."

"Having grown up in Savannah, he knows the city well and thought it'd provide a lot of local color."

"It does have that," Roxi agreed.

"I can't wait to visit and see it all for myself. Anyway, given the lucky coincidence that you just happen to be living there, as well, Gabriel and I were hoping you'd be willing to meet with him."

"You wouldn't be trying to fix me up with this Hawthorne guy, would you?"

"Why would I want to do that?" Emma countered. "When we both know you're more than capable of getting any man you want?"

It did not escape Roxi's notice that Emma hadn't answered her question directly.

"Even if that were true, which it isn't, how about the fact that now that you're so happy in your little oceanside love nest, you've fallen prey to the dreaded MWS disease?"

"MWS?"

"Married Women Syndrome. Being perfectly content in your gilded institution of marriage, you now want to lock up every other woman in there with you."

"Don't be silly." The answering laugh was merry and bright. And, Roxi thought darkly, fake. Emma never had been able to tell a lie. "I seem to recall you telling me that you never went for a man with the entire package. That you just went out with men with a below-the-belt package."

"Yeah, I vaguely remember saying something like that."

She'd been lecturing about the need to separate emotions from sex. A warning that had come too late for Emma, who'd already fallen head over heart in love with Gabriel. Which had been a very good thing, given how well things had turned out.

"Well, if you truly meant it, then you definitely won't be at all interested in Sloan. Because the man defines a complete package."

"If he's such a paragon of perfection, why hasn't some woman snatched him up?"

"Perhaps because from what I've witnessed in the few months I've known him, he's every bit as commitment-phobic as you are. Which, by the way, blows any theory about me wanting to play matchmaker between the two of you right out of the water."

Unless, Roxi considered, she was using reverse psychology.

Which was crazy. There wasn't anyone in the world as straightforward as Emma Quinn Broussard.

Emma pressed her case when Roxi didn't immediately respond. "We really need your input, Roxie. Gabriel doesn't want to back out of the project, especially since he and Sloan have a verbal agreement, and he's always felt strongly about keeping his word, but—"

"Okay." Roxi threw up her hands, both literally and figuratively. "When's this full package paragon due to arrive in Savannah?"

"Tomorrow evening." Unlike her husband, Emma Broussard was no actor. Which explained why she couldn't quite keep the satisfaction from her tone. "He's staying at the Swansea House," she said, again a bit too quickly. "I told him I'd ask if you'd be willing to meet him for dinner."

"So now you're his social secretary?"

"No. I merely felt uncomfortable giving out your number without checking with you first," Emma said mildly.

"I'm sorry." Roxi blew out a breath. "It's just been a crazed morning." After a frustratingly restless night.

"Well then, a lovely dinner with an attractive, interesting man sounds like just what you need."

Actually, if her reaction to that dream was any indication, what she needed was to get fucked, but since an elderly Swedish tourist was approaching the counter with a silver Viking dragon brooch in hand, Roxi kept that thought to herself.

Besides, as always, the quintessentially practical Emma had a point. The past few months, with her life in such flux, Roxi hadn't taken time to actually relax and enjoy herself. The Swansea House boasted one of the best restaurants not just in

Savannah, but in the entire Lowcountry region. An expensive dinner on someone else's dime sounded more than a little appealing.

And if the evening ended in one of those antique four-poster beds the inn used in its advertising campaign, so much the better.

Five

"Well." Out on the raised deck of her Malibu home, which looked out over the vast blue Pacific, Emma Broussard hung up the phone and eyed the man seated across the white wrought iron table. "I've done all I can. Whatever else happens is up to you."

"I owe you, darlin'." Sloan lifted his glass to her. "Big time."

Her smile faded and a warning glinted in moss green eyes. "If you hurt her—"

"I know. You'll have Gabe rip out my lungs."

"That might be an option," she agreed mildly. "But only after I hack your balls off with a rusty knife and feed them to that shark that was spotted offshore last week."

He blew out a breath as just the suggestion of the threat had his testicles shooting up into his tonsils. "Wow. Who'd guess an expectant mother could be so harsh?"

"I like you, Sloan. A great deal. I also enjoy your artistic vision and believe that you're one of the few people who understands and appreciates my husband's complexities enough to draw an amazing performance from him. I'd like to believe that's because, although you do appear to have a bit of a Peter

Pan complex, you're not a typically shallow, egotistical Hollywood movie prick."

"Thanks. I think."

"It was meant as a compliment. Roxi's been my best friend
since we were in kindergarten." Her expression softened and
her eyes drifted back over the sun-silvered waves. "We met the
day she put a spell on a boy who'd called me fat."

"I hope she turned him into a frog."

"Nothing that dramatic. But he did fall off his bike riding
home from school and broke his arm."

"Let's hear it for the witches," he said with a grin, then
sobered. "Kids can be mean."

Sloan knew, by some standards, especially Hollywood standards, the adult Emma would be considered overweight, as
well. Personally, he found her lush and ripe and sexy as hell.

"It was the truth," she said with a shrug. "I was, as my
mother insisted on pointing out, a 'butterball.' But you should
have seen the way Roxi lit into him. She was a five-year-old
warrior." She smiled at the memory. "Thinking about it now,
although the books hadn't been written yet, she's always reminded me of Morganna."

She slanted Sloan a knowing look. "I believe you see her
the same way."

"I've never met the woman."

He'd been in the Sahara when Gabe and Emma had gotten
married, and a damn sandstorm had kept him from getting to
Louisiana and acting as his friend's best man.

"Yet here you are, planning a trip all the way across the
country to be with her. After asking me to lie for you."

"And I appreciate it, Emma. But it wasn't exactly a lie."

She lifted a bright russet brow, reminding him yet again
that the lady was no pushover.

"More like a sin of omission," he qualified. "Number one,
I really did grow up in Savannah." He began counting off on
his fingers. "Second, I *am* going to be scouting shooting sites

there." A third finger went up. "And finally, meeting with someone who believes herself to be a real witch will help flesh Morganna out."

Believes herself to be a real witch. That qualification did not escape Emma's attention.

"Do you believe in destiny?" he asked suddenly.

"Of course."

"I never did. I always figured we made our own destiny."

"Perhaps it's a bit of both," Emma suggested. "We all have free will, the ability to make choices, take different paths. Take advantage of opportunities."

She crossed her legs and took a sip of herbal tea. "Gabe and I knew each other back in Blue Bayou growing up," she said. "We'd been friends for a lot of years. Well, to be perfectly honest, I'd been a friend who had a major crush on him. But things didn't work out."

From the shadows in her expressive green eyes, Sloan sensed that was an understatement. "He moved to Hollywood. Then my marriage broke up, and Gabriel had his little problem—"

"His scandal, you mean."

The sunlight returned to her eyes when she laughed. "Ah, yes, let's hear it for kinky sex scandals . . . Anyway, after he decided to return home to hide out from the press until things blew over, a friend of both Gabe's and mine pulled a few strings, forcing us to spend some time alone together. The sparks were still there, so . . ."

"You lit yourself a fire."

"More like a conflagration. But yes. Either one of us could have backed away. In fact, I tried to. But Gabe had other ideas."

"I don't blame him. Hell, sugar, if I'd have seen you first, I would've given your movie star husband a run for his money."

"That's sweet." She patted him on the knee. "But getting back to the point of this conversation, are you suggesting you believe Roxi may be your destiny?"

"That's probably an overstatement. But I gotta tell you, Emma, it's the damnedest thing. The minute I saw that e-mail of your wedding picture, I felt poleaxed."

"Roxi has that effect on men."

"It's more than just her looks. Hell, this is L.A. You can't throw a stick on a beach here without hitting a dozen women probably just as beautiful."

"Who undoubtedly wouldn't enjoy getting hit by flying sticks, but I understand what you're getting at."

"The point, and I do have one, is that the woman's been flat out driving me out of my mind. She's all I can think about. All I can dream about."

"I know the feeling," Emma said dryly. "Very well. But have you considered that it's because you've been so caught up in this new project, and she does resemble Morganna?"

If that wedding picture was any indication, she was the crime-fighting witch in the flesh. He wondered if she owned a catsuit.

"Sure I have. And that's probably all it is. But if I'm going to be able to keep my mind on work long enough to get this project in the can, I need to find out."

Surely taking Roxi Dupree to bed would get her out of his system once and for all. And let him get on with his movie. And his life.

"I can understand that, as well. May I offer a word of advice?"

"Sure."

"I've never been one to involve myself in other people's personal lives, but since it also occurs to me that if it hadn't been for Nate Callahan, Gabriel and I might not have had a second chance, I'm going to risk a bit of meddling.

"If, after you get to Savannah, you begin to suspect whatever you're feeling is more than just understandable lust for a beautiful woman, don't tell Roxi."

"O-kay." He knew his skepticism was written all over his face.

"I know what you're thinking. That deep down inside, no matter what they might say to the contrary, most women are looking for commitment."

"Far be it from me to make sweeping generalities. But just going by my own experience, that seems to be the case more often than not."

Although he'd always told women right up front that he wasn't the marrying kind, after a few months, or even weeks, most suddenly started talking about silverware patterns, and bridal magazines would magically show up on bedside tables.

"Roxi's the exception. She's always up for a good time, but if you let her think you're getting serious, she's going to run. I've seen it happen hundreds of times."

"Hundreds?"

Emma nodded. "At least. But I'll let her tell you about her rule of three herself. If things get that far."

"I know about the rule of three," he said. "It's the Wiccan code about whatever you do comes back to you threefold."

"That's one version," Emma agreed. "But Roxi's got her own take on it."

"Well now, sugar, I have to admit you have indeed piqued my interest. But if she's into threesomes, I'm afraid she's going to be disappointed."

Emma laughed. "I can't swear to know everything about her, but I'm pretty sure that you're safe there." She touched a fingertip to her lips. "But that's all I'm saying."

Emma was still smiling long after Sloan had left for the airport.

"I believe," she told Gabriel later that afternoon, "that things in Savannah could get very interesting."

They were lying in bed, bathed in the warm afterglow of passion after making love. It still amazed her that after all these months together, she still couldn't get enough of him. And, amazingly, if his behavior in the past half hour was any indication, her husband, who undoubtedly could have any woman in the world he wanted, felt the same way.

"*Mais*, yeah." He pressed his lips against her temple. Skimmed a wickedly clever hand down her side, from her shoulder to her thigh. "Sort of like nitroglycerin and a flamethrower are interesting."

She laughed, enjoying the image even as heat bloomed beneath his caressing touch. "I suppose it's only fair." She twined her arms around his neck and lifted her face for his kiss. "Why should we have all the fun?"

Emma's last thought, just before her husband took her back into the mists, was that her two favorite commitment-phobic people might have finally met their match.

Six

They'd agreed, during their brief phone call, to meet at the restaurant. Although he'd offered to pick her up, Roxi had thought that a foolish waste of time and effort, especially since he was already staying at the inn.

She'd heard the hum of jet engines during the call and wondered what it must feel like to actually be able to pick up one of those phones in-flight and pay the outrageous charges.

"Of course, when you're rolling in dough, I guess there's nothing you can't buy," she told her cat, La Betaille, who was lying on her bed, watching her get ready for the dinner date. "Undoubtedly even women."

Ignoring her with a feline elegance that belied the fact that the eighteen-pound former stray was missing one ear and had a diagonal scar across her nose, La Betaille began fastidiously washing her huge black paws.

"I wonder if the casting couch still exists?" She reached into the small enameled box on the dressing table and took out a pair of earrings shaped like crescent moons. They might be rhinestones rather than the diamonds Sloan Hawthorne was undoubtedly accustomed to women wearing, but Roxi liked the way they sparkled.

She studied the results in the full-length mirror standing across the room. "Though I'll bet a man like Sloan Hawthorne probably doesn't have to hold out walk-on roles in his movies as a carrot to get women to go to bed with him."

She'd spent the better part of the morning shopping for an outfit designed to knock off the Hollywood hotshot's socks, and if she was lucky, various other pieces of clothing.

She turned sideways and ran her hands down the front of the dress. Her breasts, which had always suited her just fine, thank you, suddenly seemed, well . . . a bit insignificant.

Since when had she started comparing herself to any other woman?

"You're an original, you," she said, looking over her shoulder at her butt, which, if she did say so herself, looked damn fine in this dress. "Besides, it'll be a new experience for him. Touching real, honest-to-god womanly flesh instead of silicone."

Apparently unimpressed by that prospect, La Betaille merely yawned.

She'd just fastened a moonstone pendant around her neck when the limo Sloan had insisted on sending for her arrived outside the small carriage house she was renting behind one of the stately homes on Chippewa Square, where Forrest Gump had sat on his famous bench and contemplated life as a box of chocolates.

"Okay," she said, as the driver rang the bell. "Showtime." Smoothing her hands over her hair, Roxi drew in a deep breath and pressed a hand against her stomach, which had suddenly gone all fluttery.

Which was just proof that she'd definitely been working too hard. Men never made Roxi Dupree nervous.

She reached down and stroked the cat's head. "Don't wait up."

As if taking her literally, La Betaille rolled over, closed her amber eyes, and immediately fell asleep.

* * *

The Swansea Inn had begun its life as an antebellum mansion belonging to a cotton broker. Three stories tall, created of the local gray Savannah brick that turned a dusky pink when bathed in the red glow of sunset, it overlooked the Polaski Monument in Monterey Square, which Roxi considered the prettiest of the city's twenty-four lush green squares.

She'd heard rumors that the inn had, for several decades prior to the War Between the States, been a house of prostitution, where wealthy planters and merchants had kept a bevy of women for their shared pleasure. There was even one bit of local lore that had General Sherman, after deciding not to torch the city, but to give it to President Lincoln as a Christmas present instead, paying a visit to the house to celebrate having concluded his devastating march across Georgia to the sea.

Like so many stories about the city, the tales were couched in mystery and wrapped in sensuality, and had been told and retold so many times it was impossible to know how much was true, and how much was the product of Savannahians' vivid imaginations.

She'd never been inside before, partly because she knew she'd never be able to afford the prices, but mostly because it was a private club. A place, yet more rumors persisted, of assignations. Even, she'd heard whispered, the occasional orgy.

She might have a liberal view of sex, but if Sloan Hawthorne had plans along those lines for tonight, he was going to be disappointed.

The moment the black car glided to a stop at the curve, the inn's glass door opened and a man came down the stone steps.

A sudden, white-hot sexual craving zigzagged through her like a bolt of lightning from a clear blue summer sky, sending every hormone in her body into red alert.

Roxi recognized him immediately. She'd Googled him yesterday after talking with Emma on the Internet, and while on all those Web sites she'd visited he'd definitely appeared to be a hunk, up close and personal he was downright lethal.

His hair was warm chestnut streaked with gold she suspected was a result of time spent beneath the California sun, rather than some trendy Beverly Hills salon. He was conservatively dressed in a crisp white shirt, muted gray striped tie, and a dark suit, which looked Italian and probably cost more than her first car.

He opened the back passenger door. His eyes, which were as green as newly minted money, lit up with masculine appreciation as they swept over her.

"Wow. And here I thought the woman was fictional," he murmured.

"Excuse me?" Her body wasn't the only thing that had gone into sexual meltdown. Sexual images of herself and Sloan Hawthorne writhed in her smoke-filled mind.

She told herself the only reason she was taking the hand he'd extended was that the car was low, her skirt tight, and her heels high.

Liar. Not only wasn't she sure she could stand on her own, she was actually desperate for his touch. Not just on her hand, but all the other tingling places on her body.

"I'm sorry." He shook his head. Sheepishly rubbed the bridge of his nose. "I tend to talk to myself when I'm bewitched."

"I see." He wasn't just drop-dead gorgeous. He was cute. It also helped to know that she wasn't the only one who'd been momentarily mesmerized.

The butterflies settled, allowing Roxi to pick up a bit of her own scattered senses. "Does that happen often?" she asked.

"This is the first time." His gaze swept over her—from the top of her head down to her Revved up and Red-y toenails, then back up to her face again. "That is one helluva dress."

"Thank you." It was a basic black dinner dress. That was, if anything that was strapless and fit like a second skin could be called basic.

"Did you wear it to bring me to my knees?"

"Absolutely."

"Well, then." He flashed a grin that would've dropped a lesser woman to *her* knees. As it was, it had moisture pooling hotly between Roxi's thighs. "You'll be glad to know that it's working like a charm."

Like so many of the fine old homes in Savannah's historic district, the Inn had several steps originally designed to keep the dust and mud from the unpaved dirt streets outside the house.

Sloan put a hand on her back as they started walking up the five stone steps, hip to hip. Although the gesture seemed as natural to him as breathing, Roxi's knees were feeling a bit wobbly as a doorman in a burgundy uniform with snazzy gold epaulets swept the door open for them.

She would have expected Sloan to stay at one of the modern brass and glass high-rise hotels that tradition-loving Savannahians loved to complain about. It would have made it easier to dislike him. Or at least keep her emotional distance.

But the minute she walked into the inn, which epitomized sultry Savannah, Roxi was charmed by the black and white marble floors, the mahogany paneling, the pink marble pillars holding up a ceiling that soared at least fifteen feet, and the grand, sweeping staircase that made Scarlet's Tara look like a poor imitation.

"It's stunning," she breathed, gazing up at the ceiling that managed to have enough gold leaf to be elegant without crossing over to tacky excess.

"My family's always been proud of it," he said mildly, waving a hello at the concierge seated behind a cherry desk polished to a mirror sheen.

She stopped in her tracks. "Are you saying your family owns this inn?"

She'd known he was rich. His family, according to Google, owned one of the largest brick companies in the country. But having grown up with a shrimper for a father and a housewife for a mother, Roxi found herself a bit intimidated by the idea of old wealth.

"No. I'm saying an ancestor built it."

"He was the architect?" Her heels clattered on the flowing black and white marble as they crossed the room.

"Actually, he laid the bricks. My family came from a long line of stonemasons. Which is how we got into the brick business."

"Ah, Mr. Hawthorne." The tuxedoed maître d' at the open doorway to the restaurant bowed as if greeting foreign royalty. "It's a pleasure to see you again."

"It's good to be back, Randall," Sloan said. "How's the family? Didn't my mother tell me your daughter was about to have another baby?"

"She gave her mother and I our third grandchild last week." His chest puffed up with obvious pride. "A beautiful little girl. Seven pounds, three ounces. They named her Elizabeth Rose."

"That's wonderful." Sloan's answering smile was, Roxi noted, every bit as warm as the ones he'd been tossing her way. She'd read a quote from Nicole Kidman, who'd called him a rarity in Hollywood, a genuinely nice man who treated everyone, from grip to catering staff to star, with equal respect.

"Give the proud parents my best," he said.

"I'll certainly do that." The maître d' beamed. If he'd had a tail, he would have been wagging it. "If you'll just follow me, we have your table waiting for you."

The restaurant floor was carpeted and the walls draped in a rich Savannah green silk, both, Roxi suspected, designed to mute the noise. It seemed to be working. Although the dining room was crowded, quiet conversation was possible.

It could have been a dining room in any other five-star restaurant. The men were all wearing suits or black tie, the women, for the most part, dressed much as she was, though she did glimpse some cocktail suits, and quite a few floaty, flowered dresses in the pretty pastels so popular in the South.

The walls were lined with banquettes covered in a rich burgundy tapestry, and as they walked across the room, she caught sight of several floor-to-ceiling draperies which seemed to close off private alcoves.

Were these rooms, she wondered, where the assignations took place?

As they followed the man toward the kitchen, she was thinking that for all the bowing and beaming, the old guy hadn't given Sloan a very good table, when he opened a door leading to some steep stone stairs.

"I'd thought we'd have dinner in the wine cellar," Sloan explained as Roxi looked up at him. "Given that the place tends to be packed on Friday night, I thought it'd give us more privacy."

He paused just a beat, long enough to let that idea and all its implications sink in. "But if you'd like to eat in the dining room—"

"The wine cellar will be fine." She hoped.

What did she really know about Sloan Hawthorne, after all? What if he was some sort of crazed sex fiend? What if the cellar was a secret S&M dungeon where members chained women to the wall and whipped them for their own sadistic gratification?

God. What on earth was the matter with her? Although Savannah, which Margaret Mitchell had referred to as "that gently mannered city by the sea," was well-known to possess an erotic, sensually adventurous side, it certainly didn't have S&M dungeons hidden away in five-star restaurants.

Besides, Emma, despite her uncharacteristic mistake with the dickhead, was a very good judge of character and never would have hooked her up with a sex maniac.

Although the walls and floor were made of the same stones she'd seen all over the city, stones that had arrived in Savannah as ballast in the holds of ships, there were no chains. No whips that she could see.

A single table had been draped in a snowy cloth, and set with gleaming crystal, china, and heavy silverware. Wall sconces cast a soft light over the room and a candle in a hurricane glass glowed. The damask napkin the maître d' had placed in her lap with a flourish had been lightly scented with lavender. Smooth and sultry jazz flowed from hidden speakers.

Perversely, although she certainly wasn't into masochism, after their drink orders had been taken—a summer melon martini for her, beer for him—Roxi experienced a twinge of disappointment that he appeared to have been telling the truth about having chosen this room solely because it allowed for more private conversation than the upstairs dining room.

"Did your ancestor lay these stones, as well?"

"He did. The cornerstone was set a hundred and sixty years ago and you'll note the place is still standing. I'm not sure how many modern-day buildings we'll be able to say that about."

"I love old buildings."

"Me, too, which is one of the things I miss in California, where it seems all the great old houses are being bulldozed down and replaced by megamansions. When I was a kid I used to have my birthday parties down here and show off to all my pals."

"That's nice."

It also took away the idea of the house being used as a sexual pleasure palace. From what she'd read of his family, his parents were respectable Episcopalians who attended Savannah's first church, which since 1733 had been designated as "Georgia's Mother Church." His father was CEO of one of the largest brick suppliers in the South, while his mother owned an antique shop on Bull Street across from the gold-domed City Hall. They did not sound like people who attended orgies. Nor would they, she suspected, appreciate their son dating a witch.

LOVE POTION #9 / 41

"My friends always wanted to go to my grandmother's shop," she revealed.

"Was she into magic and spells and such, too?"

"She was a *traiteur*—that's Cajun for a healer. But she also had some Caribbean heritage, so she was active in the voodoo religion, as well."

"Religion?"

"Despite the way it's often depicted in movies, what with people biting heads off chickens, making blood sacrifices, and dancing naked, voodoo is a very structured religion."

"Damn." One brow lifted. "And here I was, really looking forward to that naked dancing part."

Arousal stirred in her belly. And lower. "Oh, I've been known to go skyclad. When there's a full moon."

She combed a hand through her hair, a time-proven gesture that lifted her breasts appealingly. Unsurprisingly, his gaze followed.

Ha! As she'd always told Emma, men were easy.

Unfortunately, despite having always insisted on maintaining the upper hand, she was proving every bit as easy. She wanted him. Here. Now. In every way there was to want a man.

"I don't happen to have a calendar," he said hoarsely. "Would you happen to know when, exactly, the next full moon will be?"

Hanging onto her ebbing control with her fingertips, she managed a coy smile as she trailed a languid scarlet nail down her throat. "Not tonight."

"Well, damn. There goes that moonlight fantasy, shot to smithereens."

He might not believe in magic and spells and things that went bump in the night, but Roxi Dupree definitely had him bewitched and as bothered as hell.

The thought of those sexy, red-tipped fingers curving around his cock was all it took to give Sloan a massive hard-on.

He was debating just ditching the Southern manners he'd been taught in the cradle and jumping her luscious, sexy bones, right here and now, when the waiter showed up with their drinks, giving him time to drag his rampant libido back into check.

Seven

"So you were sharing a religious experience with your friends by taking them to your grandmother's shop?"

"No." Her laughter was rich and warm and curled around him like satin ribbons. "To be perfectly honest, they just wanted to see all the gator heads and teeth."

"I imagine gators beat foundation rocks any old day when you're a kid."

"Perhaps. But wasn't it in Savannah that that fictional pirate gave Billy Bones the map of Treasure Island?"

"Yeah. Some of the background for that novel supposedly came from the Pirate's House restaurant, where pirates supposedly hung out."

"Maybe they hung out here, as well," she mused.

As she glanced around at the gray stones, he imagined her a captive, chained to the wall, naked. Hot. Wet. Forced to do his every bidding.

He wondered what she'd do if she knew that the cellar had been originally built to hide smuggled pirate treasure. And stories persisted of Blackbeard having spent several weeks hiding out here with a woman he'd taken prisoner who'd become one of his fourteen wives.

"So, your family's from Savannah originally?"

"No, they landed in New England in 1630."

It was proving harder and harder to carry on a civilized, getting-to-know-you conversation when in his mind, she'd climbed onto his lap, her dress up around her waist as she straddled his thighs and gave him the lap dance of his life.

"About sixty years later, a group who didn't exactly buy into Puritanism broke off and moved south. And immediately became known as the black sheep branch of the family tree."

That was putting it mildly. Though, to his mind, building brothels was a lot more respectable than hanging women falsely accused of witchcraft.

"My family's story was much the same," she said. "Oh, not the Puritan thing. Which would have been unlikely, given those people's attitude about the only good witch being a dead witch."

So, here's your chance, a little voice of reason in the back of his mind counseled as she picked up the tasseled menu and began leafing through the pages of listings. *Tell her. Now. Before you get in over your head.*

Don't be a damn fool, said another voice, which seemed directly linked to his hopeful dick. *You think she'd be willing to go to bed with you if she knew the truth?*

Trying to ignore them both, he took a long drink of Guinness.

"Your name's French," he said, shifting the conversation away from his family heritage.

"Acadian." She put down the menu and took a sip of her martini. "My father's people were kicked out of Nova Scotia in the eighteenth century for refusing to convert to Anglicanism."

"And ended up in the bayou because they figured it'd be the last place in the country anyone would want, so they'd be left alone and finally allowed to settle down," he said.

"That's right." She sounded surprised.

"I had to read that Longfellow poem about Evangeline and Gabriel back in high school." He did not mention the family lore about Longfellow having been inspired to write the poem about the Acadian maiden and her lover torn apart on their wedding day, by a story told to him at a dinner party at author

Nathaniel Hawthorne's home. "I've always thought the story would make a great movie."

"There have already been two made, back in the 1920s," she divulged after their orders had been taken. "In fact, Delores Del Rio, who starred in the second one, had a statue made of herself and placed on the site where Evangeline's supposedly buried."

"But she wasn't real."

"Try telling that to some of the people down in the bayou. The Evangeline Oak in St. Martinville is actually the third oak designated as the site where Evangeline and Gabriel were united. Tourists continue to flock there, decade after decade, which is why I strongly doubt moviegoers would enjoy having the heroine find the hero in an almshouse after years of separation, then the two of them dying in each other's arms."

"That could present a problem," he agreed. "Given that moviegoers these days mostly prefer their love stories to come with a happily ever after guaranteed ending."

"Fiction always sells better than truth," she said knowingly.

He arched a brow. "Sounds as if you don't believe in happy endings."

"I suppose it depends upon your meaning of happy." Her tone definitely closed the door on that topic.

Not wanting to press, Sloan switched gears. "What about the other side of your family?"

"They came over on the coffin ships from Ireland about a hundred years later and ended up in Louisiana building the levees."

"With all those Catholics in your background, it's interesting you'd decide to become a witch."

"I didn't decide anything. Other than to practice the Craft. I have Druid blood from my mother's side of the family. And, as I said, my father's great grandmother was a Haitian voodoo priestess, which carried through the women's side of his family."

"Which makes you a two-fer."

"I suppose you could put it that way."

"Are you into voodoo like your grandmother?"

"No. I suppose I'm more like your ancestors in that way."

"My ancestors?" His gut clenched. And not in a good way.

"The ones you told me didn't make it as Puritans? The religious aspects were just too structured for me, which is why I'm not Wiccan, either."

"There's a difference?"

"Wicca is a neopagan religion. Not all witches are Wiccan, and not all Wiccans practice magic," she explained as the waiter delivered their dinners and discreetly disappeared.

"Anyway, though I'd been drawn to the Craft all of my life, I'd never thought about actually earning a living with it until my grandmother Evangeline died and left me her voodoo shop. I gave away all the gator heads and teeth and was planning to dissolve the business entirely, but people kept showing up at the day spa I'd opened up with Emma, wanting spells like they'd bought from Grand-mère."

She took a bite of crab cake and closed her whiskey-hued eyes, looking like a woman in the throes of ecstasy. Actually, Sloan realized, she looked exactly the way the witch had in his dream, when he'd ridden her hard and fast beneath the icy winter moon.

Although the stone walls kept the cellar insulated, and additional cooling kept the room at an optimum temperature for wine storage, air-conditioning going full blast, his internal temperature spiked.

Sloan pulled at the starched collar of his shirt and was seriously considering yanking off his tie when another, equally provocative image flashed in his mind.

A mental image of Roxi Dupree, naked, his discarded tie lashing her ankles to the legs of the chair, holding her legs open for him as he knelt on the stone floor, painting those smooth, taut thighs with his tongue, lapping up the warm cream flowing from her cunt, taking her engorged clit between his teeth . . .

"What?" she asked when she opened her eyes again and found him staring at her.

In his unbidden fantasy, she'd been writhing against his mouth, her screams bouncing off the stones.

"Nothing."

He hadn't creamed his jeans since he'd been sixteen and Danielle Davenport had dry-humped him in the backseat of his Dodge Charger one steamy summer day they'd been parked out on Tybee Island. But he'd just come damn close to a repeat performance without this woman so much as laying a hand on him.

"You were telling me about after your grandmother died," he reminded her.

She gave him a look that let him know he wasn't getting away with anything. Then shrugged her bare shoulders.

"I didn't want to turn the people down, so I dragged out all my grandmother's shadow books—they're sort of like a witch's cookbook—learned the ones she'd been doing for her clients, then started blending up her recipes for the various lotions and oils, which fit in nicely with the spa concept."

"But you don't have the spa anymore?"

"No. Katrina did it in. As Margaret Mitchell might say, it went with the wind." She took another bite. "Oh God. This is so amazingly delicious."

He'd never before realized that the ordinary act of swallowing could be so fucking sexy. "Randolph, the chef here, has always had a deft hand with seafood."

She cut off a piece and held it out to him. "You have to try it."

She might as well have been Eve, holding out that shiny red apple. Like Adam, Sloan found himself unable to resist temptation.

"May as well. Given that you've already got me eating out of your hand. But I gotta tell you, sugar, pan-fried crab is sure as hell not what I'm hungry for."

He curved his fingers around her wrist and, with his eyes on hers, he closed his mouth over the fork's tines.

Watching her closely as he was, he didn't miss the way her eyes darkened at the movement in his throat as *he* swallowed. Beneath his thumb her pulse had trebled its beat.

"Good," he decided. He kissed her knuckles. "As far as appetizers go." He trailed his fingers up her arm, allowing the back of his hand to brush against the side of her breast. "Makes me anticipate dessert all the more."

She licked her lips, which had his mutinous penis leaping in response. "I hear the key lime pie's to die for."

"It's good, sure enough. But tonight I seem to be craving something sweeter." His caressing touch slid over her shoulder. "Smoother." Lower, to skim along the crest of her breasts. "Warmer."

Her nipples were pressing against the black silk. "Maybe topped with some nice, ripe berries," he decided.

She pleased him by laughing at that admittedly over the top sexual metaphor. He was less pleased when she lightly slapped his hand away.

"You are so bad."

"Sweetheart, you've no idea." He cupped the back of her neck. "But you're about to find out."

Encouraged when she didn't back away, Sloan gave her the warm, seductive smile that had always been one of the most devastating weapons in his arsenal.

Then lowered his head.

Eight

Roxi was not inexperienced. She'd been kissed hundreds of times before. Thousands. But never had the mere touch of a man's lips against hers caused her world to tilt on its axis.

Amazingly, it was just like she'd dreamed. His mouth was firm and hot and outrageously clever, just skimming her lips, drawing forth a ragged sigh, before moving on.

His warm breath fanned her cheek. Her temple. Her other cheek.

"Sloan." Her voice sounded far away, as if it were coming from the bottom of the sea.

"What, sugar?" He nipped at her bottom lip, just hard enough to make her shiver.

"Kiss me."

"I am." He soothed the tender flesh with the tip of his tongue. "Do you have any idea how long I've been wanting to do this?"

"All of thirty minutes?" She realized she'd totally lost track of the time since arriving at the restaurant.

"Longer than that."

"An hour, then." Her breath was clogging in her lungs. Which was ridiculous, since he hadn't even properly kissed her yet.

"Longer." His tongue slid silkily between her parted lips, tangling with hers, engaging it in a slow, sensual dance.

"That's impossible."

"Nothing's impossible." His mouth skimmed down her throat, across her collarbone. At the same time his hand glided tantalizingly up her leg. "When you're talking about magic."

Her skin felt hot. Her dress, suddenly too confining.

"I fell in love with Morganna back when I was in film school at USC," he said conversationally as his fingers traced seductive figure eights on the inside of her thigh.

"If I'd known she actually existed, I would've dropped out and hightailed it down to Louisiana and proposed."

"It would've been a wasted trip," she managed in a ragged voice choked with need. How did he do it? His stroking touch was making her nipples ache and her clit pulse, yet he was chatting away as if they were having an ordinary dinner date conversation.

"You sure of that, are you?" His Georgia drawl had thickened to that of whiskey-drenched bread pudding. Roxi could've eaten him up with a spoon.

She closed her legs, capturing that roving hand between them. "As sure as I'm sitting here talking with you."

Trying to talk when what she wanted to do was strip off her dress, and climb into his lap, and have him take her aching breasts in his mouth and . . .

"Not that I'd want to go braggin' on myself or anything," he was saying as a red haze shimmered over her mind and her blood boiled and thickened in her veins. "But I've been told that I can be irresistibly charming." Those treacherous fingers crept higher. "When I put my mind to it."

"I've not a single doubt of that." She gasped when he pinched the flesh at the inside of her thigh, hard enough to leave a bruise.

At the same time her body arched toward his wicked hand. Wanting.

No, dammit, *needing* more.

"But back when you were sitting around your dorm room, lusting after a comic book witch, I was a mere girl of fifteen."

A virgin who, despite all those erotic novels she'd hidden beneath her mattress, had no earthly idea that someday she'd actually meet a man who could have her on the verge of orgasm with such a tantalizing, feathery touch.

"And since even down in the swamp we girls didn't marry at fifteen, Daddy and *Maman* never would've allowed me to accept your proposal."

"Fifteen might have been a bit young," he allowed. "Though I'll bet you were hot even back then."

She nearly screamed when his hand, mere inches from her clit, which had begun to burn with need, reversed direction.

"Fortunately for us," he continued, "that six-year age gap doesn't make a difference anymore."

His fingers were now massaging the back of her knee, which she'd never realized was an erogenous zone.

Roxi heard a ragged whimper, only to belatedly realize that it'd been ripped from between her own suddenly parched lips.

She drew in a breath to steady her breathing. "I think it's that time of the evening where we set some ground rules."

He leaned forward again. Touched his mouth to hers. "I've never been all that fond of rules."

"Neither am I." The kiss was light. Almost tender. But it still had her lips tingling. Along with the rest of her. "But they do help keep things civilized."

"That may be. But I have to tell you, sugar, I'm not feeling all that civilized right now."

He was looking at her as if he'd like strip her naked, drag her off to his cave, and ravish her. Once again she considered how cavelike this cellar actually was.

She wondered if that thought had occurred to him when he'd made the reservation. Wondered if he realized that if he actually dared to try to take her right here, right now, she'd help him.

"There's something you need to know before this goes any further."

He lifted a dark brow. His hand, which had been moving back up her leg, paused.

"I'm not in the market for marriage," she said.

A smile quirked. Wicked laughter sparkled in his green eyes like sunshine on a tropical lagoon. "I believe that's my line."

"It may be." She sighed prettily. "But believe me, *cher,* I've heard those words before. Yet, invariably things between a man and a woman get complicated. Especially once sex gets added into the mix."

"Are you telling me you're not in the market for sex, either?"

She tilted her head. Studied him. It would be a little hard to claim that now. Without seeming like the world's worst prick-tease, but she had to ask. "Would if make a difference if I wasn't?"

"Like you said, sex always makes a difference."

He retrieved his hand, took a long drink of water, and eyed her thoughtfully over the rim of the crystal goblet.

"But I've moved beyond thinking with my glands. At least I thought I had until you climbed out of that limo. You are the most stunning woman I've seen in I don't know how long, you smell fabulous, and"—his appraising gaze skimmed over her—"until you decided to have this rules discussion, I was about ten seconds away from biting your thigh. And that was just for starters.

"But even if we back away from what we're both feeling, I'd honestly like to hear your take on Morganna. Maybe get some background on this witch business you've got going."

"Hex Appeal."

"That's it." When he smiled again, she had to restrain herself from nipping at his square, manly chin.

"The thing is," she said, trying to keep her mind on what she needed to say, "as much as I like you, *cher,* inevitably relationships get fucked up."

"Maybe you've just gotten involved with the wrong men."

"That's been true enough. On occasion."

God, could she screw things up any more? She'd come here tonight prepared to go to bed with him. There was nothing wrong, to her mind, about wanting to scratch an itch without having to deal with the time and energy of a committed relationship. So why in hell was she insisting on talking it to death when what they should be doing was fucking each other's brains out?

"But it wouldn't matter if you were Prince Charming in the flesh and the sex between us was gold medal, world class—"

"Which it's going to be," he promised with sublime self-confidence.

She couldn't argue that. The sexual vibrations between them were so strong she was surprised this entire building wasn't in meltdown.

"All the more reason to agree to call a halt afterwards. Before we get to that pissed-off point."

"So, are you saying you're only into one-night stands?"

"Of course not. I mean, I've nothing against them, and they can certainly be pleasant—"

"If we end tonight with you even thinking the word *pleasant*, I sure as hell won't have done my job."

She felt herself shudder. Knew he'd seen the involuntary response by the satisfied gleam in his gaze.

"What I meant," she said, as his hands cupped her breasts and began plumping her nipples, "was I believe they can be . . . very . . . oh God . . . empowering."

"You know, I'd applaud that idea." He tugged the dress down, exposing the black lace bustier she'd bought this morning with him in mind. "But my hands just happen to be a little busy at the moment."

As if to back up his words, he caught one erect nipple between his thumb and index finger and squeezed. Hard. She gasped at the stab of pain/pleasure, but rather than back away from the stinging touch, she arched her back, inviting more.

Much, much more.

"The waiter," she remembered reluctantly.

"Isn't going to come down here unless I call him." He bent his head and soothed the tingling flesh with his tongue.

Her hands felt inordinately heavy as they lifted to comb through his hair. "You planned this." Her head fell back. "All along."

Roxi wondered if Emma had known about Sloan's intentions.

"Let's just say I was hopeful." He drew the nipple into his mouth with a deep, wet suction that caused her pulse to beat painfully in that hot and liquid place between her thighs. "I'm also going to tell you, darlin', that female empowerment aside, one night with your sweet body isn't going to be nearly enough."

She had the same feeling. "That's why I have my three-date rule," she gasped as his teeth closed down on the flesh his tongue had tormented.

His breath was a hot breeze against her breast as he sighed. And drew his head back.

"I'm getting the feeling this isn't about that witchy Rule of Three that states three times what thou givest returns to thee."

She was surprised he knew about that, then remembered she was here tonight because he really had read the Morganna books. "No, not that one." Though she not only believed it, but practiced it.

"Nor the usual female one about putting off sex until the third date."

He was now openly frustrated. Roxi suspected he wasn't accustomed to a woman setting the rules. Especially when it came to sex.

"Actually, it's just the opposite. I never go out with a man after the third date."

"Seems that would be a bit limiting."

"Perhaps." And one problem she was just discovering was that she couldn't imagine wanting any limits where Sloan Hawthorne was concerned. "But the problem is that after three dates it's possible that someone's going to start feeling something—"

"I'm feeling something already." He leaned back in the wooden chair and spread his legs, revealing the thick weight of his erection thrusting against the zippered placket of his slacks.

"Come here." His patted his knee, his green eyes glittering with a masculine sexual challenge.

Nine

Roxi lifted her chin. "I'm not a dog you can call whenever you want attention."

A rough, harsh laugh burst out of him. "Sweetheart, that's one word that no one would ever use to describe you. But, you know, now that you mention it, tonight you're going to play my sweet, obedient pet."

"You make it sound as if I have nothing to say about it."

"So far, you've been setting all the rules," he reminded her mildly. "But here's one from my side of the negotiating table. If we're only going to have three fuck dates, tonight's will be on my terms." His penetrating gaze narrowed, burning into hers. "My rules."

She'd never been into submission. Which was, she admitted, why she'd also chosen men who were more willing to be led. Men who were, well, malleable. Controllable.

There was nothing the least bit malleable about Sloan Hawthorne. On the contrary, he was suddenly revealing a dark and dangerous side Roxi reluctantly found wickedly exciting.

"So much for Southern charm," she murmured.

He rubbed his jaw. "Now see, it's the accent that throws

people off. Some people hear my Georgia drawl and mistakenly believe I'm a pushover.

"If you're looking to hook up with some mealymouthed, sweet-talkin', roll over and pee on himself Ashley Wilkes type, you've got the wrong fucking man."

The drawl hardened, like steel wrapped in black velvet. "But if you're lookin' to explore the dark side of your dreams, well, I'm your man."

Her body responded to that suggestion, becoming more aroused, even as she struggled to maintain some vestige of control.

"What makes you think I've been even having that sort of dream?"

"Of course you have," he said with an arrogance that would have annoyed her had it been any other man. "Same as I have."

"Emma didn't mention you were psychic."

"I've never claimed to be. But something happened when you got out of that car tonight. I recognized you, same as you recognized me. We've already done it in our sleep. Lots of times and lots of ways. Seems we may as well see what it feels like with our eyes wide open . . .

"I'm going to take you, sugar. I'm going to make you beg. And then I'm going to make you scream. And you're going to love it.

"Now." He patted his thighs again. "Come here."

His words—his dark and erotic threats—had her drenched. Telling herself that she really wasn't giving in, that it wasn't really surrender if she ended up getting what she wanted—a mind-blowing orgasm—she stood up and started to straddle his thighs.

He shifted her so she was sitting sideways on his lap, her legs dangling over his. "You put that sweet hot pussy against my groin right now and there's no way I'm going to be able to control myself."

He cradled her head against his shoulder and slid his hand

beneath her skirt. Since he'd been gentle with her so far, she sucked in a harsh breath as his short square nails scraped a stinging path up the inside of her thighs.

"You like that?"

"Yes." It was half sigh, half moan.

"It's just the beginning." He rubbed a fingertip against the crotch of her silk panties. "You're wet." His exploring touch slipped beneath the elastic band. "And hot." He combed his fingers through the triangle of curls as if he owned them. "Is that for me, sugar?"

She flinched as that treacherous touch brushed against her clit. "What do you think?"

"I think you're the most responsive woman I've ever met. Even more than I'd imagined."

As if to prove his point, he skimmed a thumb over her clit and drew a ragged moan from between her lips.

"You are so slick." She sucked in a sharp breath as his finger penetrated her. "And ready for me."

He inserted a second finger. Opening her. Preparing her.

"That's it, darlin'." He murmured encouragement as her body clutched at him. His treacherous thumb pressed down on the tangled knot of hot nerves. "Let's see you ride." His fingers thrust into her. Withdrew. Then plunged harder. Deeper.

Her hips bucked. She drenched his hand as she rode him faster and faster, lifting her hips to press against his fingers, gyrating around his demanding touch, her hot, wet flesh making a harsh sucking sound on each upstroke.

When his fingers suddenly arched inside her, and pressed against a secret spot at the roof of her passage, she cried out, stiffened, and exploded over him.

"You definitely liked that."

It was not a question, but Roxi struggled to answer it anyway, which wasn't easy with the top of her head blown off. "Y-yes." She'd never believed the G-spot really existed. Sloan had just proved her wrong.

Her inner muscles were clenching at him like a hard, wet

fist. "Oh, God, yes." *Like* didn't even begin to describe the sensation.

"Good. Let's try it this way." When his wickedly clever thumb found her clit again, she climaxed with a smothered scream, stiffened, then collapsed like a rag doll, sprawled bonelessly on his lap.

The top of her dress was down around her waist, and somehow her skirt had ended up there, as well, as he'd hand-fucked her. Her panties were drenched and his powerful erection pressing against her bottom was driving her mad.

"Sloan." Her body moved restlessly, needing more. His fingers slid slickly out of her, leaving her cunt feeling abandoned. And empty. "Please." She would have, if physically possible, split herself open for him. The climaxes he'd given her had only whet her appetite for more. "I need you."

"I know." He stroked a hand down her hair. "And you'll have me. We'll both have each other. Later."

He tipped up her face with a fingertip beneath her chin. Touched his lips to hers, at first lightly, then deepened the kiss degree by devastating degree until she trembled and moaned against his mouth.

"Amazing," he murmured again.

She could feel his satisfied smile and felt a spark of irritation at herself for making this so easy for him. "You really are a wicked, wicked man."

"Absolutely." He slid her off his lap onto her feet. "And you're about to find out exactly how wicked I can be."

Wanting to take his time, he debated tugging the dress back over her breasts, which were so enticingly displayed by the spiderweb thin lace of that corset she was wearing, then decided to stay with the theme of the evening.

"As much as I really, really like that dress, right now I want you to take it off."

It was a test, and they both knew it. They also both knew that she wanted what was about to follow every bit as much as he did.

Which was why he wasn't all that surprised when she reached behind her back. The whispered sound of the zipper lowering sounded unreasonably loud in the hushed room.

The dress slid down her body, pooling in a black, silken puddle at her feet. She stood before him wearing that lacy corset that lifted her breasts, erotically offering them up for a man to look at. To touch. Taste.

She was—thank you, God!—also wearing a matching black garter belt, lace-topped stockings, and that drenched pair of panties that were so miniscule, he wondered why she bothered with them.

"You look," he said, drinking in the exquisite sight, "like you should be on some Victoria's Secret runway."

She folded her arms. Shook her head. "Why does it not surprise me you'd watch that show?"

"What can I say. Men are pigs." The show was admittedly one of his guilty pleasures. He figured most men in America would watch if their wives or girlfriends let them.

He started to instruct her to hold her hands away from her body, then decided to wait until they got upstairs before laying on the orders. Instead, he took hold of her hands and held them out for her.

Apparently she got the idea because when he let go, she continued to hold them out, inviting him to look.

He made a little twirling motion with his finger.

She turned around slowly, like a girl showing off a new party dress, though there was nothing girlish about either the outfit or the woman. He was also impressed as hell that she was able to move so smoothly on four-inch, fuck-me-big-boy stilettos.

"You look," he murmured, "good enough to eat."

She looked up at him through her lashes. It was, Sloan thought, the same look Scarlet had flashed at Rhett when she'd shown up wearing curtains and trying to coax him into giving her the money to pay the taxes on Tara.

"That's something to look forward to," she said.

A laugh burst out of him. He might have cast her in the role of his pet submissive tonight, but Roxi Dupree was definitely his equal. Intellectually, emotionally, and, he suspected, sexually.

"Absolutely." He scooped up the dress from the floor. "Let's go."

"Go?" He thought she paled a little at that idea.

"Upstairs. Where I intend to have my wicked way with you."

Ten

He wouldn't.

Wouldn't make her walk through an entire dining room of Savannahians in the barely-there underwear and high heels.

He wouldn't treat her like a sexual slave in front of people she'd run into on the street, in the grocery store, people who might even be Hex Appeal customers.

Would he?

No. Roxi blew out a short, head-clearing breath. Even if Emma hadn't vouched for him, she knew he wasn't into humiliation.

"There are a set of back stairs to your room, aren't there?"

For a long, suspended moment Sloan was very still. He rubbed his chin. Frowned down at her. "What if I said there wasn't?"

She smiled. Serenely. Confidently. "You'd be lying."

His lips twitched. Just a bit. "You think you know me that well?"

"Yes." Although it didn't make any sense, she did.

He gave her another of those long deep looks that made her think he could see all the way inside her heart. Her soul.

Then he put his hands on her shoulders and turned her around, pointing her toward the door.

"You'd be right," he allowed.

She let out a surprised squeal when he slapped her butt.

"Now, let's get going," he growled. "I've plans for you."

That thought, combined with the rough and hungry tone of voice, made her shiver.

At any other time she might have felt self-conscious as she walked up the secret stairway in front of him. The lingerie that had seemed so alluring in the dressing room of Sensual Essentials this morning could seem a bit sluttish while parading around in it in front of a fully dressed man, but the entire evening had taken on a somewhat dreamlike quality, just like those hot and sexy dreams she'd been having night after night, so it seemed perfectly normal.

The stone steps ended at a thick wooden door with heavy iron hinges. She glanced back over her shoulder to see what he intended to do to her now, and saw him take an old-fashioned key from the inside pocket of his jacket.

He reached past her, slipped the key into the brass lock, and turned the handle.

"Come in."

"Said the spider to the fly?" she asked.

His grin was quick and wicked. "Of course."

The walls of the room were draped in a deep burgundy silk, which wasn't unusual for older homes in Savannah. But it was the art hanging on the walls that captured the eye and stirred the senses.

While unabashedly erotic, the paintings did not feature the familiar airbrushed, vacuous girls from the pages of men's glossy magazines or porn flicks.

These women were strong, confident, powerful in their skin, whether dressed in dominatrix black leather and wielding a whip, or kneeling blindfolded on a stone floor—much like the one in the wine cellar, Roxi noticed—hands clasped behind her back, about to take an engorged penis, which was only a breath away, between her parted, glossy red lips.

Another painting featured a woman seated on a table, a

dark and swarthy man pressed against her, fastening a pair of handcuffs around the wrists he was holding behind her back.

"Well." Having to remind herself to breathe, Roxi exhaled. "We're definitely not at the Hyatt, Toto."

He chuckled as he tossed her dress over the back of a chair covered in a dark brocade. It was only when Roxi looked closer that she noticed the pattern was taken from Japanese Netsuke woodcuts depicting a dizzying variety of sexual positions. "Good guess."

"Am I allowed to look at them?" Or were they, she wondered, going to get straight down to business?

"That's what they're here for."

He took off his jacket, yanked the tie off, slipped the onyx links out of his cuffs and put them in a ceramic box shaped like one of Georgia O'Keefe's flower pictures, which, of course, everyone, even people who knew nothing about art, understood immediately were meant to depict vulvas.

"Would you like something to drink?"

"No, thank you." Her earlier orgasms, along with anticipation and the blatant eroticism of her surroundings, already had Roxi drunk with feeling. She didn't want to risk adding alcohol to the mix.

He unbuttoned the top two buttons of his shirt, poured a glass of brandy for himself, then leaned against the desk, legs crossed at the ankles. She could feel him watching her.

"It's quite a remarkable collection." And extensive. She glanced down at the ivory chess set on the table and realized that the depictions of the ancient gods were anatomically correct.

"Thank you."

Surprised, she glanced back at him. "You own them?"

"I've collected them over the years. And yes, to answer your next question, this is my suite."

"Did you bring your little friends up here back when you were celebrating your birthday?"

"No, because at the time it was merely an inn and restaurant with a rather interesting past."

"As a whorehouse."

"You make it sound so shoddy," he chided. "But yes, sex was for sale here. As it was in other places. Swansea was just"—he trailed a hand over the back of the chair—"a sumptuous cut above the rest.

"When my first film hit it big a few years ago, I had some funds to invest. Since I'm a Savannahian at heart, when the building came on the market I bought it, dumped a bundle into restoring it to its former glory, with some admittedly modern touches like soundproofing the rooms and some state-of-the-art video equipment, and turned it into a private club.

"And yes, I also returned the focus to eroticism. But if money is being exchanged between consenting adults, business is taken care of before anyone arrives at the door."

"I didn't read anything about you owning a place like this."

"That's because the deed's in the name of a real estate development company I founded with friends. And my managing partners, who take care of the day-to-day running of the premises, are very discreet, which is a must given our clientele."

"I suppose it would rock the social order if people found out about all the rich, lecherous old movers and shakers swinging with their young mistresses on the chandeliers," she said dryly.

"Would it surprise you to know that approximately one third of our memberships are owned by women? And that I'm told that many of our guests are married couples who enjoy having a place away from home where they can indulge their fantasies without worrying about mothers-in-law calling or children walking into the bedroom at inopportune times?"

"Sort of like a sexual Disneyland for consenting adults."

"Everyone needs a hobby." Amusement touched his eyes. "I prefer to think of Swansea as a five-star date destination."

"Well, it's definitely a level above pizza and a chick flick," Roxi said. "You must come to town often."

The door to the bedroom was open, revealing a lake-sized,

hand-carved bed that claimed the center of the room. She was surprised as something twisted inside her. Something that felt uncomfortably like jealousy.

"Apparently not as often as I should." He sipped the brandy. "An oversight I'll have to correct."

"You're forgetting my three date rule."

"Sweetheart, I doubt there's anything I could forget about you."

"Then you're ignoring it?"

"Let's just table the topic for now." He put his glass down on a mahogany desk next to a brocade chair and wagged a finger. "Enough chitchat. Come stand in front of me and let me look at you."

This time she didn't argue. Just crossed the room and stood, the toes of her spindly black heels touching the front of his shoes as she waited for what would happen next.

"Good girl."

It was more than a little chauvinistic. Strangely, at this moment, she didn't care.

He skimmed his fingertips down her throat with tantalizing slowness, his touch leaving a trail of sparks.

His stroking fingers moved over the bodice of the corset. "Take this off."

Gladly, given that it had been hours since she'd been able to take a full breath.

Roxi reached behind her back and worked the hook and eye fasteners open, one by one. Which wasn't easy. She would have appreciated some help, had actually anticipated him taking it off her when she'd handed over her Mastercard this morning, but apparently for now, anyway, she was on her own.

She might be playing submissive, but that didn't mean she had to play dead. When the last hook was unfastened, she held the corset against her chest with one hand. Her eyes lifted to his. And held.

She waited.

He waited.

When she took her hand way, it fell to the floor.

"Nice." He took her breasts in his hands, as he had down-stairs in the cellar. "A perfect handful."

Ha! So much for worrying about not owning a pair of sili-cone D-cup boobs.

He frowned when he took in the red indentations left by the corset boning. "As sexy as that little bit of froufrou is, you won't wear it again when you're with me," he said.

"Not tonight," she agreed. "But we're on Cinderella time, *cher*. After midnight, you don't get to call the shots."

"Emma hinted you might not be the type of woman I'm ac-customed to." He traced his fingers over the faint red lines. "She's right." Roxi sucked in her stomach as he pressed an open kiss against the skin his fingers, and his eyes, had already warmed. "I don't want anything marring this tender flesh."

He picked up the glass again. Took another sip of the brandy. "Now take off those panties."

She slipped her fingers beneath the elastic riding low on her hips, did a little shimmy, and sent them sliding down her legs.

Then stepped out of them and stood there, hands behind her back, breasts thrust out, inviting his study.

"Incredible," he murmured, seemingly more to himself than to her.

He framed her waist with his broad, long-fingered hands. Expecting him to kiss her, she tilted her head and allowed her eyelids to drift closed.

When he lifted her off her feet, her eyes flew open.

He sat her on the desk. Then used his knee to coax her stocking-clad legs apart.

"I want to see you."

She knew exactly what he meant. But because she didn't want to hand him everything he wanted on a silver platter, she pretended otherwise. "I'm right here, *cher*. Nearly naked."

"Good try." He lifted the heavy glass in a salute. "I want to see those lower lips that proved so sensitive earlier this evening. And then I want you to make yourself come."

She felt the blood rush into her cheeks. Her breasts. Across her stomach, spreading like a fever.

"I don't think I can."

"Of course you can," he said reasonably. "Unless you expect me to believe a woman who's reached the ripe age of twenty-five, a woman of your intense passions, has never masturbated?"

"Of course I have."

In fact, she'd brought herself off just the other night, while reading much this same scene in *The Story of O*, when Sir Stephen had brutally punished his new slave for not doing what Sloan was instructing her to do.

Which was scary, thinking of how she was alone here in this sex suite with a man she didn't know. While she might be intrigued by the occasional kink, she definitely wasn't into pain or humiliation.

He cupped the snifter between his palms and took another drink, eyeing her over the rim of the glass. "If it eases your mind, I'm not into hurting women."

"I know that." His aura might be blazing red, but she didn't detect a bit of danger. While she wasn't in the habit of masturbating in front of a partner, this wouldn't be the first time. But she was suddenly feeing uncharacteristically self-conscious. "I just need a minute."

"Take your time." He smiled, showing her that while the circumstances might seem similar, he was nothing like the brutal Sir Stephen. "I'm enjoying the view."

She touched her hand between her legs, in that same place it had been again this morning when she'd awakened. Then she flinched. It was still slick from her orgasms, swollen and painfully hypersensitive from the earlier deep thrusts of his fingers.

"That's it."

She lifted her head and met his eyes, which had darkened to a deep emerald flame and were watching her every movement.

"Now open yourself wider." His dark voice wrapped around her like velvet bonds. "Let me see the lovely rose bloom."

She did as instructed, parting her swollen lower lips, like separating the petals of the rose he'd suggested.

"Does that feel good?"

"A bit."

"Does it hurt?"

"Not too badly." It was getting better. Closing her eyes, she slipped into a warm, sensual fog of need.

"Tell me exactly how it feels."

"Lonely."

He chuckled. "We'll take care of that soon enough." She heard something rustle, but unwilling to risk losing the fantasy, didn't open her eyes. "Now lift that tender little bud."

It pulsed like a hot little heart against her fingertips as she obeyed.

"That's excellent."

His voice sounded as if it was coming from far away. Like right after Katrina, when a post-traumatic stress therapist hypnotized her to help her overcome the nightmares that had plagued her. The difference was, the therapist's goal had been to soothe her. Sloan's voice was doing exactly the opposite.

"Now let me see you make yourself come."

By this point, she was so turned on he couldn't have stopped her. Leaning back on her elbows, she lasciviously rubbed her fingers over her soaking clit, driving herself closer and closer to the brink.

She was panting, one hand on a tingling nipple which had turned diamond hard, the other between her legs, two fingers pumping fast and deep.

She heard herself begin to moan, and couldn't care, so caught up was she in her desperate need for release.

"That's it, baby," Sloan encouraged on a ragged groan that

had her looking up at him through slit lids. He'd left the chair and was standing over her, naked and gloriously erect.

All it took was the sight of those long dark fingers curled around his sheathed, rampant penis to push Roxi over the edge.

She came with a shudder and a sound that was half cry, half sob.

But before she could come down, while she was still scattered into a million little pieces, she felt his hands against her trembling thighs and he was pushing her legs apart.

"More."

"I can't."

"Want to bet?"

She cried out when his hot and hungry mouth clamped down on her painfully sensitive clit.

"Oh, please." Her hips bucked. "Sloan." She'd fallen back onto the desk and was writhing beneath the mouth that was sucking on the fiery nub. "It's too . . . I can't . . ."

His fingers dug into her thighs, pinning her to the glossy wooden surface as he continued to feast, devouring her with lips and teeth and tongue.

Just when she was sure she couldn't endure another moment, another orgasm ripped through her, more intense than any she'd ever experienced.

"Again," he said over her scream, not giving her a second to recover before driving her up the steep peak again, even higher this time, to where the air was thin and her eyes went darkly blind.

The entire world spun away. There was only the painful pleasure between her legs, the thrust of his tongue plunging in and out, and in and out, his teeth tugging on her swollen, throbbing clit, creating a pleasure so acute she could only scream and plead, in a voice that sounded nothing like her own, for him to stop. To never stop.

Her bare hips were slapping the desktop in a way she knew

on some distant level would leave bruises. She was moaning. Sobbing. Cursing, then begging in a way she never would have imagined she, a sexually liberated woman of the twenty-first century, would ever do.

And then she was coming in a burst of heat and light, a super-nova of a climax that had her shattering into a thousand brilliant pieces.

And even then, even as her screams were still reverberating in the silk-draped room, he wasn't ready to let her come down.

"My turn," he said, lifting her limp and drained body off the desk. Holding her up by her sore bottom, he plunged into her, all the way to the hilt.

Somehow, she managed to lock her legs around his waist as he carried her into the adjoining bedroom, working her back and forth from the root of his penis to the tip, her soaked pubic curls slamming hard against his groin.

Once. Twice. A third time.

She heard the groan rumbling deep in his sweat-slicked chest. Felt the shudder deep in his loins.

The bed was a four-poster, draped in the same wine silk as the walls. Bracing her against one of the posts, he thrust his hips one last time, his cock surging deep, all the way to her womb, a feral shout of release ripping from his throat as he came with a bone-racking shudder, triggering yet another deeper, longer climax that rolled over her like a tidal wave.

"Oh my God," she gasped. "I think you've killed us."

"You'll be fine." He dragged her down, his hot and heavy body pressing her deep into the mattress. "Better than fine." He kissed her, a long, deep kiss she could feel all the way to her toes. "You're fuckin' fabulous."

He pulled out of her, rolled over, and wrapped her in his arms, holding her while the tremors subsided and her breathing began to return to something resembling normal.

"Fuckin' fabulous," he repeated against her throat. "And as good as that was, things are about to get a whole lot better."

Roxi was too spent to argue with that outrageously confident statement. Which was just as well. Because, she was to discover, as the waxing white moon moved across the night sky, Sloan Hawthorne was definitely not a man given to exaggeration.

Eleven

Having grown up enjoying the tales of pirates using the underground tunnels throughout Savannah to smuggle their stolen booty, Sloan found Hex Appeal, located on the city's Riverwalk, to be an absolute treasure trove.

The small space was packed from gleaming wood floor to rafters with a dizzying array of New Age stuff. Claiming the center of the bay window that extended out onto the cobblestone sidewalk was what appeared to a maypole, festooned in colorful ribbons, surrounded by earthenware bowls of crystals that captured the spring sunlight and bounced rainbows around the room.

Colorful glass shelves lined two of the walls and were crammed with bottles of herbs, candles, and figurines of various gods and goddesses he couldn't begin to recognize. An overstuffed couch covered with gaily patterned pillows claimed the back wall, and was flanked by two comfortable chairs. A tea set and wicker baskets of what appeared to be home-baked cookies sat on a small brass table, inviting shoppers to linger, while a pretty little sign above the sofa gently warned that unaccompanied children would be turned into toads—or given a free kitten.

The crush of customers kept Roxi from hearing the brass

bell that had announced his arrival, allowing him to watch her undetected from the shadow of a display of handmade straw brooms in the corner.

Unlike the sexy witch he'd spent the night with, she was surprisingly, briskly efficient. But she certainly hadn't traded efficiency for the personal touch. On the contrary, proving herself a deft juggler, she somehow managed to pitch the eclectic merchandise, answer questions, ring up the flood of sales, and package the purchases in hot pink Hex Appeal shopping bags.

She was, as he'd already decided long before he'd dropped her back at her house a little after dawn, spectacular. And, although she might not know it yet, she was his. Not just for last night or today, but forever.

Reminding himself of Emma's cautionary words, which had been underscored by Roxi's own ridiculous three date rule, Sloan decided to keep his intentions to himself. For now.

If the lady wanted to believe their relationship was all about sex, he wasn't going to dissuade her. At least not until he'd managed to work his way around, over, or through those emotional barricades she'd erected around her heart.

As if sensing his thoughts, she glanced up. And amazingly, after all they'd shared last night, blushed.

He found the tinge of pink brightening her cheeks endearing. Found her actually dropping a pewter unicorn encouraging. She could deny it all she wanted, but he'd gotten to her. The same as she had to him.

"Well, this is a surprise," she said as she wrapped some pink tissue paper around a fist-sized piece of quartz.

He crossed to the counter. "I don't suppose you'd believe I was in the neighborhood."

She shrugged, shoulders bared by a snug pink knit halter top. "And just happened to be in the market for a love spell?"

"That's not such a bad idea." Not that he believed in such things, but so long as she did, maybe that might be the means to achieve his ends. He dipped his hand into a bowl of small tumbled stones. "I actually came in to get some perfume blended for my mother—she has a birthday coming up—but a love spell would be cool, too. What would you suggest?"

"Roxanne." A woman wearing a flowing purple tunic and ankle-length skirt shoved him out of the way. "You haven't put out any *cannariculi*."

"Those cookies need honey for drizzling and dipping, which gets messy in the store," Roxi said mildly. "Which is why I chose oatmeal. Which," she tacked on over the woman's snort, "are also a traditional Beltane food."

"Perhaps where you come from," the harridan sniffed.

"I like oatmeal," Sloan said. Then, to prove a point, he took one from the tiered plate she'd put by the register with a calligraphic little note that read: Help yourself.

"Hmmm," he said around a mouthful of oatmeal and golden raisins, "delicious."

The woman looked up at him as if noticing him for the first time, then shrieked. "You are Sloan Hawthorne."

"That's me," he agreed. "And you are?"

"Martha Corey." She glared up at him. Poked him in the chest. "A name you should know well."

"I'm sorry." Sloan exchanged a glance over the top of her head with Roxi, who shook her head and rolled her eyes. "I'm afraid it's not ringing a bell." He flashed her a winning smile. "Do our families know each other?"

"You might say that. In another life."

"I see," Sloan said, not seeing anything at all. They were, however, beginning to draw a crowd.

The woman turned toward Roxi. "This man is a Hawthorne."

"I know," Roxi replied, appearing as puzzled as Sloan himself was.

"I wager he's changed it!" The way she was pointing at him, Sloan expected her to next say, *And your little dog, too!* "His name!"

Ah, hell. He'd known he was going to have to tell her, but hadn't wanted it to come out like this.

"It was undoubtedly *Hathorne*," Martha told Roxi, as well as the customers who were now standing around watching the show. "The judge from the witch trials," she shrieked again, when Roxi's only response to that allegation was a blank look.

Roxi looked up at Sloan, clearly startled by the news, as he'd known she would be after she hadn't made the connection when they'd been discussing their heritage last night. He'd been going to tell her. Really.

"*Those* Puritans?" she asked.

"I'm afraid so."

"Well." She blew out a breath. "You're just full of surprises, aren't you?"

"At least you can't say I've been boring."

"That's true enough."

"How about you come to lunch with me and we can discuss it."

"I'm busy. This is a holiday weekend for us and—"

"Oh, for the Goddess's sake." A tall, gorgeous woman with braided and beaded black hair, smooth brown skin, and a body that could've walked off a *Playboy* centerfold spread came up to them. "You can be such a workaholic. Hello. I take it you're the famous Sloan Hawthorne."

"I don't know about famous, but that's my name," he said.

"I'm Jaira Guinard." She held out a beringed hand. "But in case Roxi proves herself to be an idiot and turns you down again, you can call me available," she said with the sugar-coated, flirtatious female aggression that was uniquely Southern. Couldn't his own mother, happily married for forty years, charm with the best of them?

He laughed, despite the daggers being shot his way from the old woman's narrowed blue eyes. "I'll keep that in mind."

"You do that, sugar." Jaira skimmed a blood red talon down the front of his shirt. "And if you need a really hot group to sing for your soundtrack, you'll be wanting to hear the Papa Legba Voodoo Priestesses."

"Would you happen to be one of those priestesses?"

"Why, yes." She fluttered artificial lashes so thick and long Sloan was amazed she could keep her eyes open. "As a matter of fact, I am."

"The group's wonderful," Roxi said. "I don't know why I didn't think to recommend them while we were having dinner last night."

"That's all right, darlin'," Jaira said silkily, her gaze going to the little love bite on Roxi's neck. "I suspect you and Sloan got so caught up in other business, you simply forgot."

"That's pretty much what happened," Roxi agreed. "Now, although it's lovely to see you, Sloan, if you'll just give me some of your mother's attributes, we'll get started on her scent. But right now, if you don't mind, as you can see we're very busy—"

"Oh, don't be such a stick in the mud," Jaira scolded. "Let the man feed you, Roxi. I'll hold down the fort here."

Roxi glanced around. Sloan was encouraged when she was clearly torn. "Go," one of the customers said.

"Go," a second echoed.

A moment later the entire store, all except his nemesis, was chanting, "Go, go, go."

"All right!" She was laughing as her hands flew up. "Thirty minutes," she told Sloan. "No more." She splayed her hands on her hips, which pulled the halter top across her breasts.

"It's a date."

"The second one," she reminded him.

"Actually, it's only the first," he said as they left the store for the cobblestone sidewalk crowded with tourists.

"I must have made quite an impression if you've already forgotten last night," she complained.

"I haven't forgotten a thing about last night." He skimmed a finger over a faint bruise on her collarbone. "Sorry about this." He vaguely recalled biting her the second—or had it been the third?—time he'd come.

"Don't apologize. I enjoyed it. A lot."

"So did I. In fact, if it *had* been a date, it would've been the best of my life. But it wasn't a date."

"Excuse me? I just happened to be wearing a dress that maxed out my credit card—which, by the way, I don't do for every guy who asks me out—underwear that cost more than my monthly power bill, and my best fuck-me heels. We had a candlelight dinner and hot monkey sex afterwards. Followed by dessert and champagne, which you ended up eating and drinking off me."

"I seem to recall you doing some fingerpainting with the fudge sauce yourself," he said, then wished he hadn't thought of that just now, being that he really didn't want to have to walk all the way down to the park with a boner the size of Texas.

"Exactly. So, if dinner, sex, and playing paint the penis with fudge sauce wasn't a date, I'd like to know what it was."

"A business meeting."

"Wow. It's true!" She looked up at him with exaggeratedly wide eyes. "Y'all really do things differently in California. If you call last night a business meeting, your Hollywood movie conferences must be full out orgies."

"We talked about Morganna over dinner." He skimmed a hand beneath the long glossy slide of hair, pleased with her faint tremor. Oh yes, they weren't finished yet. Not by a long shot. "So, technically it was a consultation."

"Good try. But it was a date." They'd already passed three restaurants which were starting to fill up with lunch crowds. "Do you have some place in mind? Other than Six Flags over Sex City? Because as enticing as the idea may be, I really don't have time for a nooner."

"I suspected that might unfortunately be the case. Though, I have to tell you, sweetheart, that shirt is damn tempting."

She glanced down at the script running across her chest that suggested, "Get a Taste of Religion—Lick a Witch."

"You've already done that."

"True. Which is why I intend to go back for seconds. Meanwhile, how does a picnic sound?"

"Lovely. But again . . ." She cast a warning glance down at her watch.

"I had the chef prepare a picnic. I thought we'd eat at the park." Which was less than a five-minute walk away at the end of the Riverwalk.

"You're got yourself a date."

He skimmed a finger down the slope of her nose. "Consultation."

"Date," she corrected firmly.

He'd always found that women were suckers for romance. Fortunately, having always been a sucker for women, it was easy to give them what they wanted. Which, in turn, tended to make them generous in return.

He'd had Roxi Dupree's body and it was everything he'd dreamed of, and more. Now he had to capture her heart. Which should've been a piece of cake.

Definitive word there, *should've*.

Unfortunately, whatever fickle fates or gods had decided he belonged with this woman must've had one helluva sense of humor because apparently Emma hadn't been kidding.

The luscious witch was definitely a hit and run artist.

It wasn't going to be that easy to convince her to see the light. As he retrieved the wicker basket from the backseat of the rental car parked across the street, Sloan tried to remind himself that he'd never truly appreciated things that came too easily.

Twelve

"I should've told you about my ancestor before that old woman had a chance to out me," he said as they sat on a bench beneath a leafy green tree on the banks of the river at the end of the short street.

"You did, in a way," she said with a shrug. "I mean, you did mention the Puritans. I just never put two and two together. I think the only reason Martha did was because she's one of those militant hard-liners who spends much of her life living in the past, suffering from ancient grievances. She took her witch name after one of the women who were hung on Gallow's Hill."

"Ouch. I can see where my ancestry might be a sore subject."

"Oh, she already hated you because of Morganna. She doesn't feel the Mistress of the Dark is a proper representation of the Craft."

"What do you think?"

She took a bite of shrimp salad on a buttery croissant that nearly melted in her mouth. "I think if I had more than three dates with you, I'd end up being the size of that tanker," she said, nodding toward the huge cargo ship making its way up the river just a few yards away.

"You'd be perfect whatever size you were."

"Flatterer."

"It's true." He took a bite of his huge roast beef sandwich. "Besides, we'll work it off."

"I'm going to hold you to that."

"I hope you do." He considered kissing her, then decided that if he began, he wouldn't be able to stop, and being that they were in a public park, that probably wasn't the hottest idea he'd ever had. "By the way, did you happen to notice that that Corey woman filched a candle?"

"A candle and a vial of dragon's blood," Roxi said. "She's a kleptomaniac. Her niece always pays up at the end of the month."

"Maybe she's just smart. Getting someone else to pay for her witch supplies."

"That thought has occurred to me."

They continued eating in a surprisingly comfortable silence.

"So," she said, gesturing toward a nearby statue with a crunchy sweet potato French fry, "do you think she was really waving for her lover?"

The statue, portraying a woman in a simple dress waving a piece of cloth, with a collie by her side, represented one of Savannah's most endearing legends. The daughter of a lighthouse keeper on the nearby coastal island of Elba, Florence Martus, who'd become known as Waving Girl, had lived a quiet and uneventful life until one day she began communicating with sailors by waving a white handkerchief as they passed. At night, she'd wave a lantern, and it wasn't long before sailors around the world began to signal her back.

Over the decades she became a beacon of the city, daily offering a joyful welcome or fond farewell.

That story in itself would have been good enough for most cities. But Savannah, staying true to its colorful self, had chosen to add speculation that Florence had fallen in love with a sailor who'd promised to return, but had vanished into the ocean's vast horizon.

"I think it's a nice story," he said. "And perhaps it began that way. But while most women are probably willing to stick a relationship out for more than three dates, forty years seems like overkill. I suspect it's more likely she lived a lonely life and waving to the ships not only gave her a connection with someone besides her father and brother, but also gave her something meaningful to do, given how, if the thousands of letters addressed to Waving Girl she received are any indication, the sailors seemed grateful."

"I suppose. It's sad either way."

"Granted." He balled up the waxed paper and tossed it back into the wicker basket. "So, I guess you're not going to stand out at the airport waving off planes until I come back?"

"Sorry. I wouldn't hold my breath if I were you."

"I figured that'd be your answer. And I've decided what kind of spell I want."

She arched a brow.

"A binding spell."

She laughed. Reached out and ruffled his hair. "That's what you say now. Trust me, *cher*. That's one helluva powerful spell and not to be used casually. If I gave you the power to bind me to you, by this time next week you'd be so sick and tired of constantly having me around, you'd start hating me."

"Think so?"

"I know so."

He knew differently. But reminded himself that patience was supposed to be a virtue.

"So," he said, deciding it was time to change the subject, "remember that scene where Brianna uses her charmed sword to behead the evil gods of Hades?"

"Of course. It was the first time she ever went over to the dark side."

"You don't think audiences will have a problem with that? She is, after all, the 'good' twin."

"They were holding her sister hostage. Of course she'd save

her. I have seven sisters and brothers, and if anyone threatened them, I'd do whatever was in my power to save them.

"But you know, as much as I really like the books, pagans don't view light and dark, good and bad, the dualistic way Western society does. Western thought, being deeply rooted in the Christian view, tends to view dualism as a battle between the good, or light, versus evil, which is dark.

"While paganism is based on monism, where light and dark exist, but as polarities, two opposite, yet complementing aspects of a whole. So, in reality, Morganna and Brianna should be equal parts of the whole. If you want to stay true to the belief system. But," she said, "I can understand how that doesn't work well when you're telling it to an audience steeped in Western thought."

"Plus there's the little matter of Gavin Thomas having written the characters that way."

"Well, there is that," she agreed with a smile. "And what a unique concept. A moviemaker actually attempting to stay true to an author's vision."

"I try," he said modestly. Not mentioning that Thomas's witch wife had threatened to turn him into a toad if he didn't treat her husband's work—and witchcraft—with respect.

"That's one of the reasons I came to Savannah," she revealed. "After Katrina blew away the Every Body's Beautiful day spa and spell shop, since I had to rebuild anyway, I was looking to spread my wings. Savannah had always interested me because, like New Orleans, it's a city that embraces its dark, midnight side right along with its light. And, as I said, that balance is what the Craft is all about.

"This time, though, without Emma to handle the spa stuff, I decided to stick with the magic aspect, and the concept seems to be working. I suppose, if the box office for your Morganna movie comes even close to *The Last Pirate*, my business should get a nice a boost from all the moviegoers who leave the theater wanting to embrace their inner witch."

"I'm all for Morganna making buckets of bucks," he said. "But how many people do you believe are actually harboring an inner witch?"

"I believe everyone's born with the power of magic. It's just that not everyone learns how to use it."

"Now you remind me of Morganna again."

She stood up, folded her arms, and looked down at him. "Let me guess. Despite making this movie, you don't believe in witchcraft. Or magic."

"You're not talking about an illusionist making a seven-forty-seven disappear, are you?"

"No."

"Then, I guess I have to say no. I don't. But don't take it personally, sugar. I don't believe in the Easter Bunny or Santa Claus, either."

She didn't respond. Just gave him a long, steady look. He could practically see the wheels turning inside that gorgeous dark head, but had no idea what she was thinking.

He wondered idly if Gavin's wife was actually telling the truth about that toad thing. Thought about the sign on the wall in Hex Appeal.

Nah.

"What are you doing tonight?"

"I was hoping to spend it making love to you."

"It's customary to ask a woman for a date ahead of time. I have a thing tonight."

"A thing. Is that like a date? With some other guy?" Like that was going to happen.

"A date. But not exactly with another man. It's Beltane. You might know it as May Day."

"Ah." Comprehension belatedly sunk in. "So I guess you'll be doing some sort of ritual thing with your coven, or whatever you call it."

"Martha would call it a coven. As it happens, I'm a solitary witch. I'll be doing my ritual at home."

"May I come watch?"

"I would have thought you had enough of a show last night."

"I'm serious. I'll admit that I'm not a believer in what you call the Craft, but I'd really like to see how a witch celebrates a sacred festival."

"For research."

"No." He thought they ought to get this point perfectly clear. "Because I want to know you better. I want to try to understand what's important to you."

She gave him a narrowed, slit-eyed look. "That's probably a mistake. The more people know about one another, the more likely they are to get involved. And I've already told you I'm not into commitment stuff."

"Are you saying you don't want to know anything about me?"

She flushed again, just as she had back in her shop.

"No." She shook her head. Dragged her gaze out toward the river where another tanker was heading into the harbor. "I mean, sure. Of course I'm interested, *cher*. It's just that I . . .

"Dammit." She turned away and began marching back down the cobblestone roadway. "You're confusing me."

The admission, Sloane thought, was a start.

He let her get a little ahead of him, enjoying the sexy sway of her tight butt in those white cotton pants that stopped right below her knees. The back of which, he'd discovered last night, were directly, erotically, connected to her pretty pink clit.

Catching up with her in two long strides, he grabbed her arm, spun her against his chest, and little caring about the tourists crowding the sidewalk, kissed her, a long hard kiss that sent a jolt of heat shooting through them both.

"Static electricity," she murmured, sounding as staggered as he felt.

"That must be it." He opted against pointing out that he couldn't recall any science class teaching about receiving electrical shocks from cobblestones.

"Are you going to let me come with you tonight?"

She shook her head. Not in denial, but resignation. "You may as well."

"Thank you, darlin'."

He'd received more generous invitations over the years, but wasn't going to quibble. Leaning forward on the balls of his feet, he brushed a lighter, gentler kiss against her tightly set mouth, encouraged when her lips parted on a soft sigh.

They continued walking back to the shop, his arm around her shoulders, hers around his waist.

"Beltane," he said, "that's a fertility festival, right?"

"It celebrates the divine union of the Lord and Lady."

Sloan grinned. "Hot damn."

Thirteen

After she went back to work, Sloan researched Beltane online and discovered it was the one festival people had been most unwilling to give up, no matter how much the Church had fought against the holiday.

Which made sense, he thought, given that it was definitely the kinkiest of all the pagan holy days, revolving around lust and passion as the celebrants honored not just the mating of their goddess and her consort, but their own bodies and the male and female physical relationship, a necessity if they wanted the human race to continue.

In ancient times they'd burn fires on hilltops, couples would make love in freshly plowed fields to ensure the success of the crops, and any child resulting from this night was considered a chosen one. A blessing from the goddess.

A nice thought, Sloan thought, at the same time making sure he stocked up on enough condoms to ensure there wouldn't be any surprise blessings from this Beltane celebration.

The moon was a silver sickle, slicing through a deep purple sky. Fog was drifting in from the sea, obscuring the stars and wrapping the silent night in a soft, misty shawl of white. Thunder rumbled in the distance.

They were sitting outside, sipping red wine in her postage-stamp backyard which was surrounded by a tall green hedge that provided privacy.

She was filling in the bits and pieces of the Shabbat he'd learned about today.

"In Celtic society," Roxi explained, "not only did the woman own all the land and cattle, she also chose who she'd marry. The handfasting contract lasted a year. At the end of that time, if she or her husband were unhappy with each other, they'd just walk away."

"No harm, no foul," he said.

"Exactly." She nodded. "It was actually a very sensible system."

"This from a woman who'd insist on renewing every three days," he reminded her.

"Times were different then," she said mildly. "Relationships were all tied up with land and property and survival. Not to mention that being tied to the earth as they were, an agrarian society, there was so much more opportunity for powerful outside forces to rule your life."

"I know how it feels to have outside forces rule my life every time one of my movies has its opening weekend," he said.

"I believe it would have been a bit more serious."

"Hey, they're both about survival. If Morganna goes bust, I don't eat."

"At least not caviar and champagne," she said dryly. "My point is that Beltane would've been the one time a year when people could let loose and celebrate the future instead of dwelling on all the things that might have gone wrong in the past."

"And fuck like bunnies."

She dimpled prettily in the light from the candles she'd placed around the yard.

"I was going to say it was when they'd make wishes for the year ahead, because their lives would be forecast by what they saw at dawn the next morning. But that fucking thing works for me, too."

As they laughed together, her eyes warmed with something richer than lust. Perhaps he was only fooling himself, but Sloan didn't think so. Despite what she might think she believed, he knew that by inviting him here tonight, by allowing him to share in something so important to her, she was opening not just her body to him, but her heart, as well.

"You know when I said you reminded me of Morganna?"

"It would be difficult to forget. Being that it was only last night."

"I was wrong."

"Oh?" Her luscious lips turned down in a little moue.

He skimmed a hand down her hair, which she'd woven with a riot of fresh flowers that smelled like a night garden. "You're worlds above that fictional witch." He touched a palm to her silky smooth cheek. "In fact, I may just be beginning to believe in magic."

She smiled, openly pleased, and covered his hand for a moment with hers.

Although he had never witnessed a ceremony in real life, he'd read enough books and seen enough movies to recognize the casting of the sacred circle, the calling of the elements. In lieu of a maypole, she'd woven ribbons of traditional white and red together and had hung them from the branches of a sweet gum tree in the center of the yard. A CD of a Celtic harp played softly.

The wide sleeves of the red robe she was wearing slid down her arms as she lifted a silver chalice in a toast.

"Behold the chalice, symbol of the Goddess, the great Mother who brings fruitfulness and knowledge to all."

Putting the chalice onto the table, she lifted a knife, the handle formed into the shape of a Celtic crane, the blade glinting in the slanting moonlight. Although Sloan knew it was only his imagination, he could have sworn he saw a shimmering blue energy swirling around the sharp steel tip.

"Behold the Athame, symbol of the God, the all-powerful Father who brings energy and strength to all."

The distant storm was growing closer, lifting her hair, tossing it in a tangle around her face. Heat lightning shimmered behind churning dark clouds as she picked up the chalice again and slowly and deliberately lowered the Athame blade into the wine.

"Joined in holy union together, they bring new life to all."

Impossibly, the wine began to bubble, smoke pouring out of the chalice like the dry ice his mother used to put in the Halloween punch.

"Blessed be."

She took a sip of the wine, then held the chalice out to Sloan, who couldn't have resisted if his entire fortune—his life—depended on it.

The wine was warm, like deep red velvet against his tongue. After he'd taken a drink, he handed it back to Roxi. Instead of taking it from his hand, she placed her palms on top of his hands and together, with her leading the action, they poured the remainder of the wine onto the ground, which immediately swallowed it up.

Returning the chalice and knife to the table, she went through the rite of closing the circle, then turned toward Sloan.

With her eyes holding his, she lifted her hands to the silver brooch holding her cape together, unfastened it, and let it slide down her shoulders to the ground.

She was an enchantress. Circe. Lorelei. Morgan La Fey. Brigid, goddess of eternal fire. She was all the goddesses of all the ancient myths in one stunning package and he wanted her more than he'd ever wanted anything in his life.

Smiling a sorceress's smile she went up on her bare toes, splayed her fingers at the back his head, and pulled his lips down to hers.

Fourteen

Sloan heard the low, threatening rumble of thunder and couldn't tell if it was coming from the midnight dark sky or inside himself as he kissed her in a deep, tongue-thrusting, branding kiss.

He felt the four winds whipping her hair across both their faces, and although he knew it was as impossible as the blue light he'd thought he'd seen bubbling in that chalice earlier, he felt as if they'd been swept into a tempest and were being dragged across the night.

She tasted of sex. Of temptation. Of magic.

As the sky opened up in a hot, drenching rain, they dragged each other to the ground, rolling on the wet grass, greedy mouths devouring raw, painful breaths, hands tearing at his clothes.

The storm broke with a clap of thunder directly overhead that shook the earth beneath them. As Roxi ripped Sloan's shirt open, sending buttons flying across the garden, neither noticed.

Lightning forked across the sky; as he sat up and yanked the ruined shirt off, neither cared.

Her shaking hands struggled with his belt buckle, but she managed it, whipping it through the loops of his slacks. There was a clang of metal as it landed somewhere on the brick patio.

Bending over him, her face shielded by her thick fall of hair, she lowered the zipper then released his rampant erection from its confinement. It jutted from the whorl of dark hair, thick and long and heavy. And for tonight, it was hers.

She curled her fingers around the suede-smooth girth and began stroking him.

"Harder," he instructed through clenched teeth. Covering her hand with his, he tightened her grip and increased the strength as he began to pump their joined hands up and down, spreading the slick fluid from root to purple-hued tip.

"That's the way, sugar." Sloan couldn't remember the last time he'd shaken from need. "That's right." He couldn't remember because he fucking never had before tonight. Before Roxi. Not even when he'd been a hormone-driven kid.

"God, you're good at this." He bucked into her clenched fist and tangled his hands in her hair. "Faster."

She did as instructed, stroking, pumping him hard and fast, her own breathing getting harsher as she got into the rhythm.

"More," she said. Dragging her head away from his grasp, she scrambled up onto her knees and bent over him, her long wet hair draping over his chest.

She kissed the tip with that same gentle touch she'd first used, making him fear she was going to drag this out. But once again she proved herself to be perfectly in sync with him sexually as she took him in her mouth, swallowing him deep, all the way to the back of her throat.

Her tongue was doing amazing things, stroking up and down and around while her head bobbed, and the slurping as she sucked him was one of the sexiest things he'd ever heard, right up there with the way she'd screamed.

"Oh, yeah. That's it, baby." He could feel the pressure building in his balls, at the base of his spine. "But you'd better pull out now because—"

"Mmmph." Her jaw was stretched wide so she could take him all in, which only allowed that mumbled protest, but she had no trouble making her intentions known.

Stubbornly shaking her head, she dug her fingers into his hips and kept pumping.

His stomach clenched. His thighs were trembling. And then he lost it, pistoning his hips violently as he exploded with a long, shuddering moan.

And still she kept sucking and licking, her lips closed tightly around his throbbing cock until he was semi-flaccid. Then, and only then, did she allow herself to collapse upon his chest.

Sometime during that world-class blow job, the driving rain had lessened to a soft drizzle that should have, in theory, cooled them off. But as the water hit their overheated flesh, Sloan imagined he could hear a sizzle, like water on a hot griddle.

"Thank you," she breathed, pressing a kiss against his wet skin.

He managed a rough, hoarse laugh. "I think you've got that backwards."

"No." A lingering bit of lightning illuminated her face as she smiled up at him, and Sloan knew he'd remember the way she looked tonight for the rest of his life. "I love your body, *cher*. All of it. Especially"—she trailed a finger over the tip and made it jump in response—"this delicious supersized cock."

"You realize, if you keep talking to me this way, you're not going to get any sleep tonight either," he growled as he felt himself growing hard already.

Her laugh as she kissed him was sexy and wicked and probably would've gotten her hung on Gallows Hill if she'd lived in old Judge Hathorne's time.

"Promises, promises."

"I've got a proposition for you," he said, much, much later as they lay in her bed, arms and legs entwined, riding the golden afterglow of a night of passion. A soft predawn light was beginning to slip through the slats of the plantation shutters, casting a lavender glow over the room.

"I don't think there's anything we haven't done," she said. Her fingers were idly trailing through the arrowing of hair on his chest.

"Oh, I'm sure we can think of a few things." Sloan ran a lazy finger down her spine.

He glanced around the room, taking in the crystals with their glittering magic from the earth waiting to be released, the candles on every flat surface, the bottles of lotions and potions, and the frilly pillows that had been on top of the bed and were now scattered all over the floor.

The scarred, one-eared cat, who looked as if it had gone ten rounds with a junkyard dog, had huffed off somewhere.

"If we take some more time to put our heads together."

"How much time?" She leaned up on an elbow and kissed his flat nipple.

"Oh, I don't know. Maybe forty, fifty years."

She stiffened as he untangled himself from her sweet embrace.

"You can't be serious."

"Actually, I've never been more serious in my life." He reached into his pocket and pulled out a black velvet box. "I'd intended to give you this earlier, but I got a little distracted."

Sitting upright now, she was looking at the box as if it were a water moccasin about to strike. "What is this?"

"You'll probably be able to see better if you open it," he coaxed mildly.

The pendant hung on a platinum chain was a stylized Celtic silver dragon on onyx set with garnets. "It's yin and yang," he said into the thundering silence. "Jaira told me it signifies the duality of Morganna, and also of the equal forces of male and female."

"You spoke with Jaira? About us? When?"

"This afternoon."

"You weren't in the shop."

The mattress echoed his sigh as he sat down on the edge of the bed. "There's this new invention. You may have heard of it. Called a telephone? We discussed what I wanted and she had it sent to the inn."

"I remember her wrapping it up," Roxi said. "But I had no idea . . . if I'd known . . ."

"You would have refused to sell it to me?"

"No. Yes. Dammit, Sloan, I don't know." She ran a finger over the dragon's silver wings. "You're confusing me again."

"If you don't like it—"

"No, I love it. I loved it when I ordered it from that jewelry dealer at a southeast Atlantic craft show. But it was too pricey for me."

"Fortunately, I'm rich. It seems a little strange buying something for you from your own shop, but Jaira assured me it was perfect."

"It is."

She didn't look pleased by that idea.

"The dragon, of course, is a fire sign for Beltane. I figure I can get you a different one for each Shabbat we celebrate together. It'll become our tradition."

He'd never had to beg for a woman before. Sloan feared he might have to for Roxi. Which wasn't a problem. He'd crawl naked on his knees through broken glass down Bull Street in front of the entire town if that's what it took to get his sexy witch to agree to spend the rest of her life with him, but he feared she wasn't going to make it that easy.

"That wasn't . . . it couldn't have been a proposal?"

"I believe it was. Though if you have some rule against marriage—"

"Of course I do! Oh, not for other people. Emma and Gabe certainly seemed happy when they left for California—"

"They're even happier now."

"I'm glad. Like I said, maybe it's okay for other people. But it's not for me."

"We're back to that ridiculous three date rule?"

He liked that she tossed up her chin. On some perverse level he even liked that she was making this difficult. He'd always preferred a challenge.

"I'll have you know that rule's always worked before."

"That's because you hadn't met me before." The calm, controlled tone cost him.

"You mean I haven't met anyone crazy enough to propose after two dates."

"That's exactly what I mean. Are you saying you don't believe in love at first sight?"

"Of course not."

"You didn't feel anything last night?"

"Well, sure. Lust."

"I recognized you. You recognized me."

"You thought you were looking at Morganna," she insisted.

"And what did you think?"

"Okay." She yanked the sheet, which had been down around her hips, up to cover her breasts, and folded her arms. "It may have crossed my mind that you reminded me, just a bit, of Damian. Morganna's lover."

Sloan arched a brow at her sudden show of modesty, but decided against getting sidetracked off topic. "And partner in crime-fighting."

"Sloan. Listen to me. They're fictional characters!"

"I know that. Just as I know we've done this dance before."

"You don't believe in magic," she reminded him.

"I didn't. But that was before. This is now." He forced a smile to encourage one in return. It didn't work.

"It's only chemistry."

"Hey, don't knock chemistry. It's what makes coal into diamonds and dead dinosaurs into oil."

"It also doesn't have anything to do with love."

"Try telling that to my parents. My father proposed to my mother the day he wandered into her antique shop looking for an anniversary gift for his parents. They've been married forty years."

"That's lovely. But—"

"And my grandparents, for whom my father bought that tea set from my mama, have been married sixty-five years. They had one of the longer courtships in our family. Gramps proposed to Nana on their second-week anniversary. He was a pilot in World War II. She came to his base in England dancing on a USO tour and broke her ankle when she tripped over his big feet. He likes to say she fell for him on the spot."

"Clever," she said dryly.

"He and my grandmother Anna seem to think so, given that they still tell the story every anniversary. They couldn't get married right away, because of that little complication regarding the German army, but they made up for lost time later. My dad's one of six kids. And my great-grandparents—"

"That's my point," she broke in, holding up a hand like a traffic cop. "Not the part about your great-grandparents, but your grandparents having six kids. I grew up in a family of eight kids. I watched my mother not have a moment's freedom. Her life totally revolved around us kids. I swore I wasn't ever going to fall into that trap."

"Interesting that you'd think of children as a trap, but I don't recall asking you to procreate."

"Are you saying you don't want children?"

"I'm saying I want you. However I can get you."

"This is crazy." She jumped out of the cozy bed and began to pace. "Just because the men in your family have this crazy tradition, or habit, or whatever the hell you want to call it, of proposing to a woman as soon as they meet her—"

"Not just any woman. The *right* woman." He caught her in midstride, linked their fingers together, lifted them, and brushed his lips over her knuckles. "How about we make this a little easier? We'll table the *M* word. And just focus, for now, on living together.

"Now, as long as I show up in California from time to time

for meetings, I can work anywhere. You've already been displaced once in the past year, and I've been getting homesick anyway, so we can buy a house here in Savannah and—"

"I'm not living with you, Sloan."

"How about going steady?" he asked. His voice was calm; his eyes were not. "Think you'd be up for that? I believe, if I ask my mother, she may still have my old high school class ring in a cigar box somewhere in the house."

"You're making fun of me."

"No." He pulled her closer and pressed his lips against her hair. "I'd never do that. However . . ."

With a deep sigh, he released her and began putting on the clothes they'd thrown onto a wing chair covered with dancing fairies. "If your mind's made up—"

"Set in stone."

"Okay." He pulled on his knit boxer briefs and slacks. "You know where to find me when you change your mind." Which he had not a single doubt she would.

"What? You're leaving?" She scooped her hair back with a frustrated hand. "Just like that?"

"Since you insist on counting last night as a date, we only have one more anyway. By your rule of three."

"So you're just going to cut your losses." *And not even try to change my mind?* She didn't say the second part of that sentence, but the words were hovering between them just the same.

"No. I'm going to go back and prepare for a preproduction meeting with some studio execs that's been scheduled for two months. Then I'm going to sit in on some casting auditions. And while I'm doing that, maybe I'll pay a visit to Venice Beach and get one of those fortune-tellers to weave me that binding spell we were talking about earlier."

He touched a hand to her cheek. Her lovely, lovely cheek. "I really do love you." Which was why walking away was the most difficult thing he'd ever done. But he'd already determined that Roxi Dupree was one hard-headed lady. The more he pushed, the more she'd back away.

Better, he'd decided, to let her be the one to make the next move.

"You can't possibly."

"Why not? You happen to be a very lovable woman."

"It's too soon."

"There you go. With that counting thing again. So how many dates do we need before it's real? Four?" He bent his head and touched his lips to hers in a light kiss. "Five?" Another kiss. "A dozen?"

Her lips clung, sorely tempting him to stay. Keeping his eyes on the prize, he forced himself to back away. Now, while he still could. "If it's not love, I guess the only answer is that you put some kind of love spell on me."

He touched a fingertip to the lips whose taste he hoped would hold him until she saw the light.

"Thanks for that Beltane party. Who knew paganism rocks? Last night's going to make a great story—censored, of course, for the PG family audience—to tell on our sixty-fifth anniversary."

"You're crazy." Moisture pooled in her whiskey brown eyes and almost broke his heart.

Hold firm, he told himself one last time. "Crazy about you," he agreed.

He kissed her again, a hard, possessive kiss that ended too soon for both of them. "Call me when you change your mind."

He did not look back as he walked out of the room, out of the carriage house. But if he had, he would have seen Roxi—who hadn't even cried after Katrina had blown away both her home and her business, and had certainly never cried over a man—standing at the window, tears streaming down her too pale face.

Fifteen

Five days later, Sloan was sitting on the deck of Gabe and Emma's Malibu home, watching the waves roll onto the impossibly golden sand.

"You sure you know what you're doing?" said the man who had, during the filming of *The Last Pirate*, become Sloan's best friend.

"I sure as hell hope so." He took a long pull on a bottle of pale ale. "Emma seems to think it's the way to play it, and if I'd stayed in Savannah and let the woman play her three date game, I'd be gone now anyway."

"What if she decides to stay single in Savannah?"

"She won't do that."

"You're that sure of her?"

"No. I'm that sure of us." He leaned forward, dangling the green bottle between his thighs with two fingers. "The thing is, she has to want this. I figure if I put on a full court press, I could convince her. But then there's an outside chance that she'll always wonder if she'd made the right decision. No." He shook his head, firmed both his jaw and his resolve. "It'll be better if she comes here to me. Without any lingering reservations."

"And if she doesn't?"

"Then I'll go back to Savannah, and tie her to my bed at Swansea until she changes her mind."

Gabe lifted his bottle in a toast. "Works for me."

Sloan's office bungalow, located at the far reaches of Baron Studios' sprawling properties, belied his skyrocketing fame and fortune. It was a small, white stucco building designed for efficiency rather than boosting the ego.

As the golf cart carrying Roxi approached, the door opened. She wasn't surprised to see Sloan. Although Gabe had gotten her a studio pass, the ancient guard had insisted on calling the office so Sloan could utter whatever magical command would open those high, wrought iron studio gates.

"Hello, sugar," he greeted her in a neutral tone that threatened to destroy the last of her already tattered nerves.

It had been two weeks since she'd last seen him. Two weeks during which she'd tried to convince herself that he was just like any other man. That all they'd shared was some blanket bingo that had, admittedly, been more earth-shattering than most. But sex was just sex.

She'd told herself that over and over again. But after two long and unbearably lonely weeks she'd decided that she'd badly miscalculated and it was time to put her heart before her pride.

The fear of commitment that had been such a deeply imbedded part of her for so long was gone. She'd never been forced to examine it until Sloan had dragged it out into the bright light of day, where, she'd discovered, it had as much substance as morning mist beneath a hot Savannah summer sun.

When just the sight of him, standing in the doorway of the building with its red tile roof, caused her previously barricaded heart to turn over, then settle back into place, as if it had finally found a proper home, she knew she'd made the right decision.

One tanned hand was braced against the doorframe, the other was stuck in the pocket of a pair of faded jeans so worn through her mother wouldn't have even saved them for dusting. The stance drew Roxi's eyes downward, to where the denim cupped his penis. The memory of him fucking her mouth while the rain poured down from a stormy sky caused heat to curl in her belly.

"Hello, *cher*." As she climbed out of the golf cart, her legs felt uncharacteristically wobbly.

He stayed where he was, watching her, his gaze narrowed against the slanting afternoon sun, which kept her from reading his eyes. There was a coiled, dangerous intensity around him that frightened her just a little. And excited her a lot.

"I hope I haven't interrupted your work?"

"Nothing important." He moved aside, inviting her in. "And I'll always have time for you, Roxi."

She glanced around, getting a vague impression of bold colors and bright movie posters, but her nerves were too knotted for her to concentrate on any one thing but her reason for having come here today.

"I brought your spell. The binding one," she said when he didn't immediately respond.

Had he forgotten? Oh God, even worse, had he changed his mind? Wouldn't that be ironic? If she came crawling to a man only to end up being the one who got dumped?

"Ah. I hadn't realized Hex Appeal had delivery service." He sat down in a chair behind a glass-topped desk, braced his elbows on the arm of the chair, and observed her over the top of his tented fingers.

"You had this delivered to the inn," she reminded him, lifting the dragon pendant from where it had been nestled between her breasts ever since May Day morning.

"So I did. But it was two blocks from your shop to my suite. This is a bit more of a trip."

He wasn't going to make this easy on her. He hadn't even

asked her to sit down. So much for her midnight fantasies of him dragging her down onto his casting couch and ravishing her the moment she walked in the door.

"True. But being a firm believer in the value of service, I've always been willing to go the extra mile to keep a valuable customer."

She took out the small, black silk drawstring pouch containing a vial of rose water made from petals picked while they were still wet from morning dew, seven vanilla beans, a lock of her hair tied with a red ribbon, and a small seashell she'd picked up on the Tybee Island beach and charged beneath the full moon.

"I've written the spell on a piece of paper. It's best that after you do it you place the package beneath your lover's bed for seven days and seven nights."

"That presupposes that I'll be anywhere near my lover's bed for the next seven days and nights."

"Well, all magic has its challenges." She echoed his neutral tone, which was beginning to make her last nerve screech.

Deciding that, having tried subtle, it was now time to pull out all the stops, she went around the desk and settled herself in his lap.

He might have been able to keep his desire for her from his voice, but the enormous erection pressing against her bottom was proof that he was no more immune to her than she was to him.

"What are you doing here, Roxi?" he asked. "Really?"

"That should be obvious, *cher.*" She began unbuttoning his shirt. "I've come to seduce you."

He sucked in a sharp breath when she pressed a wet, open-mouthed kiss against his chest. "I do so love the taste of your skin." Her lips skimmed over him, reveling in the rich male flavor she'd been dreaming of ever since he'd been gone. "It tastes so dark. And warm." She circled his nipple with the tip of her tongue and felt his penis leap. "And forbidden. It's the dark side of the dream."

He thrust his hands through her hair, burying his face in the sleek black strands. "You've changed your scent."

"Because I've changed. I blended it up special to help me seduce you." She pressed her lips against the hollow in his dark throat, thrilled that his pulse echoed the trip-hammer beat of her own heart. "Is it working?"

He caught hold of her waist, shifting her on his lap. "You know damn well it is."

His hand slid up her bare thigh, slipped beneath the sherbet pink, yellow, and green skirt, and discovered hidden delights.

"Damn, sugar. You must've been in one hurry this morning, leaving Savannah without your underwear."

"I haven't worn panties since you left," she revealed. "I've been walking bare-crotched all around Savannah, feeling the river breeze and the heat on my pussy, imagining your hands and your mouth on me there, remembering how you felt inside me."

"I've been thinking the same thing." He dipped a finger into the moist cleft, causing a secret thrill. "Doing the same damn thing and it's been driving me fuckin' nuts."

He shifted her slightly again, giving him access to the fly of his jeans, opening the metal buttons with hands that were not nearly as steady as Roxi remembered them.

Her eyes went dark and warm as she took his freed cock in one silken hand, brushing her thumb over the drop of pre-cum.

Her gaze, when she lifted it to his, shone with a heady mix of lust and what he knew to be love. "I've never felt this way with any man," she murmured wonderingly. "Oh, I've had sex before. Good sex. Even great sex."

"Well, that does a helluva lot for my ego."

She laughed like the sexy, seductive witch she was, then anointed the thick and throbbing head of his penis with her lips. "It's another world with you." She looked up at him again, her heart in her eyes. "You've got a dark and dangerous aura at times that both scares me and thrills me. But at the same time, whenever I'm with you, I feel totally safe. As if I'm exactly where I belong."

"I've felt the same way. From the first. The dark and light." He skimmed a finger over the pendant he'd bought to symbolize it. "All in one."

"Yes." She smiled. Lifted her face for a long, deep, soulful kiss. "I thought it would be hard."

"It is."

"No." This time her laugh was merry, reminding him of sunshine on water. "I meant submitting. Not sexually, which is exciting on occasion, but giving myself—all of me—to another person." She framed his face in her hands. "But once I made the decision, it was not only easy but exactly right. Because Beltane was all about looking ahead, not back, and I realize that whatever the future brings, you'll be there with me."

"I know the feeling." His own laugh was one of pent-up relief. "Very well."

Her nerves settled, she glanced around the room, her gaze settling on the black leather sofa.

"Is that your casting couch?"

"Why?" He arched a sardonic brow. "Do you feel like auditioning for a part?"

"Actually, I do." She slid off his lap and pulled her dress over her head. Then stood before him wearing only a pair of strappy pink Manolos and perfumed and powdered skin. "I want to audition for the part of your wife."

Desire. Lust. Gratitude. And love. She could read them all on his beautifully sculpted face.

"That's a very important role," he said. "It's important I choose right."

"Oh, Mr. Movie Director, I so agree," she said in a breathless little Marilyn Monroe voice she'd practiced back in junior high. It had worked then. It worked now. "I'll do anything to get the part." She trailed a hand across the crest of her breasts. Around her taut and tingling nipples. "Absolutely anything."

He stood up, crossed the room and locked the door. Then scooped her into his arms.

"I hope you didn't have any other auditions scheduled for today, sugar," he said as he carried her over to the couch. "Because this may take a while."

A full moon rode high in sky, casting a warm and benevolent white light over the Southern California coast, illuminating the man and woman.

"Mine." He needed to say the word out loud. Needed to hear her response.

She didn't hesitate. "Yours," she agreed on a soft, shimmering breath.

For all time.

Clinging to him, her body bowed, her slender hands racing up and down his back while she chanted words from an ancient time, the witch opened completely. Utterly.

As the man opened to her.

And together, moving to music only they could hear, they surrendered to the magic of the night.

Midnight Plane to Georgia

E.C. Sheedy

One

Kent drained his beer and waved the empty can in the direction of the kitchen. "What do you think they're doing in there?"

The eyes of the other man left the Seattle Seahawks game—damn commercials!—and followed the beer can.

"They're trying to talk her out of it," Cal said, taking the game break to load up on nuts and bolts. "What's in these things anyway? Damn things are addictive."

"Only when they're Tracy's. Lark's taste like aluminum filings." Kent reached past Cal and loaded up.

"They're wasting their time," Cal said, taking a swig of Coors. "The way I see it, Tracy's mind is made up."

Kent squinted at the tiny screen, tried to make sense of the bold techno-sketch outlining the moves in the last play. "Why are we watching the game here, anyway, when I've got a plasma forty-incher in my den? Or better yet why the hell aren't we at Qwest Field." He frowned. "Damn, they're bringing in Hanson. Can you believe that?" Kent shoveled in some bolts. "Her mind's made up about what?"

"Going to Georgia."

"When?" Kent shot him a quick glance before regluing his eyes to the TV.

"In a couple of weeks, I think. Never, if Ginger and Lark have their way." Cal leaned forward, glared at the screen, shook his head. "This is going to be bad. Real bad." He dove for some chips. "They think she's making a mistake."

"What do you think?"

"I think they tend to underestimate Tracy. Always have."

A thirty-yard pass!

"Did you see that, like a goddamn missile," Kent hollered. "And that new kid? He's got hands." He took a swig of beer, watched the replay. "It's Tracy's business. Mistake or not, they should butt out."

Cal grinned, arched a brow. "You want to go in there and tell them that?"

Kent laughed. "Not unless I want this to be my last ever football game."

"Coward." Cal's eyes went back to the tiny screen. "Jesus! Would you look at that!" He shot to his feet, shook a fist in the air, then sat down again and pawed up a fistful of nuts and bolts.

"Hell of a game. Just a goddamn hell of a game."

In the kitchen the game wasn't going so well, but Tracy Allson was holding up . . . so far, although she was sure the worst was yet to come. But, damn it, if they started in on what they called her "masochistic niceness," she'd get crazy.

Ginger Cameron leaned against the counter, wineglass in hand, arms crossed over her chest, and fixed her attention on Tracy as if she were the only receiver open for the game-winning pass. Her friend Lark sipped her wine and watched from the bench.

Here it comes . . .

"I still say what you're doing doesn't make sense, Trace. Leaving all this"—Ginger lifted her wineglass, waved it to encompass the mini kitchen, with its ancient fridge, scarred countertop, and stained porcelain sink—"for some crapola house in—where is it again?"

"Parasol, Georgia. Not too far from Atlanta, according to Uncle Tommy. He says it's beautiful." Tracy picked a pretzel from the dish. "And what exactly am I leaving? A computer graphics art job I tolerate, a worse than 'crapola' loft in a not-so-good section of Seattle—with dented car to match—and a very big, very *empty* bed." She crunched on the pretzel, both glad and sad at the thought she had no special someone to leave behind.

"You should go back to your art—seriously. I mean, all those years in art school, all that time you put in . . ."

"And we all know where that got me." A couple of good shows, a feature in *Art-Magic* magazine, and a damn scary bank balance. No, circumstances dictated she leave her Van Gogh period for later in life and figure out what to do here and now. "I'll be in Georgia six months tops. It'll be fun, and besides, Tommy needs the help."

"That 'need' thing gets you every time, Trace. Remember Christopher?" Ginger added ominously.

"Yeah. I also remember the Alamo. Both are history." She straightened a little. Ginger was right; that TLC roll she'd slipped into with Christopher was one of her more memorable male missteps. She'd let his needs—of which there were many—overpower her. But she'd learned from it, and her do-gooder days were over. Her time in Parasol, Georgia, at the Eden B&B was all about her. "Besides, what I'm doing for Tommy is nothing like that—"

Lark, the lawyer, spoke. "You're responding to a plea for help, Tracy. There are parallels." She slid her disapproval in with courtroom slick.

"You guys are harsh." Tracy frowned.

"We love you." Lark nodded at Ginger, who nodded back.

"Humph, hard to tell." She took a breath. "But argue all you want. Me? I can't think of one good reason not to go."

"How about Tommy himself. Isn't he the uncle who's started about six million businesses in his life and failed at them all? Isn't he like the family . . . loser?" Ginger looked apologetic at the last. "I don't mean to be blunt, but—"

"Really, I didn't get that," Tracy said, but knew she couldn't call her on it, because Ginger was right, mostly. "Tommy's had his, uh, problems, I admit, but he's more dreamer than anything."

Kind of like me, Tracy thought, and wandered to the fridge to get a bottle of water. Taking a drink, she thought of the zillion years—well, five at least—she'd been trying to cut to the corporate chase with her art; finally settling for the job with the computer graphics studio. Her real reason for going away was to come up with a new plan for her life—her own plan. Not Ginger's and not Lark's. They were both beautiful, bright, and seriously successful—and she loved them—but living in their shade was getting the tiniest bit depressing. She wanted a new perspective on her life, and she'd decided to find it in Georgia. On her own. Tommy needing her help right now was simply good timing.

"And in his current dream," Lark went on, "Tommy's made the shift from a poultry farm in Florida to the Eden B&B in Georgia." She shook her head, her straight, shining hair sliding over her shoulders like hair did in one of those TV shampoo commercials. Tracy would kill for Lark's hair, or at least maim. Anything would be better than her own too-thick, too-curly mud brown hair that allowed for only one style, short. Let it get an inch below the ear, and it took on a life of its own. Unless she were to opt for hair management as her life's work, short was her only choice.

"Don't forget the mood rings for the nose," Tracy said, smiling, in an attempt to change the subject.

Ginger brightened. "You know, I think I still have one of those. I wore it in my nipple, though."

Tracy cringed.

Lark lifted her brows.

Ginger didn't notice. "I should get it out again. It would make Cal crazy."

"Stay on point, would you?" Lark said, before rounding on Tracy. "You've done some impractical things before, but giving up your life here for the Georgia . . . outback gets the blue ribbon."

Ginger saved her from answering. "We've all done impractical things, Lark," she said, adding, "And really, Georgia's a great state—all pine, peaches, and plantations." Ginger squiggled her eyebrows. "Not to mention some *very fine* southern gentlemen. Who knows, Trace might even catch herself one."

Tracy didn't bother reminding her friend she was going to Georgia to help Tommy get his B&B started—and think hard about her own next step—not catch herself a "fine gentleman"—southern or otherwise.

Lark shot Ginger a legal-beagle glare, one of those acidic ones she used for quelling purposes. "Do not tell me you're going along with her plan."

Ginger didn't quell. "Actually, it's beginning to sound like fun." She gazed into the distance, waved toward the great beyond somewhere to the southeast. "Especially the southern gentlemen part. Of course, there'll be the dirty linen to change, getting up at six to bake bread, all those toilets to clean. Other than that it should be swell."

Tracy Allson, aged twenty-eight and rising, sighed her last sigh and straightened her shoulders. "Tommy has a neighbor woman coming in to do that. All he wants from me is decorating advice—he says the place needs some updating—and maybe a few promotional ideas." She looked at her friend Ginger, who ran a successful ad and PR business in Waveside Bay, a few miles out of Seattle. They'd been roomies there before Cal Beaumann came and scooped her up for his own. Lucky Ginger. "On that score, you'll be hearing from me, Ginge."

"For the usual fee, I assume," she said dryly.

"Absolutely, your prices can't be beat."

"Hmm. I can see it now. A perfectly aligned row of zeroes."

Lark pushed away from the counter. "In the end you'll do what you want, Tracy, and we'll support you, but think how hard it will be, pulling up stakes, moving to another state . . . doubly hard to come back. Start all over again."

"Lark, you forget, I've got nothing to start, nothing to lose, and at least a minor adventure to look forward to." And, God help her, she needed a change, a place to regroup. Six months in warm, sunny Georgia would be perfect. And it would be rewarding, helping her uncle make the Eden B&B successful.

Ginger set her wineglass on the counter and faced her. "The thing is, Trace . . . what we're saying? It's all about caring." She gestured toward Lark, who now stood beside her to form a wall of gloom. "We know how soft-hearted you are, how quick you are to say yes when a *no* would save your own butt. We just hate to think you might be taken advantage of." She paused, and her expression darkened. "Plus, we'll miss you something awful, won't we, Lark?"

Lark nodded. "Something awful, Tracy."

Tracy's throat tightened. "Well, you can stop worrying. No one's going to take advantage of me. And"—she walked to her dearest friends and hugged them—"it won't be forever, because I'll miss you, too."

And when I come back, I'll have a new focus for my work, my art, and my life.

Three goals, but hell, if she managed one out of three, it was better than feeling Useless in Seattle.

Two

Colson Jones stepped out of the Seattle Sheraton front doors into a drizzling August rain and hailed one of the waiting cabs.

He watched the driver stow his bags, then got into the backseat. He settled his carry-on beside him and brushed some dampness from his thick hair.

"Where to?" the driver asked, giving him a brief glance.

"SeaTac. Northwest Air."

The driver set the meter. "Doing a red-eye, huh?"

"Yeah." And Colson wasn't looking forward to it. It seemed he'd logged a million miles in the last five years, but he still hadn't learned how to sleep on a plane. Doze, yes. Sleep, no.

He gazed into the night beyond the cab window. Nice. Rain-slicked streets, the city lights bouncing off their shine in all directions, making a prism of colors. A few soggy leaves were jumbled and bunched against the curb, and people, their heads down and umbrellas up, hurried along the sidewalk. Where they were all going this late at night, he couldn't guess.

He put his head back against the seat, closed his eyes. He was tired to his bones. He might not sleep well on planes, but he figured this time, if he were lucky, he'd sink into a coma.

One good thing about this Atlanta trip, after his meeting, he'd scheduled time for the book. Hell, it'd feel like a damn holiday, just him and his laptop holed up at the best hotel in Atlanta. There was even a chance he'd make his deadline.

And somewhere in there he'd call Sarah . . . Blade. No, Slade. That was it. They'd go for dinner, and she'd tell him how she'd *love to see his room* while she ran her hand up his thigh and squeezed where a nice southern gal shouldn't be squeezing. Then the night would take its inevitable course, a thought that depressed him more than he wanted to admit. Sarah was hot, great body, great . . . everything, if he remembered right. Hell, he should be hard thinking about her. He wasn't. Not a tingle, not a twitch. And that pissed him off.

He was thirty-seven years old and running on empty.

His cell rang. "Colson, here."

"Hi, sweetie, sorry to bother you this late. If I didn't know your schedule, I wouldn't—"

"It's okay, Melissa. What's up?"

"Nothing's up. At least not for you in Atlanta."

Colson knew Melissa didn't have ESP and wasn't referring to the libido shortfall he'd been mulling over. Still, what she'd said rattled him. Maybe some kind of goddamn omen. "What's the problem?"

"John Carter's wife called. She said he's got himself a virus and won't be in his office tomorrow. Because of his heart—and his age—his doctor had him admitted. Says he won't let him out till this thing runs its course. Maybe a week, he said."

Shit! "A week? You're sure." Dumb question, Melissa was always sure; that's why she worked for him.

"That's what she said. I'm glad I caught you before you boarded."

"Yeah, me, too." Colson ran his hand behind his neck, gripped it, while his spent mind made an effort to rearrange his complicated schedule. "Pull over, would you?" he said to the cabbie.

"I know what you're thinking," Melissa said, "but nothing's going to work—not unless you charter a plane and reorganize both the London trip and the India one."

Christ, he couldn't even wrap his head around the logistics required for that kind of maneuvering. And he'd be a zombie if he tried. "No." He waved the cabbie to get going. "I'm going to Atlanta anyway. I'll work on the book in the early part of the week and hope John's okay before I have to leave for London."

"Sounds like a plan." She paused. "Have you come up with a name for the book yet?"

"Never Tell a Lie: The Outsourcer's Handbook."

She snorted. "Oh, yeah, that'll sell by the truckload."

"Good night, Melissa."

"Good night, Colson."

She was still laughing when she hung up.

A half hour later Colson joined the SeaTac march of tired, cranky night flyers. The way he saw it, anyone having to travel at this time of night was entitled to be cranky. He sure as hell was.

He checked the board. His flight was on schedule, but a quick scan told him another dozen were either late or cancelled. He didn't waste neuron power trying to figure out why. When it came to air travel these days, what was . . . was. No point bitching about it.

He cleared security and found his gate with twenty minutes to spare. He knew first-class was full because despite his trillion frequent flyer points, the agent couldn't beg, buy, or borrow him a seat there. But it looked as if economy was equally jammed. Add to that there was a stop in Charlotte, meaning he wouldn't make Atlanta until after ten in the morning EST. Almost eight hours on a packed midnight plane to Georgia. Things were getting better and better.

Suck it up, Colson, he said to himself. *This is your life.* He took the only seat available, next to a heavyset woman with enough cabin baggage to fly solo on FedEx, and set his carry-on between his feet. He didn't bother pulling out the paperback that had been his constant companion for a month without being finished; instead, irritated and bored, he looked around.

At first his sweeping gaze bounced right off her, then . . . *Whoa!* . . . It backed right up and settled—on the best view in the terminal.

Tracy sat on the floor beside her bag. She'd already finished her book, read two papers from cover to cover, done the crosswords, and written in the diary she was determined to keep about her time in Georgia.

Since arriving at the airport seven hours ago, she'd been shuffled from one holding area to the other, a victim of cancelled flights and nonstop gate changes. It was eleven-fifteen P.M., and she was flat out of activities other than people watching.

She popped a sour lemon drop in her mouth, bent her knee, rested her arm on it, and studied the waiting passengers. She started playing the who'll-be-my-seatmate game. Her eye snagged on a big woman with fifty tons of baggage, all of which she apparently planned to stow under, around, in and over her seat.

Tracy shuddered. *Please, God . . . no.*

At first she missed him, probably because she was in the shoe phase of her horde scan, and when you've seen one pair of top-line Nikes, you've seen them all.

Then something prickled along her hairline, and she looked up—then away—then back. Took him in. Took him all in. And all of him was excellent in the extreme. Thick dark hair, probably fabulous in the morning. Intelligent, arrogant, amazingly vivid blue eyes, and he wore his jeans—no, his jeans *wore him* in all the right places, loving every inch of his long legs, lean hips, and other...body parts. He wore what looked to be a well-worn but expensive sports jacket with his jeans, and a gray tee with a Celtic knot emblazoned on the front. A computer bag and soft leather carry-on sat at his feet. He looked tasty, offering the whole package. Seductive, confident, and—even sitting stone-still on a hard airport lounge seat—forceful.

Eye-chocolate.

A climax waiting to happen.

And he was looking back, and letting what he saw put a very intense light in his vivid blue eyes.

Across a crowded room . . .

She tilted her head one way; he tilted his the other. Their gazes met, held. They smiled.

The ten feet that separated them evaporated, trailing off into a mist, shrouding the hundreds of people spread out among the gates. The mist muted their chatter, deadened the blare coming from the constant reportage of the PA system, and, when she finally got her lungs pumping again, brought the scent of gardenia to her nose.

A group of tourists stepped into their lust line.

Tracy let out an uneven sigh and slumped back against the wall. Okay, maybe the gardenia scent did come from the girl who'd taken a seat on the floor beside her, but as an olfactory backdrop to first sight of a man who knocked your socks off, and would probably knock off anything else he wanted if he got close enough, it worked for her.

The tour group moved off.

Eye-chocolate was gone.

Her world ended. And she smiled.

"That guy was a walking orgasm," the girl bedside her said, her voice holding a touch of awe.

Tracy shot her a surprised gaze, then smiled. "That's one way of putting it," she said, leaving out her own sexual-fulfillment analogy of moments ago.

"How would you 'put it'?" she said.

Tracy stared at the seat he'd abandoned and did a little conjuring, waiting for her tummy to settle and her breathing to quiet enough so it didn't sound like a gale-force wind in her ears. "I'd say he's fine, *very* fine—and he probably has a wife and kids at home who think so, too."

Her companion in thrall nodded, her expression wistful. "Yeah, you're probably right."

The formation of their mutual admiration society was aborted by the call to board their flight. Finally.

Forty minutes later, having been loaded, stowed, and serviced by the flight crew with the efficiency of a SWAT team, the pilot had them airborne. After a cursory greeting to her seatmate, a slim man in a golf shirt who smelled vaguely of too many scotches in the airport bar, she gave her attention to the airport hustle outside her window. Fortunately the scotches took golf man off to the first tee within seconds of takeoff—and he didn't snore. Twice blessed.

Her neck sore from craning and swiveling to look for Mister Eye-Chocolate, Tracy finally concluded that hope was lost; he wasn't on this flight.

Not that she had time to mess around with anything but the business at hand: getting to Parasol, Georgia, and helping out Tommy. She was a woman on a mission, and good-looking guys capable of sex by telepathy didn't figure in it.

She took off her hat, pummeled the airline's bite-sized pillow into submission under her short curls, and decided to sleep, "perchance to dream" of blue eyes and denim-coated thighs. That'd be one way to pass snooze time in the air. Grinning and wishing, she closed her eyes.

When a slash of light came through under the blind she'd pulled over her window, Tracy squinted, then stretched.

"They're serving breakfast—you might want to wake up."

"Hmm." She closed her eyes. Golf man could eat alone.

"We'll be landing in about an hour and a half; if you don't wake up, my taking this miserable seat next to the heads for half the night will have been a waste of time."

Tracy opened an eye, then another. It was eye-chocolate! She blinked. "Where did you come from?"

"Seattle."

"No, I mean you weren't on the plane when I looked fo—" She grimaced. *Tracy the cool one strikes again.*

"You looked for me?" he asked, with the innocence of Darth Vader.

She wasn't going to answer that; instead, she pulled the cotton ball she'd used for a pillow from behind her head and onto her lap and kneaded it. Of course, her hands should be working on her hair, but that would be hopeless. She considered shouting for the attendant, demanding a style replacement due to pillow malfunction. No doubt her hair was mashed, compacted, and lopsided—and she probably had ruts on her cheek.

"I told the attendant you'd be awake, ordered you coffee and orange juice. That okay?"

"How long have you, uh, been sitting there?" *Watching me.*

"About a half hour after you went under."

"Don't you sleep?"

"Not on planes. But you do."

She screwed up her face, hoping it would hide the heat in it. Heat meant pink, scorching pink.

"You sleep like an angel, by the way. Mouth closed, no snoring, the occasional long interesting sigh, maybe a stretch or two."

"I snuffle like a pup, stretch like a caged giraffe, and flail like a grounded trout. You're lucky I didn't take your eye out."

"Whatever you do, I like it." He looked at her hair. "But I'll admit you could use a comb."

"And give in to my vanity, because you look as if you've

just stepped out of a hotel spa? No way." She ran her fingers through her mangled hair, gave it a few tugs and pulls, and grinned at him. "*C'est moi le matin.*"

He frowned at her splatter of French.

"This is me in the morning," she translated, again tousling her hair. Mainly because it kept her from looking at him, staring at him. *I mean, a girl needs to breathe.*

"You speak French?"

"A little, thanks to a French-Canadian grandmother. I use it when I'm—I don't know, ill at ease, I suppose."

"Like now?"

"Like now."

"What does it mean . . . what you said?"

She risked meeting his eyes. "Never been absolutely sure, but Grand-mère always said the morning light was the true light."

"Ah . . ." He smiled at her for the first time, his "ah" long and thick with undertones. His eyes weren't merely vivid; they were brilliant, she decided, like cobalt with flame in it. But weary, she registered. This man was wrung out—and if it was true he hadn't slept, the effort to flirt with her was costing him. And he was definitely flirting.

When her stomach started jigging, she made a big deal out of stuffing the pillow to her side so as not to look at him, then said, "If you'll excuse me, I'd like to use the little girl's room before breakfast."

"Full name and address first. It's a big plane. You could get lost in it." He stopped smiling. "I wouldn't like that."

She opened her suddenly dry mouth, but her brain wouldn't supply clever repartee in either French or English. "Tracy Allson. Of no fixed address. At least not in Georgia."

He offered his hand. "Colson Jones." He lifted his other hand to encompass the cabin of the plane. "And for now at least, this is as close to home as I generally get. When I do land long enough for a visit, it's Chicago." When she took his hand, it was big and warm, and his fingers were strong. He didn't shake, he held. "Nice to meet you, Tracy."

She nodded, pulled her hand back, suddenly not exactly comfortable with her over-the-top attraction to a complete stranger. "Me, too."

I think.

Three

Colson wondered what the hell was the matter with him. He never accosted women in airports, restaurants, or any other goddamn place. Okay, so he was lucky; they usually accosted him—if they didn't, he didn't bother. Yet here he was coming on like the stereotypical out-of-town sales guy looking for an easy lay.

He must be more tired than he thought. But, Jesus, what the hell had happened in that airport waiting lounge.

Like some kind of weird trauma. One look, one across-a-crowded-lounge look, and he'd reacted like a fuzz-faced teenager. He shook his head. He hadn't taken a sex hit like that since he was fourteen and Judy Ann had groped him in the pool house.

All that was okay, but what really got him was his following up on it, and probably looking like a lecherous idiot in the process, by asking the guy beside her if he'd change seats at three in the morning.

Definitely trauma. But when he'd spotted her, sitting on the floor, wearing torn jeans, a patchwork velvet jacket, and looking cat cool, he couldn't take his eyes off her. Hell, he even liked her hat, kind of a baseball-styled thing with rhinestone letters on the front saying, I AM ART.

And she was. All color, bold strokes, and . . . illusion.

Like all women, he added, his cynical self growing stronger with every second the female focus of his attention stayed out of his sight. Colson liked women, delighted in them, as long as they kept things light and were good in bed, but on some level he distrusted them—or was baffled by them. He had the sense women weren't always what they seemed on the surface, that they were all layers and secrets. Never the real deal. Not that he didn't mind peeling away those layers.

But peel one too many and you'd sure as hell find that ever-after thing. He hadn't met a woman yet who wasn't into that—big-time. Which he definitely was not. He'd spent years getting his business to where it was now. It exhilarated him, and it consumed him. Ever after? Hell, promises for the *week after* took a month of advance planning. Neither "accommo-dating" nor "spontaneous" were in his lexicon. Women re-quired both.

"Excuse me." I Am Art slid past the sleeper in the aisle seat and managed to step on his foot while she was at it. "Sorry. I'm so sorry."

The guy grumped and closed his eyes.

"I'm a klutz," she said to Colson when she got herself set-tled into her seat beside him. "What can I say?"

"He's got big feet," he said.

She smiled. She'd brushed her hair, and she smelled minty, like toothpaste.

"I'm famished," she said. "If they don't show up with some curdled eggs, limp toast, and watery coffee soon, I won't be re-sponsible." She grinned at him, as if not expecting an answer, then turned to look out her window.

Lights popped on throughout the cabin, and a few people raised their blinds, letting in some southern sunshine. In little more than an hour, they'd be in Atlanta. If Colson were lucky, she'd either live in Atlanta or be staying in town for a few days—a few days, thanks to John Carter's unfortunate virus and Colson's Rubik's cube of a travel schedule, he had to spare. And, thanks to Tracy Allson's bathroom break, the rogue wave sent his way by that testosterone surge in the airport lounge had ebbed; he had his wits back. He was in control. They'd now have a friendly, but engaging airplane conversation. He'd get her number; then they'd go their separate ways. They'd meet when it was convenient for him, and his world would go on as before.

He shifted in his seat, faced her. "So," he said, giving her his most effective smile. "What takes you to Atlanta, Tracy?"

She met his eyes, grinned back, and his stomach did an Olympic-worthy flip. "Not Atlanta exactly," she said. "I'm going to Parasol, Georgia. I've got an uncle who opened a B&B there. It's called the Eden. I've never been to Georgia before, so I'm looking forward to . . ."

Turned out her smile was a hell of lot more effective than his, because two hours later, Colson Jones, hard-headed successful entrepreneur, and Tracy Allson, soft-hearted not-yet-successful artist, were loading their luggage into the rental car Tracy had arranged for, heading to a dot on the Georgia map called Parasol, and her uncle's B&B.

Colson had no idea how he got here.

One minute they were talking about his work in reverse outsourcing—how using management techniques and technology to make American labor forces more competitive in the global market would bring jobs home, a full ten-minute speech in which she actually looked interested—and the next she was telling him about her plans to help her uncle with his B&B. About two seconds later, and he really couldn't remember whose idea it was, he and his laptop were booked in for a week. Fate, she'd told him, synergy at work; he needed to rest, relax, and write, while her uncle needed paying guests for his fledgling business. Perfect.

Colson couldn't figure out who had hustled whom, and while that momentarily confused him, he let it go, convincing himself a well-run B&B—especially one operated by this sexy, curly-headed brunette—beat out the Marriott any day. Plus he was exhausted. Hell, even his bones were tired. Some small-town quiet would be great, and after he'd slept for twenty-four hours, he'd be a new man.

With a new woman just a few feet away.

And a goddamn book to write, he reminded himself, wondering again why he'd taken on the project when his schedule was packed already.

When they were both seat belted into the excuse for a car she'd reserved, she shot him a serious look, and said, "You're okay with this, aren't you? I mean *really* okay. Tommy will be ecstatic having the business, but I didn't mean to push too hard." She eyed him. "You've still got time to cut and run."

"Is there a bed at the Eden. A very big, very soft bed?"

"I'm sure there is, but—"

"Then I'm 'really' okay with it." He lowered his head, looked out the windshield. The day was white bright and blistering hot. He hoped the air conditioner in this tin can was up to the challenge. "The Eden sounds great, exactly what I need right now." He put the key in the ignition and slanted her a gaze. "What about you? You second-guessing this arrangement?"

"Me? Oh, no. I'm good with it, except . . ."

"Hm?"

She grinned. "I feel like I'm doing some reverse outsourcing of my own."

"Not getting that."

"Picture Little Red Riding Hood, dragging the wolf to her lair and eating *him* all up."

The eating part got his attention. "You think I'm a wolf?"

"Of course. It's biological. When it comes to women, all men are wolves—to a degree."

"And it's the 'degree' that matters, right?"

"You got it."

He didn't turn the key; instead, he turned to study her.

"And on a scale of one to ten—the really Big Bad Wolf being the top of the heap—what's your wolf preference."

"Eight," she replied promptly. "Past eight and the guy belongs in a cage."

He couldn't help the smile that pushed through his exhaustion. "Eight, huh. Good to know, good to remember."

"Not really, you'll be whatever you are. Can't change the wolf meter."

"Yeah?" He turned the key, and the tin can clinked to life. The air conditioner blew out some boiled air, then started cooling down. "Sounds like you've got us guys all figured out."

"Don't I wish." She fluttered her eyelashes at him, openly theatrical, then flattened the map over her knees. "I'll navigate—and don't worry, I'm good at it."

For some reason he doubted that, but he let that go, too. Ever since his gaze collided with Tracy Allson in Seattle, he'd been doing a lot of letting go. Not like him.

Colson eased onto the airport exit road, where the traffic snarled, stalled, and pumped out exhaust fumes and impatience in equal measure.

Tracy put a finger—its nail color an odd silvery pink—on the map, and said with a note of triumph in her voice, "Easy. All we need to do is head for Savannah. Parasol is maybe eighty, ninety miles this side of it. There'll be a sign." She folded the map and put it in the glove compartment. "When we get closer, I'll start watching for it."

End of navigation. *Okay.*

"Two hours tops," she added.

The car was shoebox-sized, the kind that used a pint of gas for every thousand miles. It seemed Tracy was into economizing. Colson had no problem with that, but his bone-weary, six-foot frame did. He hoped to hell she was right about the time.

She wasn't.

Parasol was thirty miles off the highway, and given traffic, wrong turns, and a stop for lunch, the trip ended up being over four hours, which, if you didn't count the fitful snoozes on the plane, took him past the twenty-four-hour mark without sleep.

"Wow," Tracy said when he—at last—pulled the car into the circular driveway and up to the front of the house. They'd barely stopped before all five feet and maybe four inches of her leaped out of the car. She did a three-sixty, twirled like a little girl in her first party dress, and looked at everything, obviously liking it. "Oh, God, it's beautiful."

While she ODed on glee, Colson unwound himself from the shoebox—slowly—stretched, and checked things out.

That beautiful thing had to be something lodged in the eye of the beholder.

The house, Queen Anne style according to Tracy, appeared to him to be a confused three-story confection of railings, posts, and verandahs in more shades of fading pastels than Colson knew existed. It might have been a plantation house in its day, or simply a bad copy made fifty years later. He couldn't tell—and didn't care as long as it had a bed.

It was shaded by ancient live oaks and a profusion of overgrown shrubbery that flounced around its base like a green tutu.

Not exactly ugly, he decided, just a big pile of deferred maintenance sitting on an unkempt acre or two.

While he got their bags, Tracy ran to the door. She was trying to open it when he got to the top of the steps.

The porch was wide, blessedly shaded from the day's clinging heat, and furnished with prewar—probably the Civil War judging from the looks of it—chairs, rockers, and swings.

Tracy banged her fist on the door. "Tommy. It's Tracy. Are you there?" She waited, then cast him a worried look. "He's not home. He said he'd be here. He knew when I was coming."

"Try again." He set down the bags.

She did with the same result; silence poured out of the house the same way the sweat was pouring between his shoulder blades. He'd forgotten how hot inland Georgia could be. "I'm assuming you don't have a key?"

"You assume right. We could wait. He'll probably be right along, or—" She chewed on her lower lip, thought a minute, then said, "We could break and enter."

He looked around. The porch had at least six or eight windows at the right height. He looked down at her. "You sure this is your uncle's place?"

"This is it. One eight six Parrot Lane."

"Okay, but how about we try to avoid the *break* part of that B&E thing you're proposing and check the windows."

The second one they tried opened enough for Tracy to wiggle through—and give him a wolf's-eye view of a nicely lush butt—which reminded him why he'd come to Parasol, Georgia, in the first place, while giving him a pick-up shot of adrenaline.

When she opened the door for him, he carried in the bags. He followed her while she opened doors and peaked into rooms before arriving in the kitchen at the back of the house. The kitchen was old and large, and the ceiling was high, so at least some of the heat had drifted upward. Compared to outside it came close to being cool.

"Look." She pointed to the ancient fridge where a note, giant-sized, was magnetized to its door. She pulled the note off the fridge and read:

Hey, sweetie, sorry I missed you, but a friend of mine took sick down in Tampa. Had to go. I'll be back in a few days. If you could handle things 'til then I'd appreciate it. Got some guests due at the end of the week, so if you could get a couple of rooms ready, that'd be good, too. You'll find the key to get in under the cushion on the second rocker from the front door.

She lifted her gaze to meet Colson's; she looked as if she'd been shaken and stirred. "He's not here," she said, stating the obvious, and not mentioning the inn proprietor's misguided directions to the house key.

Colson pegged Uncle Tommy for a bungler, sight unseen—and maybe an exploiter when it came to his niece. He kept his opinion to his weary self, and settled on saying, "Seems so."

"And that means we're here . . . alone." She didn't look alarmed; she looked bewildered, as if the gods had reordered her universe and removed the exit sign.

Colson held back on the smile. "Yeah, just you and the wolf." He reached out and placed one of her curls behind her ear. "And what this wolf wants to do more than anything else right now"—he ran his knuckles over her cheek—"is go to bed."

Four

Tracy's stomach stumbled, and she was sure her face was the color of that gawd-awful pink someone had painted the third floor of the house.

The way Colson Jones had touched her hair, looked at her, his tired eyes with that simmering after burn . . .

He didn't mean—

He couldn't mean—

Did he?

She met his gaze, and while he watched her, she worked to make sense of things. She was alone in a strange house, in a strange town, in a strange state, with a strange man. Hell, even for her that had to be some kind of rashness record.

She barely knew Colson Jones; maybe he made a habit of taking midnight planes to Georgia, picking up susceptible women, and having his way with them. Not that she was susceptible, of course. Not anymore. That particular period in her life was over—had ended with crybaby Christopher.

Her traitorous mind spun to Colson having his way with women, then warmed at the thought of what that *way* might be. He flashed into her artist's mind. Naked. *Dear Lord, all that chocolate.* Her knees weakened.

She attempted to get a grip on her hormones by dredging

up the age-old woman truth, those words first passed around a campfire lit by bashing two rocks together, the warning handed down to generation after generation of the female sex: a girl can't be too careful.

But her hormones proved surprisingly resistant.

Something in Colson's intelligent eyes, something in the curve of his mouth, added to the *something* inherent in the word "bed" coming out of it had utterly unnerved her. Best she set things straight and not waste any time doing it.

"I didn't bring you here to, uh, you know. This is all business and I . . ." *Oh, God, this isn't coming out right at all.*

His mouth quirked, even as he lowered his head to study her face, looking at her as if she were speaking in Congolese.

"Merde!" she muttered and straightened her shoulders. "What I'm trying to say is that I'm not going to bed with you," she blurted out, her cheeks and neck salsa hot.

Colson, who remained standing within touching distance, gave her a speculative look. "I'd say that's a wise decision on your part, because right now I wouldn't be at my best." He headed for the door. "I'll take the first room I see with a bed in it."

Oh, my God, he hadn't meant . . .

Colson stopped at the door. "But about that not-going-to-bed-with-you thing? I consider that a temporary lapse in your judgment." He grinned at her, but she couldn't miss seeing how exhausted he was. "Hell, we've been heading for a bed since we eye-locked in that airport lounge. It's inevitable, Tracy."

Then he was gone. She heard him climb the stairs, a door close, then silence.

When her face cooled enough to touch it, she covered it with her hands and leaned against the wall beside the doorway. She was an idiot, a complete dolt. Worse, she was in thrall to a man she'd picked up on a plane.

"You did not pick him up, Tracy Mae Allson," she said through the hands still covering her face. "You were simply trying to help out your uncle by bringing Colson Jones to his B&B as a paying guest. If you were a man, this would be strictly business and all perfectly normal."

"Nope. If you were a man, I wouldn't be here," he said from immediately behind her. "And I sure as hell wouldn't want you in my bed."

When her jump-started heart settled, and she could open her eyes, she glared at him. "I thought you were upstairs." Lord, she was full of suave conversation.

"Yeah, I figured that—and I was. But as you are the proprietor of this charming place—your uncle being AWOL—I came down in the hope you could scare me up a towel." He headed back to the stairs. "I'll be in the shower." He stopped about three steps up, looked back, and added, "And when you make the decision as to whether I'm 'strictly business' or 'pleasure,' I'd appreciate being notified."

He was definitely goading her. "First I have to decide whether or not I even like you, Colson Jones."

"Do you usually drag men you don't like to out-of-the-way inns in Georgia?"

"Of course not, but—"

"There you go. Decision number one is already made. The second decision, whether or not we sleep together before this week is over, we'll consider tabled." He yawned, covered his mouth, then rubbed at his stubbled jaw. "Just a towel for now, Tracy. That's all I want, a towel." He closed his eyes. "Please."

When he was out of her sight, Tracy searched the sorry premises and found a linen closet on the second floor, where folding had morphed into rolled and shoved; she dug out a towel.

The sound of running water drew her to an upstairs bedroom; its door was open, and steam drifted from under the bathroom door.

"I brought your towel," she said. "I'll put it on the bed."

"Toss it in here," came the reply.

She had a brief battle with her inner bad girl about whether or not to sneak a peek, then opened the door, tossed in the towel, and yanked the door shut behind her.

She leaned against the door, breathing as if she'd tossed a hod of bricks rather than a soft terry towel.

The word "Chicken" wafted from under the door, joining the steam, the smell of soap, and her image of hot water rushing over wide straight shoulders, hard muscle, a tight male butt, and . . . everything else that Colson Jones seemed to have in abundance.

Telling herself to derail her sexual train of thought, she looked around the large room. Colson's bag sat on a chair upholstered in pale pink and purple flowers, like the paint outside, the chair was badly faded. The room was dusty, a stack of boxes sat under the window, and the bedstead held a bare mattress, not a sheet or blanket in sight.

And she was in charge of this . . . situation. So enough with the sexual fantasies she'd woven around the gorgeous man in the shower, she had work to do—thanks to her errant and very absent uncle.

She headed back to the hall linen closet and ferreted out some sheets, pillow cases, and a patchwork quilt. There wasn't time for a major clean, but she'd at least provide her guest with a decent bed. And if she hustled her butt, she'd have it done and be out of his blue-eyed sightline before he got out of the shower.

She failed.

She was on her last tuck when he strode back into the room, in a wash of bathroom mist and wearing nothing but the towel she'd tossed into the bathroom—she gulped— around his neck.

Okay, her eyes dropped—and she got a little breathless.

He stopped in his damp-footed tracks. She froze in hers, the heat in her burning face threatening to peel off her skin. "I'm sorry, I was—"

He smiled and, without a sign of embarrassment, casually dragged the towel from his neck and wrapped it around his waist. He looked at the freshly made bed. "Thanks," he said, and moved toward the bed—toward her—or to be absolutely exact, toward a woman who had marbleized where she stood.

When he was close enough for her to smell the sex punch he used as an aftershave, close enough for her to see every pore in his recently shaved face, he lifted her chin and stroked her cheek with his thumb. "You know . . . I think there's one more thing I want before I crash onto that bed."

"Uh-huh." She knew what he wanted; it was in his eyes—and there was nothing a marble statue could do to stop it.

"This." He brushed his thumb over her lips, then replaced his thumb with his mouth, his easy mobile mouth that touched hers so softly it was more a haunting than a kiss, more a dream than reality. Only their lips touched, but she heard his breath quicken, sensed his muscles tighten.

He moved his lips from her mouth to her cheek, her jaw, to her neck below her ear, where he whispered in a husky voice, "Later, Tracy, when I can do us both justice."

Touching her hair, then stroking it, he stared down at her in total silence, his eyes dark and hot at the same time. She knew the same need was reflected in her own and didn't try to hide it. "This is fast," she said, "and more than a little bit crazy, you know."

"Yeah." He twisted one of her curls around a finger, looked at it, then into her eyes. "That's what's so great about it. About us." He paused, kept his gaze fixed on her. "I don't know about you, but I haven't done anything 'crazy' in a long time."

She thought about what he said, thought about saying she wasn't about to start now; instead, she said, "Me either," and walked toward the door, stopping to add primly, "Which means I need to think about it." All that woman lore about being careful wasn't easily ignored.

"Fair enough." He didn't smile, but looked as if he might, then added, "While you think, I'll sleep—and probably dream."

She gave him a curt nod, and with her head set to straight, her body on pulse, and her heart eerily tilted in her chest, she left the room, quietly and firmly closing the door behind her. She didn't breathe normally again until she'd made it to the kitchen.

Once there, she sat at the table, stared out the window, saw nothing, and attempted to make her second decision.

It wasn't easy.

She liked Colson, was drawn to him in the lusting sense; he was right about that, but a week of . . . craziness with him? She alternated between cringing back and the urgent desire to leap, sans net, into the void of impulse.

A sexual pickle, that's what she was in, flailing about like a fish scooped from a bowl by a playful—very hungry—cat.

Tracy might be too friendly and too obliging, even rash on occasion, but she wasn't careless about relationships—or sex. Not anymore. So far all that friendly and obliging crap had only managed to attract men who wanted to take more than give. If a girl didn't learn from that, she went beyond rash and into the realm of seriously stupid. She wasn't stupid.

Still . . . Colson attracted her, and not only physically. There were other things: his personality, his easy smile, his serious approach to his work. His ambition.

She just wasn't sure it was enough. She also wasn't sure she could ignore the hot, heavy, and very ready feeling that overcame her every time she was within ten feet of him—at least not for long. There was something frighteningly magnetizing in the way he looked at her.

Roughly, she pushed her hair back from her face, shook her head.

She couldn't decide; she simply couldn't. Tomorrow. A la Scarlett O'Hara, she'd think about it tomorrow.

Looking around the big empty kitchen, she sighed at all the work that needed doing. Hell, she'd be lucky to find time for sex. Maybe mini-Tara, being so demanding, would make the decision for her.

For the first time since arriving in Parasol, a wash of weariness overtook her. Unlike Colson, she had slept on the plane, but not long, and not well. She could use some under-the-sheets time herself.

First she'd clean up the kitchen, see what supplies they needed; then she'd do exactly what Colson had, shower and hit the sheets. She got up and headed for the cupboards, hoping to Wite-out the decision-making process in a short burst of activity. She wished she had a daisy; *I'll sleep with him, I'll sleep with him not . . .*

What she had was a ringing phone.

Five

When the phone rang, its clatter made Tracy's heart jump. Putting her hand on her chest, she pressed on the thumping there and looked around the room. The phone was a black dial-up type, seventies-style, mounted on the wall by the fridge. She went over and picked up the receiver.

"Hey, Trace. How's it going?"

Ginger! Lark couldn't be far away. "Wow, you're fast. I haven't even unpacked." She smiled, pleased to hear the sound of her friend's voice and grateful for the diversion.

"We wanted to make sure everything was okay. Lark's here, she says to say hi."

"Hi, back."

"So . . . what's it like?"

The phone cord was long enough for her to carry the receiver to the kitchen sink and look out the window. "It's wonderful. Warm. Lush. Friendly people." Okay, so she hadn't met any people yet except the gas attendant who filled the car, and Colson, who was from Chicago, but she was sure they were all nice, so why not say so. "And the house is fabulous. Kind of a miniature plantation house. A bit shabby, but a real southern belle. Some paint and paper and she'll be a stunner."

She picked up a bowl from the sink; splotches of black furry scum clung to its rim. She made a face and set it down.

"How's Tommy?"

Tracy took a second, knew this was a loaded question. "He's down in Tampa visiting a sick friend. I'm on my own for a few days, which is great. Gives me time to get the feel of the place. It should be fun," she said, stuffing her tone with perkiness. *And exhausting.* Everywhere she looked there was something to do. And she couldn't forget there were guests due within days. All of which—after their speech about her being taken advantage of—she intended to keep to herself.

"Good."

"Good?"

"Yeah, because Lark and I are coming to visit." She sounded as if she'd announced Tracy had won the state lottery. "We want to help."

"No!" Tracy clapped a hand over her mouth. She didn't usually blurt the word "no" to her friends. To anybody. But as blurts went it was unstoppable. She visualized Ginger's frown, her shaking her head as she turned to look at Lark. But her main vision was of the man upstairs—all that . . . potential. Suddenly light-headed, she knew instantly her "no" to Ginger was a "yes" to Colson—in her own time, of course. But a yes all the same. She let out a breath.

Hell, that decision was easier than I thought.

She came back to earth and noticed there was a giant load of silence churning down the line.

"That was definitely a no I heard, right?" Ginger said in her careful, suspicious voice, the one where she enunciated each letter as if it were being polished.

Tracy tightened her grip on the phone. "Yes, it was a no."

"Okay. Why?"

"Because, uh, the place is . . . filled up. There's no place for you to stay."

"We could get a motel."

"There aren't any."

A slight pause. "We could rent an apartment."

"None available."

"Buy a house."

"None for sale."

"Sleep in our car?" Ginger said, sweet as acid.

Silence.

"What's going on, Trace?"

Tracy crossed the kitchen, peeked through the doorway, and looked up the stairs to the second floor. She thought of the man sleeping there. "Now's not the time, Ginger. That's all."

This time the silence coming down the line was so thick it clogged her ears. The only thing getting through was the growing chorus of cicadas doing whatever cicadas did in the trees outside.

"I think I'm hurt," Ginger finally said.

"No, you're not. You're confused."

"I am?"

"Yup, because I don't usually say no, to you or anyone else." She loosened her grip on the phone, unwound the frayed cord from her fingers, and smiled—the image of Colson Jones' towel-wearing entrance claiming center stage. "The thing is, in the coming week, I've got a . . . lot to do. And it isn't anything you can help me with. So, how about I call you next week, okay?"

She visualized her friend nodding, her face sober, her lips twisting the way they always did when she was thinking hard. "Okay," she finally said; then there were muffled words between her and Lark. "But I'm with Lark on this; whoever he is, he'd better be worth it."

Friends! A blessing beyond value—and damned scary when they guessed your secrets from across a continent. "I don't know what you're talking about," she said, striving for prim.

"Yeah, right," Ginger muttered. "And now that you've alienated your two best friends, quite likely forever, why don't you turn down the volume on those Georgia tree bugs and get some sleep. If he's any good, you'll need it." She hung up.

Tracy grinned and put the old receiver back on its perch. Damn smart those friends of hers, worth every penny she didn't pay them.

She glanced at the clock. Closing in on seven P.M. and a Georgia sundown. She set to work cleaning the kitchen, accompanied by the sound of the backyard cicada chorus. To her Pacific Northwest ear it sounded metallic, like someone shaking sheets of tin.

An hour later, she was driving the car into the parking lot of Parasol's only strip mall. But it had the Thriftway Market and a decent-looking hardware store, which was all she needed.

When she got back to Parrot Lane, the house was quiet—not a breeze, not a singing insect—only a calm evening stillness.

Giddy from lack of sleep, work, the rare experience of saying no to her friends, and having made her decision to enjoy the company of Colson Jones—in every possible way—Tracy stowed the groceries and headed for the stairs. All Colson had to do was be . . . obliging.

A hot August morning followed the hot August night, and Colson woke to the smell of coffee and frying bacon—and with a major hard-on. It was six-thirty.

He swung his feet to the floor. A quick cool shower, shirt, jeans, and sport socks, and he was heading for the kitchen—and the innkeeper—prepared to pick up exactly where he left off with a lot more gusto than last night, when he'd gone comatose on that bed she'd made up for him.

She wasn't in the kitchen, but the coffee was, so he helped himself.

He found her on the front porch, sitting on one of the swings, sipping coffee, and nibbling on a piece of toast.

She was wearing white shorts, a bright blue top, and no shoes. Her legs were long, sleek, and pale, and her toenails were the same shade of silvery pink as her fingernails. Her hair, still shower-damp, formed a thousand tight, glistening curls on her head. She was fantastic. And the gnarl in his solar plexus surprised him.

"Hi," he said, musing on what it meant when a woman looked better from one day to the next.

"Hi," she said back, giving him the female version of the once over, interested but noncommittal. "I thought you'd never wake up."

"Over twelve hours. Most I've slept since a vacation I tried to take three years ago." He sat beside her and stretched out his legs. "I'm a new man."

She cocked her head, grinned. "Now, that's too bad, because I kind of liked the old one."

"You flirting with me, Tracy Mae?" he said, putting a southern spin on her name.

"How'd you know my middle name?"

"Yesterday, in the kitchen, when you were talking to your hands, telling them how you didn't *really* pick me up, that I was *really* just business." He paused, slanted her a glance. "I don't think they believed you. I know I don't."

"I did not pick you up."

She was getting pink again. She was dangerously tempting to tease. "Moot point. Here I am. At your service."

"I'll bet you got an A in cocky when they flunked you out of high school."

"You know, I don't think I'll go anywhere with that 'cocky' remark. I think that's kind of a show-don't-tell thing."

There was a little more pinking of cheeks before she said, "Are you hungry?"

He lifted a brow. "Another leading question and it's barely seven. I love it."

"That wasn't *leading* anywhere. I was talking about breakfast," she said. "Now that you've had your sleep, I think the next best thing is for you to eat. I intend to be very demanding, and I don't want you running out of energy."

What the hell . . . "Now, this is getting interesting."

"I thought you'd think so." She got up and headed for the screen door. "I'll call y'all when breakfast is ready, 'cause I'd dearly love to get started before I get any hotter." She went in, and he sat there listening to the screen door bang behind her.

Colson took a swig of coffee, feeling on top of the world, hot weather, hot coffee, and hot woman. This was going to be one hell of a holiday.

He planted his foot on the porch, set the swing to swinging, and put his head back. He couldn't wait.

After one of the best breakfasts of his life and another strong coffee, he looked up at the object of his desire.

"Breakfast okay?" she asked.

"Perfect. Thank you."

"Glad you enjoyed it." She stood. "We'll get right to it, then. I'll go get . . . what you need."

Colson liked the words, but not the look in her eye. And if she was talking about condoms, he never traveled without them.

She was back in seconds, standing in front of him holding a . . . goddamn paintbrush.

He eyed it with deep suspicion.

From behind her back, she brought out a can of paint. Pale Apple, the can said. She held it out to him, but did not speak.

Neither did he—for about two seconds. "You've got to be kidding."

She shook her head, held out the paintbrush. He snapped back as if she were handing him an open-mouthed cobra. "Would you like my speech now," she said, "or can it wait?" She dropped the paintbrush to her side.

"Now. Absolutely."

She set the paint crap on the table, then sat herself on the chair across from him. "It's like this. I have a reputation—as a softie. As the girl who never says no. That's what my mother says, and it's what my friends say. 'You're too kind, Tracy.' 'You always let people take advantage of you.' 'Want a helping hand, you'll find one at the end of Tracy Allson's arm.' Get the idea?"

He nodded, not getting it at all.

"I came here to get away from that people-pleasing paragon, and what did I find? Same old, same old. Tommy skipped, leaving this mess"—she waved her hand—"and some incoming guests for good old Tracy to attend to. I'm sure he never thought for a moment I wouldn't do it. And, of course, he's right. I won't let him down."

"Okay, I'm with you so far, but how does this scenario involve me and that." He jabbed a finger toward the paintbrush, careful not to touch it.

She eyed him. "I want you to consider me a . . . not-for-free woman."

"Definitely not getting that."

"You want to sleep with me—and I *think* I want to sleep with you."

He didn't like that "think" part. "Go on."

"But I won't know for sure if you're worth sleeping with until you help me out." She lifted the paintbrush again, waved it around. "Here."

"Painting?"

"And general clean-up."

"Did it occur to you that I'm a guest at this illustrious establishment."

"It's not illustrious, and you can be a guest if you choose."

"And as a guest, you won't sleep with me."

She shook her head. "I'll consider it a doctor/patient relationship."

"You're nuts."

"So I've been told." She didn't look as though the description bothered her. She looked determined.

He studied her for a time, looking for dents in what was obviously newly donned armor; what he saw was conviction—and resolution. Along with a hot body, great legs, and a lush mouth that when it smiled turned his gut to gruel.

But, paint? Damn it, he had a book to write, and he'd planned on spending his days doing that and his nights—well, he'd planned on spending his nights steaming up the state of Georgia with the innkeeper. He hadn't planned on the innkeeper staring him down and relegating him to handyman status. And he hadn't planned on seeing, behind all that determination, a drift of fear deep in her eyes. As a man who had no trouble going after what he wanted and expecting to get it, that hint of panic got his attention.

"You're really not used to this, are you?" he finally said.

"Used to what?" She tightened her grip on the brush.

"Asking for what you want. Getting something for yourself."

She didn't answer right away. "No. What you're dealing with is a whole new Tracy Allson."

"Lucky me," he said dryly, thinking the old one would have probably been a lot easier to get into bed.

"Well?"

"What you're telling me is you're willing to have sex with me for a can of paint. Do I have that right?"

"No, you don't. I'm willing to *consider* sex with you for about . . . four cans of paint. I am not making a guarantee."

He saw her swallow, lift her chin, and knew this planned scenario was about a lot more than painting. He might be male, but he wasn't slow. And he'd learned enough around a million boardroom tables to understand agendas had surface and depths.

He took the brush. "Deal. With one added suggestion."

"I'm listening."

"About that no-guarantee thing. You might want to reconsider that." He smiled, ran his finger along the clean varnished handle of the brush, into the hairs of the brush's working tip. "I'm a hell of a painter."

She handed him the can of green paint. "Suggestion considered . . . and denied."

"You're a hard woman, Tracy Mae." He stood. "But given

that I'm a hands-on kind of guy, I'm up to your challenge."
And fully intend to toss out one or two of my own along the way.

"You'll do it?" She looked as surprised at hearing his answer as he was saying it.

"Where do I start?"

She smiled, her expression triumphant, then lifted a hand and whirled it to encompass the grimy kitchen. "Here looks good."

He grasped her hand, pulled her close, ran the soft hairs of the paintbrush over her cheek. "You're right about that. Here, for example, looks extremely good." He kissed her lightly, or at least intended to . . .

When he deepened the kiss, she offered no resistance, coming soft and flush to the hardest part of his body, nestling against him until he groaned his frustration at being denied. He nuzzled close to her ear. "God, you taste good. Smell good." He breathed her in, wanted more. "What is that, anyway?"

She pulled back, but stayed in the circle of his arms, looking dazed and confused. Her breathing, he noted with male smugness, was erratic. "Probably bacon grease," she said, and ran her tongue over her lower lip as if it were dry, instead of glistening with the moisture from their kiss. She took a visibly deep breath. "You're not going to make this easy, are you?"

"Now, that's where you're wrong; I intend to make your going to bed with me as easy as possible. As a man, I see that as my sacred duty." He stepped back, stripped off his shirt, and picked up the can and brush. "And while I'll admit painting as foreplay is an entirely new concept, a guy has to work with what he's given."

Tracy's gaze attached itself to Colson's broad chest, long, lean muscles, and perfect biceps as if Super-glued. She sighed inwardly. It seemed to her this particular man had been *given* more than his share. Her mouth went dry.

And he was going along with her plan; he was going to help out. She ignored the weakness that came with her relief. She'd not only organized the help she needed, but she'd held herself back, given herself time to consider what—if anything—she was getting herself into with Colson Jones.

Weird, really, because she already knew she was going to sleep with him. What she didn't know was what that meant. She hoped it was nothing more than fun and games, but she sensed that underneath their instant attraction something else lurked, and she hadn't yet decided whether it was the pot of gold at the end of the rainbow or a nasty troll, sitting on a pile of bones, intent on having the last laugh.

Six

They worked steadily, stopping only long enough for a quick ham and cheese sandwich for lunch.

After lunch, Tracy found herself slopping green paint on the white trim, because she couldn't keep her mind on the job or stop herself from continually peeking over at Colson's muscles. And when those same muscles started shining with sweat in the sizzling afternoon heat, she opted to paint the entry hall. Alone.

Add to that, Colson surprised her. Throwing himself into the task at hand with concentration and skill, he worked fast, and he worked quietly. When he did stop, it was to take long drinks of water from one of the large Evian bottles she'd stocked in the fridge last night.

She peeked at him through the hall doorway. He was at the sink. She watched him bend over it, run the cold water and splash his face, neck, and chest, then shove his thick straight hair back with his still wet hands.

When he flexed his shoulders and, eyes closed, rolled his head, she felt a stab of guilt. The sun was almost down; it had to be after seven. She put the lid on her paint can, cleaned her brush, and went back into the kitchen.

Propping a hip against the counter, she crossed her arms, and said, "You're tired."

He smiled at her. A man who smiled while doing chores had to be a saint in a sinner's skin. "I'm okay." He gestured toward the back kitchen wall. "I'm done when that's done. Half an hour tops." He walked toward her, touched her face, then tapped his index finger on her chin. "I like to finish what I start."

Their eyes met in one of those paralyzing electrical moments that made her brain fog. "I'll make us some iced tea, then start some dinner," she croaked. Yes, it was a croak, husky, sharp, and unlovely to the ear. This man brought her to her knees with one look—and she had him painting. God knew, there were a thousand other uses for those strong hands and long fingers.

"I'm more of a cold beer man myself." His tone was steady and low, his eyes hot as the sinking Georgia sun.

She cleared her throat, but wasn't so lucky with her hormones. "Done. There's some in that old fridge on the back porch." And getting them would give her the chance to put some distance between them, lower the heat.

When she made to turn, he caught her arm, pulled her hand to his bare chest. "Feel that?"

What she touched was water and sweat-slicked skin, heat, and the roughness of chest hair . . . and the heart beneath them beating solidly. And very fast. Her own heart worked in a bumpity-bump rhythm that made her think of an old car about to either surge full-speed ahead or stop cold on the side of the road.

"Yes," she said. "I feel it." She dropped her eyes, brought her other hand up to his chest, and skimmed his nipples. Her reward was his sharply indrawn breath. Her stomach coiled and dropped; she swallowed, tried to ignore its curling, combustive roll. She felt him all right. She felt him to her bones and beyond.

"And?" His chest expanded and contracted under her

hands, and he dragged her against him, close enough for her to feel another rhythm, the one behind the zipper of his jeans.

"And what?" she whispered, wondering what the question meant even as it spilled from her arid mouth.

"You still want *food* for dinner?" His slow smile bore down on her, teasing, taunting, and suggesting . . .

God, no, she wanted him, and she could have him. Right here. Right now. She took a step back. "I, uh, think so."

Her hesitant answer amused him, and his eyes glittered, telling her he knew damn well he'd made major progress toward his getting-her-to-bed objective.

You're a fool, Tracy Allson, an utter fool. First for extorting painting for vague promises of sex, and now for letting him have his way with you. Well, almost his way. She tore her eyes from his pecs and straightened her tee. "We both need to eat to—"

"Get our strength up for what comes next?" He lifted a brow.

"Something like that."

"Fair enough." He didn't look smug exactly, but he definitely looked pleased.

"I'm not saying—"

He touched her mouth to shut her up. "I know exactly what you're saying, Tracy."

Good thing someone did, she thought, riffling through her roiling brain to find the last of her common sense, because she sure as heck didn't. She shook her head, at him, at the situation—at unreliable hormonal surges. *"Je suis un imbecile,"* she muttered to herself.

"If I remember right, your using French means I'm making you feel awkward." He wrapped a hand around the back of her neck, pulled her close, and lowered his head so he could level his gaze with hers. "Right?"

"A little." She dropped her gaze. Damn, she was transparent. When she was thirteen she'd wanted to be a *femme fatale*, dark, mysterious; a woman with an enigmatic smile who could ensnare a man with the arch of a brow, the mere twitch of an eyelash; a woman every man adored but never knew because he could never see into the secret depths of her. Romantic day dreams, as it turned out, because Tracy Mae Allson was as mysterious as a beached jellyfish.

"You're not the only one feeling awkward, you know," he said, his expression sober. Too sober. His eyes too wide. "I'm always . . . uncertain around beautiful women." His thumb played idly, erotically, under her ear, the sensitive place where her lobe met the column of her throat.

Colson uncertain? His hand hot, possessive, and still half circling her neck said otherwise. When she looked at his mouth, saw it quirk, saw he was teasing her, she laughed and shook her head. "You're rising awfully high on the wolf meter, Colson. You better watch yourself."

"I'll take that under advisement," he said, and brushed his lips over hers. "But making you smile was worth the risk."

"The truth is, you're never uncertain, are you?" She posed the question seriously. "You always know exactly what you want and just go for it."

He took a moment to answer, stared at her long and hard. "When I've decided the goal is important, yes, I go for it."

"And right now I'm the goal." The thought stalled her breathing.

His eyes glinted. "Yes, you are. We're going to be good together, Tracy Mae. Very good. But it won't happen until you want it to happen. Are we clear on that?"

She nodded, and he kissed her again, quick and hard, then slid his hand from her neck. "Now, how about I finish up in here," he said, "then grab a shower while you rustle up that dinner you mentioned. Deal?"

"Deal."

She let her hand drift to her mouth and watched his straight, naked back as he stooped to pick up his paint can. Suddenly, she didn't feel awkward at all; she felt like Xena the Warrior

Princess, Wonder Woman, and Madonna all rolled into one girly Amazon.

But like it or not, they did need to eat.

Only now, they needed to eat fast.

Colson Jones had done his share of seducing; it was time for her to do the same. If she really wanted to take charge of her life, sexually and otherwise, the time was now.

Thank God, Colson worked fast. In under an hour, he was back in the kitchen, dressed in fresh jeans and a soft denim shirt.

When they were settled at the table, Tracy made a big deal out of yawning and trying to look exhausted. As she picked at her food—not hard because she didn't have a shred of hunger—she kept the talk between them small, and the distance between them large.

Her plan was simple. Get dinner over with. Get Colson otherwise occupied for a time and head to her room. There, she'd have a long bath, do some female enhancement chores, like repaint her toenails and slap on moisturizer, then later, show up in his room, smelling of magnolias—or whatever she had that was southern.

Colson eyed her speculatively a couple of times, particularly when she slipped from small talk to ridiculous social drivel—like the price of Seattle real estate of all things. After that he went quiet for a while, but overall he let her carry the ball and went along with things, finally complimenting her on the dinner, a simple one of fried chicken and gravy, then offering to help with the dishes.

"No way," she said. "You're my guest."

"Yeah, when did that happen?" He looked around the kitchen he'd sweated in for most of the day.

"When you went upstairs and came down looking like you stepped out of a movie-lot trailer." She eyed him across the table, but resisted sighing aloud. "It's scary how good looking you are."

For the first time since she met him, he looked uncomfortable. "Thanks, I think." He stood then and picked up his dishes.

"Why don't you go out on the porch and enjoy the cicada serenade. I'll put these"—she gestured grandly toward the dishes—"in the dishwasher. Then I'll come right out and join you." She'd tried for casually perky, but sounded more like a Stepford wife on a housekeeping high.

"Are you all right? You've been weird since we sat down to dinner."

"I'm perfectly fine. Never better. Now, you run along. Go set a bit."

" 'Set a bit'?" he repeated, cocking one of his amazing brows. "You been into the mint juleps, Tracy Mae?"

She ran a hand through her hair. Things weren't going as well as she expected. Damn, this seduction thing wasn't easy. She blew out a noisy and frustrated breath, got up, and stood in front of him. Grabbing his biceps—which was like gripping molded steel—she attempted to direct him toward the door. "Just go, Colson. Damn you, go. Find something to amuse yourself with, something other than me for a while."

He didn't move, of course. All he did was stand there, like the masculine god he was, and look her up and down. "What's going on?"

"Nothing as long as you hang around the kitchen."

His expression fell somewhere between sharp and suspicious; he didn't take his eyes off her face. "Why exactly do you want me to leave?"

"Because I need some time to do stuff."

"What kind of stuff?"

"Stuff. You know . . . before we—"

His brow furrowed.

Oh, hell, why not just say it? "Before we sleep together, Colson." Okay, she didn't say the sex word, but she'd come close.

He made a move toward her, the grin on his face pure sin—laced with determination.

She stepped back, held out a hand, palm toward him. "Damn it, I had a plan, and you—with all your questions—have ruined it."

He did something with his mouth, kind of tightened it as if he were holding back a grin. "Let's hear the plan."

"Pretty simple, really. I planned to go to my room, have lipo-suction, lose twelve pounds, give myself a chemical peel, then attack you in your room."

"Sounds painful—and time-consuming." He put his hands on her waist and pulled her body flush with his. "And I can't wait."

"I'll settle for a shower."

"I've got a better idea."

"I'm listening."

"You go upstairs, take your clothes off—"

"Now, why didn't I think of that?"

"It's a guy thing," he said.

"Go on . . ." She touched the shell of his ear.

"Take your clothes off—"

"You already said that."

He ignored her. "And crawl into that big claw-footed tub I spotted in the main bathroom. And then—" He gave her one of those soft kisses he was so damn good at—at least it started that way—then it turned wild, his tongue meeting hers, play-ing and dancing in her mouth, until she couldn't think, and he'd somehow managed to back her against the counter and brace what felt like a glorious erection between her thighs.

Then she had her hands in his thick, shiny hair, pulling his head to bring his heavenly mouth tighter to hers, his tongue deeper, until she couldn't breathe. Didn't want to breathe. She wanted to suck . . . so she did. And Colson let her know how much he liked it by groaning, almost purring against her mouth.

"Jesus," he muttered finally, his forehead propped against

hers. For a minute she thought he was going to say more, but all he did was inhale and exhale, as if he'd popped up from a thousand feet below sea level.

She found some words between her gulps for air and the hot pulse between her legs, and forced them out, "You were saying?"

His eyes were dazed. "I was saying something?"

"About the claw-footed tub."

"To hell with the tub." His darkened eyes smiled into hers, the hint of a question lurking there.

She sighed. "I really should have a shower . . . or something." Which would mean she'd have to take her hands off him. And that would be hard. Very hard.

Like Colson was hard, against the part of her needing him the most. "I'm for the 'something.' " He opened the button on her shorts, pulled down the zipper, and slipped his hand in—found what he needed, what she needed, with the precision of an A-list surgeon.

"Oh, that feels good." She closed her eyes and leaned back, her breasts warm, her nipples jutting against her shirt. All she wore were shorts and a tee, but they suddenly clawed her skin as if they were wool underwear.

"It gets better." He stopped long enough to pull off her shorts and panties, lifted her to sit on the edge of the counter. She kicked away her discarded clothes, anxious for him to have those magic hands back where they belonged. He didn't waste any time, and she spread her legs; his access was clear. She moaned when he separated the lips of her vulva; groaned when her wet slick covered his fingers and he used it to lubricate her in long, easy strokes.

His mouth was at her throat, hot and busy. "Take off your shirt, Tracy," he rasped out. "I'm busy here." He slipped one hand around her, squeezed her buttock, and held her to his other hand. He slipped one finger into her, deep and with pressure, then another, using his thumb to press on her clitoris.

If it hadn't been for the counter, the strength of his grip, she'd have slid, boneless, to the floor.

"The shirt, baby. Please."

She ripped it off.

"The bra, get rid of the bra." He started playing with her, rolling her nub under his thumb, slow and easy.

"I . . . can't. I'm going to . . ." She was going to come. He was getting her off with the art of a master. She grasped his shoulders, dug her nails in, and hung on. Bra be damned.

"It's okay," he soothed, nibbled on her lobe, and stilled the work of his thumb, held it in place. "I want to see your breasts. I want you in my mouth." His fingers quiet within her, he said, "Now. Do it now." It was the eye of the storm.

Her hands were useless, and there was no way she could undo the clasp, so she dropped the bra straps over her shoulders and pulled the bra down to her waist, leaving it to cling there like a limp flag of surrender. Resting back on her hands, she felt the warm night air sift over her exposed breasts; her nipples peaked, aching dully—in the best possible way.

Colson looked but didn't touch, and his voice rumbled, low and distant, when he said, "Nice. Very, very nice."

He met her eyes, then dropped his head and took a nipple between his lips, then deeper, suckling luxuriously.

When his fingers again started their probing teasing game, her eyes closed as did her throat, and she let her head fall back. She didn't need to see or breathe while Colson made fire over her body.

His fingers, deep inside her, joined the rhythm of his mouth on her nipple. Easy, enticing, inducing. Relentless. She strained, arched, pulsed . . . opened.

His thumb rubbed over her center, once, twice, then a firm, direct pressure as he drew deeply on her nipple.

The ache became a shuddering, building wave, then . . . release. Grand, wild, and consuming.

Tracy imploded, weakened, then moaned long and low. She

reached for Colson's head and drew it between her breasts, holding him as the tremors faded, tightening her trembling body around the last pulsing, the final shiver of orgasm.

Colson's hand rested on her pubis, stroked softly. He didn't seem to mind that she had his head in vise and couldn't see letting it go anytime soon.

She drew in some air, loosened her death grip on him, and lifted his head to look into his eyes. He smiled crookedly, but he looked as if he'd just completed a decathlon.

"That was . . ." She didn't know what it was, life-altering or life-threatening, but either way, as orgasms went, it was a supernova. "Probably a bit, uh, painful for you," she finished.

"Define pain."

"Unsatisfied." She stroked the thick ridge behind his zipper, and his stomach contracted.

"Yeah, there's always that, but"—he took her face in his hands, his hot eyes serious—"there was nothing 'painful' or unsatisfying in what I just did with you. You were open to me, spontaneous. Beautiful. And one hell of a turn-on."

"I was spontaneous, all right," she mumbled, glancing away. Which was why she was now sitting bare-assed on a hard kitchen counter, naked as a porn star, wearing her bra for a belt, and had her legs wrapped around a fully dressed man she'd known for less than three days. And who would be out of her life by the end of the week.

No promises.

No commitments.

No relationship . . .

She gulped. What could be better?

"Do not second-guess what happened between us," Colson said. Typically male, he'd misread her female angst with macho imperfection. His tone preacher style, his eyes dangerously narrowed, he added, "It's a waste of your time and"—he smiled—"it denigrates some of my finest work."

He was dead right about the wasting-time part. "Some of

your best work?" she repeated, forcing a smile. "You mean you can do better?"

While she tamped down her post-coital angst, Colson plucked her off the counter and hefted her easily into his arms. "It's bath time. Watch me."

Oh, I will, Mr. Chocolate, I will.

Tracy wrapped her arms around his neck, said a prayer he wouldn't put his back out, and prepared for her bath.

Seven

Colson ran the water, watched Tracy take off the bra still hanging from her waist and step into the tub. When she was settled in, he left her long enough to get some protection from his room—a short intermission that did nothing to cool him down.

He couldn't remember the last time he'd wanted a woman this badly. And that bit of business in the kitchen had seriously ramped up the need. If he had his way, this bath would be the shortest in recorded history. He wanted a bed, and he wanted Tracy in it. Pronto.

She was deep in the tub when he returned, and when he stepped back into the room, she grinned at him. "I missed you," she said, making waves in the water with the back of her hand, as if making room for him. "Get in?" She opened her legs.

The water was clear enough for him to see the dark curls at the apex of her thighs. He started unbuttoning his shirt.

Somehow amidst the steam generated by sex and seduction, he'd missed what a great body she had, or at least the details of it. She was short, but perfectly proportioned, with long legs, a small waist, and with what his mother would have called child-bearing hips—and a rap artist would have called booty.

He liked everything he saw, and he sure as hell had liked everything he'd touched.

When she poured something called Evening of Magnolia oil into the tub, he grimaced, but didn't stop stripping off his clothes.

"Now, that," she said, pointing to his erection, which was beginning to feel like a permanent condition, "is impressive."

"Glad you like it."

He sniffed the heavy flower scent drifting from the warm water and rolled his eyes at her. "Please tell me the Fab Five aren't lurking outside in a stretch limo with a plot to rearrange my love life." Damn good thing he didn't have a business meeting to worry about.

"Don't look so distressed, Colson. Think of it as exploring your feminine side."

He joined her in the tub, taking the opposite side to face her. Their legs tangled, then settled, his outside of hers. "The only feminine side I'm interested in is yours, Tracy Mae."

"Good to know, and for you to discover." She leaned back, looking all soft and satisfied. Something wickedly male in him took credit for both, particularly the satisfied part. God, she'd exploded for him, and he'd felt every muscle and sinew contract around his fingers, pull on him, a million tiny, quivering contractions. He'd damn near come in his jeans.

And the juice . . . His cock hardened even more, so he shifted a bit in the tub and reached for the soap as a distraction. *Easy, boy . . . easy.*

If there was one thing Colson prided himself on, it was patience, when it came to business negotiations and when it came to sex. If you controlled the need, you controlled the situation. The part of his upper brain still functioning hopscotched to another, not so rational truth. He hadn't controlled much of anything since he'd spotted I Am Art in that airport lounge. And he didn't much care, which was an even more troublesome thought than the first. He had the quick, fading thought that he was in water a lot deeper than was contained in this old tub.

"And about those Fab Five guys being outside? No way," she said, soaping a washcloth and running it over her breasts. Great breasts, two perfect handfuls. "You think I want all that competition?"

"You've got no competition, trust me. What you've got is my full attention." And that was God's honest truth. He couldn't keep his eyes off of her.

Her gaze settled on him, warm but quizzical. "You surprise me." She soaped herself, running the cloth over her shoulders and down her arms. Then leaning forward she pulled it under the water and ran it slowly over his calves and knees, inching it toward his personal south.

He managed to say, "How's that?"

"You're a more patient lover than I would have thought."

She touched him then, and he closed his eyes—his vaunted cool taking a direct hit by her heat-seeking missile. If she expected an answer, she wasn't going to get one, because Colson was deep into the moment, the feel of her hands on his aching length. She cupped him, stroked him, and squeezed him, until his brain shut down. He stopped her hand, said roughly, "You clean enough yet?"

She laughed. "I think so. I definitely think so."

She gripped the sides of the tub on her way out of the bath, getting to her knees between his legs. His hands went to her breasts as if they were on goddamned autopilot, and it was his turn to stroke and squeeze. She was glistening with bathwater and magnolia oil, smelled like sin, and looked even better. He licked one rosy nipple, took it briefly into his mouth.

She ran her hands through his hair, purred close to his ear, when she said, "Oh . . . that's good." She took his earlobe between her teeth, nipped gently, her breath gusting warm into his ear. A breeze that hit his body like a gale-force wind.

He moved his hands to her waist, applied enough pressure

so she knew he meant business. "Out of this tub. Now. I'm fresh out of patience."

She took her hands from his hair, rested them on his shoulders, and smiled. "Whatever you say."

"Don't I wish."

As she climbed out of the tub, he did a few seconds of deep breathing to bolster what sexual control he had left, then followed her.

They hit her bed wet and ready, the only light in the room a sliver of gold cutting in from the partially open bathroom door. He kissed her long and deep, the ache in him building until he knew he'd have to take her hard and fast. He pulled back from the kiss enough to look into her eyes, run a hand into her hair, tight and coiled by the bath's moisture. "I like you, Tracy Mae. I like you a lot."

"I know," she said, meeting his gaze, her own hazed from their kiss. "I like you, too. Or"—she ran her hand down between them, gripped his straining erection—"I wouldn't be doing this." Her hand circled him, and she squeezed, rubbed.

His eyes closed, and he swallowed. When he could speak he said, "I can't . . . wait." Fuck! If she kept working him, he'd blow in her hand.

"I know that, too." She released his cock and ran both her hands over his chest and clasped his head. She pulled his mouth to hers, kissed him with a tongue from heaven, and breathing heavy, in tandem with him, murmured, "Just do it, Colson. Do it fast and hard." Her eyes met his as she put her hand between them and stroked herself. "I'm more than ready."

He fumbled for protection—he never fumbled—and when he was sheathed, he did exactly what she'd told him to do. He went in fast. He went in hard. He filled her with everything he had, and she rose to meet him, arching to take him in, her inner walls contracting around him.

He heard her moan, felt her tighten around him, and he released on a growl in one long, powerful thrust, deep. Deeper. To her far reaches. One blinding spill of himself that took his breath and stopped his heart, leaving his muscles slack and turning his bones to rubber.

He rolled off her, covered his eyes with his forearm, his damn lungs chugging like a train on a mountain pass. He worked to find a rhythm so he could breathe.

"You okay?" she asked from beside him, her voice barely a whisper.

"Better than okay. Don't move." When he knew his legs would work well enough to take him to the bathroom, he got up and dealt with the condom.

Back in bed, Tracy shifted closer to him and put her head on his chest, and his hand moved to her hair, rested there. "That was—" he started.

"Excellent," she finished for him, kissing one of his nipples, then licking it with one sweep of her tongue. "Absolutely excellent." She snuggled closer as if they'd made love a hundred times, as if she belonged there.

And he liked it. Another surprise, because he generally switched from the heat of sex to the cool required to strategize his exit from the bed—no matter how good the sex. So why was he this time running his hand down her back, over her sassy ass, while stroking her hair and playing with her curls with the other? Not an answer in sight, just a tiny jolt of panic.

"I'm so glad I picked you up on that plane," she murmured, yawning against his chest.

He knew she was smiling with the last. "Me, too," he said.

She yawned again and slackened against him. She was falling asleep, curled against him like a contented kitten.

He smiled into the darkened room, continued to stroke her hair, then lifted his head enough to kiss it. "Me, too," he whispered again. "Although I think it's the guy who's supposed to fall asleep after sex."

"Hmm . . ."

She was gone, and in under two minutes, so was Colson, his heart beating slow in his chest, his mind pulling the woman beside him into his dreams.

* * *

Tracy woke disoriented, her head tucked against Colson's shoulder, her ear hot against his skin, her arm resting over the relaxed rise and fall of his chest.

Colson's chest. She was in bed with Colson Jones.

She ignored the thumping of her heart—a thumping that felt a lot like panic in hiding—and told herself to calm down, not go where her thoughts would inevitably take her. Into the land of second-guessing. It was far too late for that.

And she was much too comfortable to mess with the status quo. What was done was done. She wouldn't fool around with regrets. Although she would have liked it if she'd had the dining room painted, too. She grinned. Ah, well, a girl took what she could get—and what Colson had given her was worth a dozen painted dining rooms. Still, she wanted to know more about him. If she was going to paint his picture in her memory book, she'd like some text for the caption.

"You awake?" he asked, his voice deep and soft above her head.

"Uh-huh."

"Good," he said, kissing her forehead. "Maybe this time we can get it right. Together." He rolled her back and loomed over her. With the bathroom light behind him, she couldn't make out his face. "Not that the his-and-her approach hasn't worked so far." He brushed her short tangles back from her forehead, then kissed it. From there he slid his hand to where her neck met her shoulder, rested it there. "But before we continue our sexual marathon, I've got something to say."

"Men don't talk after sex."

"Like women don't fall asleep?"

"You've got me there." She reached up and stroked his cheek, letting her fingers play over his chin, the clear skin of his face. "Okay, shoot."

"In a few days, I'll be gone."

The directness of his statement, the truth of it, stopped her heart, and her stomach furled. "I know."

"This"—he kissed her lightly, ran his hand over her shoulder and down her arm—"thing between us will be a memory."

She refused to look away. This wasn't news; all he was doing was mirroring her own thoughts, stating a fact they were both aware of. No reason to get hurt, irritated, and depressed because he saw things the same way. "I know."

He lifted her chin, looked directly into her eyes. "Are you really okay with that?" The question hung there, a sharp icicle on a snowy eave, the temperature rising. She couldn't read his face, but saw it shift from questioning to something she couldn't define. Concern? Caring? Relief he'd been honest?

"Absolutely," she stated firmly at the precise moment her bones jellied and her mind refilled with ancient woman lore, and she realized she'd broken the sacred law—again. The one about how a girl couldn't be too careful. It'd been okay when it had been her yammering to herself about this being some time-out-of-time, sex-with-a-stranger fantasy, but somehow hearing him confirm it was a knife wound. "I wouldn't have it any other way. I've got work to do here, lots of work. I don't have time to get starry-eyed because we made lo—had . . . one night of great sex." The number one came with the fresh wound. She wouldn't risk more. More would be madness.

"One night?" He slid his hand to her waist, across her tummy, and every butterfly in her body was set loose to flap and fly. "I was planning a few more than that," he said, bending to kiss her nipple.

"Uh-uh." She shook a negative even though it killed her—and his hand was slipping down toward her danger zone. "Any more than one night and it could get . . . messy. I might start thinking about white fences and golden years." She tried to sound flippant, but wasn't sure she pulled it off, so she stopped, the words and her breathing. Being cool when it wasn't your talent didn't come easy. She swallowed. "You don't want that—"

Silence. A moment of stillness.

She took it as a no.

"And I sure don't." She covered his unmoving hand with her own, took it to her mound, and arched into it. "So, tonight it is, and all this talk is taking up a lot of it."

He stroked her, his hand slipping down her inner thigh, then back to where she ached for it. "You sure about that . . . the one-night thing?"

"I'm sure." She might be late grasping the be-careful concept, but she had it now, and if the idea of his leaving hurt her after one night, a week of him loving her body, her loving his, would bring on serious soul pain. She wasn't setting herself up for that. No way.

"Then I'll have to set about making you unsure."

"You can try." She forced herself to smile at him, determined to lighten things up. There would be only this night, and she'd make the best of it—if it killed her. "But you'll fail."

"Ah . . . a challenge." He ran his finger along her crease, and she closed her eyes. His touch was heated magic, playful and confident. "Then let the game begin," he murmured against her ear, before nipping her lobe. "And you should know, sweetheart, I *hate* to lose." He kissed her before she had a chance to answer, his tongue sweeping her mouth as his fingers opened her, then slipped inside, moving in and out to the rhythm of his tongue.

Colson was a man who knew what to do and when to do it. In another time, another place, she thought, as she drifted into a sensual fog, he might have been the man of her dreams. The man of her life. But he wasn't. He was a man who was leaving.

But not tonight.

She opened for him, lifted to his hand, the promise in his touch. Tonight he was all hers.

He took her slowly, patiently, drawing her forward, then back, his voice whispering in her ear, words about her heat, her moisture, the softness of her skin, the silkiness of her—inside where his fingers worked expertly—before he moved down her body, silently pressing her knees apart, then the lips of her vulva. He gave her one deep stroke of his tongue, then lifted his head to look up at her. "I want it all." He touched her nub, rolled it, his eyes, dark in the dimly lit room, fixed on her. "Everything you've got to give. Can you do that?"

She nodded, her mouth dry, and grasped at the sheets on either side of her, balling the linen in her hands.

Colson again bent his head to her center. And in seconds, in one blinding, body-numbing rush, he had exactly what he wanted. Everything.

Tracy woke slowly, and pleasantly, with Colson's body spooned against her back, his even deep-sleep breathing soft against her hair, his arm draped over her waist.

His erection pressed against her naked butt.

Her eyes popped open, and she froze. A check on the travel clock at her bedside told her it was seven-fifteen A.M., which meant their one night together was officially over. Now all she had to do was extricate herself from the hard body wrapped around hers—and the other, even harder thing that should he waken and discover, would make nothing but trouble.

But, oh, what trouble . . .

When she sensed herself weakening, she rallied her skinny army of resources and gave herself a good talking to: *You made a promise to yourself, girl, so start keeping it. There's no good to come from letting yourself get any closer to Colson. You're already in deep lust and heavy like; you've already followed your same old pattern, saying yes when a no would serve you better. All Colson wants is a few days of recreational sex between flights. There's absolutely nothing in that for you.*

Okay, that was kind of a lie . . .

She rephrased. *There's nothing* long-term *in it for you.* Yes, that was better.

Either way, continuing a sexual relationship with a man hopping the next plane out of your life was . . . masochistic. Last night was fantastic and achingly memorable, but more time in a bed with a giant GOODBYE! looming over it like the Ghost of Christmas to come would ruin everything.

She'd end up wanting more of him—*damn it, she already did*—even though he'd told her "more" wasn't in the cards, and she'd get hurt. A smart woman would back off now. And she, Tracy Allson, Queen of Yesville, false starts, and numerous beginnings, was definitely a smart woman. Starting now.

Lying still as a plastic mannequin, she considered how to get out of the bed in a way that wouldn't wake him. Slowly, carefully, she shifted her lower body away from the danger zone, sliding her hips forward toward the edge of the bed.

She'd barely gained an inch before his hand pressed into her tummy, then slid up to cup her breast. He kissed her shoulder. "Mornin', Tracy Mae."

She drew in a deep breath; not easy when a strong male hand, amazingly deft for the early hour, was toying with one of your nipples—and you were loving it.

Bolting from the bed, she stood, breathing heavy, and looked down at him. She wasn't sure what showed in her eyes, but a good guess would have been panic. Lord, she had four days more to hold out, and she weakened when he breathed on her neck. Not good. Not good at all.

"Good morning to you, too," she said, grabbing her red cotton robe from the post at the foot of the bed. She put it on and pulled the tie tight around her waist. "Coffee, coming right up." She turned on her barefooted heel and started for the door.

"Whoa . . . hold on a minute."

She looked back, saw him pull himself to a sitting position, his back against the padded headboard, one knee bent. His dark hair was mussed, his jaw was dark, and his eyes were a burning blue in the fresh morning light. God, he was beautiful! He made her mouth water and her heart fire in staccato, like one of those tommy guns you saw in old gangster movies. He made her elbows sweat.

"Do you want some toast—or the full breakfast thing?" she said, her tone bright and competent. "I can do either."

"What I'd like is you back here." He ran his hand along the empty bed space beside him.

She swallowed. "Not going to happen, handsome." She took a step or two away from the bed. "I've had my way with you." She managed a weak smile. "Now I've got new worlds to conquer."

"Which are?"

"Getting this B&B in shape for those guests Tommy has arriving." She searched the floor for her terry mules; anything was better than looking at Colson casually ensconced in her bed . . . waiting. She didn't find the mules, but the search took her closer to the door. "And another thing. You've got a book to write, so you'd best get on it."

"You were serious. About the only-one-night thing." He frowned slightly, but his blue eyes had a speculative gleam.

"Glad you picked up on that. It will make the rest of the week go a lot easier."

When he didn't say anything, just rested on the bed like a fox selecting his next chicken, she added, "So, what's it to be? Just coffee, or a full meal, eggs, bacon, the works."

He didn't answer right away; then as if reaching a decision, he smiled. "Definitely the full meal. I'm a hungry man." He tossed the quilt that had covered his lower half and stood—his erection saying a good morning of its own.

Tracy's eyes dropped—*I mean, where else would they go?*—and his smile—hitting number seven on the wolf meter—widened dangerously.

"You're not going to make this easy, are you?" she said.

"It'll be as easy for you as it is for me. I guarantee it."

She was afraid of that, but she had no answer, so she opened the door, saying over her shoulder, "Breakfast in half an hour."

Eight

Colson took the whole half hour to shower, shave, and think. It looked to him as if his hot little innkeeper meant what she said and had definitely drawn a line in the sexual sand. He'd been dumped, after one night. He grinned at his face in the mirror.

Interesting . . .

He shaved the final swath of beard, ran the razor under the water, rinsed the last of the foam off his face, and toweled off.

She was probably right—and smart—to call it quits. After his business meeting in Atlanta, he'd be gone for over a month. After that? More of the same. Meeting Tracy Allson on a powerful surge of attraction and having heart-threatening sex with her hadn't changed his schedule.

But it had changed something, and he knew the exact moment it happened. It was when she'd bolted from the bed, stood staring down at him, her face pale, her brown eyes filled with panic—and resolve. His hand went to his bare chest, rubbed it idly. Damned if he hadn't felt some of that panic himself.

Yeah . . . she was smart to keep her distance. Hell, he'd set the rules—brought up that crap about his goddamn schedule, his leaving in a few days—it shouldn't bother him that she was keeping to them. But, damn it, it did.

He wasn't only turned on by Tracy; he was caught in some kind of force field—and he liked it. She might not be the first woman to make him hard below the belt, but she sure as hell was the first one to make him soft above it. No way was he going to let what was happening between them go. Let her go. And keep his hands off her? Not have her in his bed again? Not doable.

He put the towel back on the rack, went into the bedroom, and shrugged into a blue cotton shirt. At the half-buttoned mark, his hands stopped, and an old voice roared to center.

Your brain is on freeze frame, Colson. All you've got happening here is a serious case of zipper-think. It's your dick talking, man. Great sex. That's all it was.

He finished buttoning his shirt, frowned. Dick talk or not, he intended to straighten things out between him and Tracy Mae. And while he did that, there was no reason for them not to enjoy each other's company, in bed and out.

He headed for the kitchen, grateful for the empty house and the uninterrupted time he'd have to put his plan into effect. This was one schedule he had under control.

Tracy had on jeans and a tee—and her hair was in some kind of clip that held the curls off her face, a face already glazed with a fine film of sweat. The kitchen was warm because it caught the morning sun full on, and her frying bacon and eggs for him added to the temperature.

"Hi," she said, and gestured to the table already set. "Take a seat." She did a double take, gave him a quick once-over, and added, "Jeez, do you always look so friggin' cool?"

He sat down. "I'm not cooking." He returned the once-over. "But I'm not cool. Not with you in the room."

She waved the spatula she was holding. "Don't start, Colson. We made a deal."

"You made a deal. I kept my mouth shut."

She dropped the spatula to her side, thought a bit, and didn't look happy. "You're right. But you do understand the word *no*, don't you?"

"Absolutely. It's the no coming after the yes I'm having trouble with."

"You'll figure it out." She turned back to the stove, filled his plate, and brought it to him.

For the first time he noticed the table was set for one. "Aren't you eating?"

"I had toast earlier."

Colson got up from the table and faced her. "This is crazy." He tried to keep the impatience from his voice, but knew he failed by the flash of fire in her eyes. "We need to talk about this."

"No, we don't. And you can stop glowering at me."

"This is not glowering. It's basic male confusion." He touched her face, but she pulled back, and he stuffed his hands in his pockets. "We're good together, Tracy. Why waste that?"

"We're good in bed together, Colson. And we have no time to get beyond that." She paused, did some breathing, and for a bit it looked as if she wouldn't say any more. "Last night, you said that in a few days what happened between us would be a . . . memory—"

"And you said you were okay with that." And he wished to God he'd kept his fucking mouth shut!

"And I am." She hesitated. "If we stop here. Stop now. You told me yourself, you live on planes. And when you're not flying to God knows where, you live in Chicago. I live in Seattle, or will when this Tommy mess is over. We've got one of those never-the-twain-shall-meet kind of situations. Plus, I've got a life to sort out—make something of." She firmed her mouth, shook her head. "Falling for a business jet-setter would only complicate that."

His brain tripped over the "falling for" part, and the back of his neck prickled. He pegged it for an alert, something like woman-looking-for-commitment around the next turn, but it felt more like satisfaction. "Is that what you're afraid of? Falling for me?"

She reddened, closed her eyes, and cursed—significantly.

Colson was impressed. "Look, we can work on this—"

The kitchen door opened with a bang.

"Tracy darlin', you're here." Uncle Tommy, and a woman almost a head taller, exploded into the room.

"Tommy!" Tracy, relieved by the interruption, glanced at Colson. Whatever he'd meant by "work on," she didn't want to know, because the only thing she wanted to work on was herself, and this tumble-down B&B. The Eden was why she'd come here, and it's why she'd stay—long after he'd gone.

"In the flesh, sweetums." Tommy dropped the two small bags he was holding and enveloped her in a bear hug.

"I didn't expect you back so soon," Tracy said, hugging back.

"We finished up early, didn't we, sweet pea?" He let go of Tracy so he could drag the other woman forward. "Meet my wife, Loralee. Loralee, meet my favorite niece, Tracy."

"You're married?" Her brows lifted almost to her hairline, her eyes wide with shock. "Wow. That's a surprise."

"Full of surprises, our Tommy." The tall woman clasped Tracy's hand and smiled her hello.

Tracy glanced at Colson, who raised a brow of his own. She managed the introductions.

"Good to meet you," Tommy said, pumping his hand. "First paying guest, Colman. A man should get something special for that."

Colson didn't correct the name mistake. "Already did," he said, glancing at Tracy. "Great place you got here."

"Can we get back to the, uh, married thing?" Tracy said.

"Loralee was my neighbor—lived"—he gestured out the kitchen window—"just yonder. She's already sold her place and"—he dragged the woman to his side, held her against his hip—"I've got a buyer for mine—as soon as we get the place prettied up."

"Prettied up?" Tracy echoed.

"Uh-huh, and I see you've got us a real start on that." He beamed at the freshly painted kitchen. "Nice, huh, Loralee? Didn't I tell you my Tracy was a marvel?"

"Very nice, darlin'," Loralee said, in a voice soft and southern. "Now, if y'all don't mind, I'll go upstairs, get myself freshened up, before we— Well, now, I'll leave your uncle to tell you the rest."

Tracy, still dazed, nodded. "Fine," she muttered. "Nice meeting you, Loralee."

"Same here, sweetie."

When Loralee cleared the room, Tracy eyed her uncle, her suspicion feeding the lump in her stomach. "I'm not getting all this, Tommy. You said you were called away to visit a sick friend in Florida."

"Hmm, sorry about that, little one, but this, uh, getting married idea came up kinda suddenlike."

"Exactly how 'suddenlike'?" The lump in her stomach started heating up; she damn well didn't like the way he was hesitating. And she hated the way Colson was standing there, like a cigar-store statue, arms crossed, face expressionless.

"I don't know, maybe a few days before you got here," Tommy said.

"And the selling the house idea? When did that bulb go off?"

Tommy rearranged his red tie, dropped his gaze. "Round about the same time, I guess. The thing is Loralee and me want to move back on down to Florida. We got ourselves a nice condo there."

Tracy shook her head, tried to bring the pieces of the puzzle together. "So . . . if I have this right, you brought me here to clean and decorate the place for resale, while you and, uh, Loralee had a honeymoon."

"Well, now, I kinda set that plan—you coming and all—in motion before all the marriage business, and because you were all booked, when things changed, I figured I'd—"

"Take advantage of me."

"Ah, now, honey, I figured it would do you good, get you out of that Seattle rain for a few days."

"You 'figured'?" The rock now low in her stomach exploded into a zillion sharp pieces. "You said six months minimum, Tommy. That you wanted my help to start an ongoing business." Her voice was tight, low. "I gave up my apartment. My car. I gave up my job." Okay, not much of a job, but at least one that paid the bills.

"A buyer came around a bit sooner than I thought." He met her eyes, barely. "He'll be by on the weekend."

Another lie. "You told me you had guests coming."

"I, uh, figured we'd do best with some kind of deadline, and I didn't think you'd be too keen on the selling idea." He stopped, and she watched him visibly straighten. "And the thing is, honey, Loralee and me? We can't stay. We have to go north a bit to her mama's place, tell her about the wedding, the move, and all. We only dropped in to, uh, get a few things, maybe see how you were doing . . . with everything."

Tracy was speechless, and her eyes were so shock wide they were drying out. God, Ginger and Lark would be I-told-you-soing into the next millennium—if they were those kinds of friends, which thankfully they weren't. Still, going home with her figurative tail between her legs to kick start her life in Seattle held all the appeal of a slug-slime body wrap. Add to that she wasn't exactly awash in cash. What a mess!

Colson stepped forward, shot Tommy a withering look, and took her arm. "You've been had, Tracy Mae. Let's go for a walk."

Outside, the day steamed, but it was cool in comparison to the heat of Tracy's outrage. Colson figured his best course of action was to keep his mouth shut and his ears open. After years sitting at negotiating tables, he knew enough about anger to know it didn't lead to rational decisions. Cooling down was a must.

They walked for maybe half an hour, while Tracy alternated between rants and stony silence.

After the longest silence of them all, she said, "I'm going back to the house and book a flight home. I'm out of here. *Today.*" She turned to go.

Colson figured that would be her reaction; he grabbed her wrist. "Is that what you want? To go home?"

"I don't see a choice. No way am I staying here and working my butt off for that . . . that man." She sealed those beautiful lips of hers, her expression mulish.

"You got what you came for, then?"

She blinked. "What do you mean?"

"You told me on the plane you were coming to Georgia to sort things out. Make some decisions. That done?"

"No, but—"

"Then why leave? Why not stay until you get what you came for?"

She looked at him as if he'd erupted in face boils. "Are you serious?"

"Look," he went on. "Even if this so-called buyer does put an offer on the place, he won't take possession for at least a month—more if you insist Tommy extend the closing period. Not the six months or a year you planned, I admit, but enough."

Her expression turned wary, but he could see she was thinking. "Is this idea—my staying—born out of some macho idea it will give you enough time to get me back in your bed."

"I'd be lying if I didn't tell you the thought crossed my mind."

"Humph." She shook her head. "Men."

"Putting that derogatory aside, your staying still makes sense."

She gave him a grudging nod. "I'll tell him three months— two for sure. But I won't 'pretty up' his damn house for him."

Colson rubbed his chin.

"What?"

"The thing is, a share of the house profits might make that worth while."

Her eyes lit up. "Damn, you're good!" She walked away from him, then back again. "I'll stay, insist he accept nothing less than a two-month possession date—if the place sells—and that I'll clean up the place and paint for a percentage of the profits."

"Sounds fair to me. And I'm betting your uncle will go along with it."

"And I'll get it in writing."

"Smart."

Walking back to the house, Colson didn't know who was happier, him because he'd bought himself some time, or Tracy because she'd done the same—for a whole different reason.

It took no time at all for Tracy to issue her ultimatum to Tommy. Her way, her time, and *her pay*, she told him, or she'd leave without doing the breakfast dishes. A half hour after he'd caved—in writing—the honeymooners piled themselves into Loralee's tidy little Toyota and headed north.

Colson had left her to handle the negotiations herself—which she was grateful for—while he'd spent the entire time on his cell phone. He walked into the kitchen, confirming, to whoever was on the line, his meeting in Atlanta for the end of the week. Then saying something she couldn't quite make out—because he turned his back on her—about some trip to India.

She tried to ignore the heaviness in her chest, concentrate instead on her coup over Tommy, but it was hard to imagine her time here alone—without Colson.

Not wanting Colson to pick up on her grim mood, Tracy looked around the once again empty kitchen. "I'm starved," she said, determined to sound brighter than she felt. "I'll make us some sandwiches so we can eat before I get started."

"Before *we* get started," Colson said.

"You don't have to paint, Colson."

"No, I don't, but I will." His phone was ringing again, but he ignored it, kept his blue gaze fixed on her, unyielding and intense.

Tracy's nerves kicked up, in tandem with her hormones. Nothing had changed between her and Colson. At the end of the week, he'd be gone, and she'd be lonely enough bumping around Eden without getting closer yet. Add to that, she wasn't sure how she felt about that look in his eye. Her wolf meter could be wrong. Maybe he wasn't a seven; maybe he was an eight in painter's clothing. Best she set the record straight. "There'll be no sex for paint. You can paint your fingers to their bony nubs, and I won't sleep with you."

He stuffed his still ringing phone in his pocket, gave her a quick grin. "Yes, you will, Tracy Mae, although maybe not tonight; bony nubs aren't much good for lovemaking." He settled his gaze on her, direct and intense. "But we'll get around to it before—"

"Before you leave?" She arched a brow.

He nodded.

"You're awfully sure of yourself, Mr. Colson Jones. Ever heard of pride arriving just before the fall?"

"You want something, you figure out a way to get it."

"You're trying to manipulate me."

"Yes. How am I doing so far?"

"You're making me crazy." *In so many ways . . .*

"It's mutual, sugar pie." He touched her chin, then stepped back. "But why don't we forget the lure of the bedroom for now, concentrate on painting the dining room. We've got a lot of work to do, and less than three workdays to do it." His hand went to the top of his shirt, opened that exciting first button, then the second . . . "Where's the paint?" he asked, freeing button number three.

She caught a glimpse of his silky chest hair and swallowed. "Outside on the back porch." She headed toward the door. "I'll get it, while you do your Chippendale thing; then you can get started while I make those sandwiches."

"Sounds like a plan."

She nodded, not bothering to tell him the other part of the plan was for her to stay as far away from his world-class pecs, soap-star abs, and to-drool-for biceps as the Eden B&B allowed. *The bathroom!* She'd work in the main floor bathroom, well out of peeking range.

The sun was already going down and casting long black shadows beyond the trees in the backyard when Tracy finally cleaned her brush and put the lid on her paint cans. Her back was aching, and her painting arm felt on fire. She was tense from the effort of avoiding Colson for the past five hours. It would have helped if he hadn't kept strolling by—for God knew what reason—about a million times. He probably thought she was rude, not even glancing up at him.

Well, there was no avoiding him now, and exhausted or not, if she wanted to stay emotionally intact, she had to face the night resisting his overpowering . . . maleness, not to mention his humor, intelligence, seductive smile, and all-around sexiness.

And his lean, hard body . . .

Which brought her to her own traitorous body's ridiculous desire for a repeat of last night's magic. God, he was good in bed, the way he'd touched her, caressed her, his hands everywhere she'd wanted them to be, his eyes—

Damn his eyes. She rolled hers, miffed at her silly, and dangerous, thoughts.

She planted her hands on her lower back, stretched, then wandered around the main floor. Colson's paint supplies were neatly stored in the corner of the dining room, but there was no sign of the man himself.

She heard a creak from the front porch, stepped out, and let the screen door bang shut behind her. "Colson?"

"Here," his voice came from the shadows a few feet away. Another creak; he was sitting on the swing.

"You slackin' off out here?" she said, determined to be appropriately friendly and gracious, when what she wanted to do was jump his beautiful bones. His head rested on the back of the swing; he turned toward her when she got closer. He was barefoot, still no shirt, she noticed, and wearing his paint-spattered Calvins. She probably owed him a new wardrobe.

"Yeah, I'm done." He patted the seat beside him on the porch swing. "Come set awhile, Tracy Mae."

"Can I get you something? A beer? Some iced tea?"

"Got it already." He lifted a beer, turned his head from her to look straight ahead into the dim world beyond the porch rail. He looked relaxed, at home, as if he'd taken ease on this verandah a thousand times. "The air's feeling heavy."

She sat beside him on the edge of the swinging seat, looked at what she could see of the sky beyond the porch. "Comin' up a bad cloud."

His foot stopped the swing. "I never heard that one before." He looked quizzical and amused.

"Me either, the old man in the hardware store said it when I was in there buying the paint. A lot more colorful than saying it's going to rain, don't you think?"

"Hmm." He held the cold beer against his chest, closed his eyes, started the swing again—this time with a hard push that made her fall backward, deeper into the seat.

She knew he'd done it on purpose, but she didn't mind. It was nice out here, nice sitting in the evening shadow with Colson. She settled back, rubbed her eyes. "Whatever it is, it's making perfume of the air. Rose, magnolia . . . and something like peppermint." She drew the scents in, put her head back, and let her tired muscles relax and twilight close around her.

Swing and creak, swing and creak, swing . . .

"You hungry?" she said after a time, thinking if she didn't move and move quickly, she'd fall asleep and not move at all.

"I'm taking you out. When we drove in, I spotted a diner about ten miles out of town. Parking lot was full, so they must be doing something right." He took a drink of his beer, slanted her a glance. "You okay with that?" He paused. "Has the advantage of being safe, too. Not a bedroom in sight."

Until we get back here ... "I'm fine with that, dinner and the safe part."

He laughed, stood. "Then get that pretty little ass of yours in gear, honey pie. Your man needs red meat"—he pulled her from the swing, hard against his chest, kissed her quickly, lightly, and let her go—"along with a lot of other things."

The kiss was playful, packed the wallop of a lightning bolt, and was so fast, she didn't have time to protest. Not that she wanted to. What she wanted—for a longer time than he had to give—was Colson Jones. And the thought made her feel bluer than blue.

They climbed the stairs together, stopped at her bedroom door, and stared at each other—the air between them hot and jagged; sharp enough to stall Tracy's breath, thick enough to clot in her lungs and obscure her vision for anything other than the man in front of her.

She wanted to drop her gaze from his, but couldn't, wanted to reach out and touch his jaw, but didn't, wanted to draw his mouth to hers, but ... denied herself.

She wasn't sure what Colson felt, but his eyes were hot and intense. Still, he didn't touch her again. "See you downstairs," he said. "Twenty minutes enough?" He didn't move.

She nodded, closed her fingers around the doorknob. "Colson I—"

"Tracy, I—"

They smiled.

"You first," Colson said.

"I wanted to say thanks ... for your help today with the Uncle Tommy business. I'd never have thought to look at things quite the way you did. I was too damn mad, I guess."

"You're welcome." He lifted one of her curls from beside her temple, watched it coil around his index finger, then dropped his gaze to hers. "That kind of thinking is what I do for a living—find advantages where there doesn't appear to be any—the 'fortune' in *mis*fortune. It's always in there somewhere, if you can get past the problem and focus on the solution." His brow furrowed, and he let her curl spring back against her face, briefly glancing away.

She tilted her head, intrigued by his deeply thoughtful expression. "Was it something you said?"

"Made me think. How with you—with us—I haven't done that. I've focused on the great sex, not the follow-up, not the mornings after."

"I'm not getting that," she said.

His gaze rested on hers, but she had the sense he wasn't quite seeing her, that his mind had drifted elsewhere. "I'm not sure I'm 'getting' it either. See you downstairs." With that he turned and walked to his room; he didn't look back.

Tracy watched him stride down the hall. She wasn't exactly sure what he'd meant to say, but she guessed he'd finally come to the same conclusion she had. Buying into great sex without a follow-up program was a bad bargain.

That thought made her even more dismal than she already was.

Nine

Colson stripped off his clothes, went directly to the shower—where he did his best thinking.

He scrubbed at some paint on his shoulder, and for a nanosecond, it kept his mind from where it was determined to go.

Tracy Allson. *Jesus! I'm in goddamn deep here.*

He wasn't usually made weak by his own deductive reasoning. But something that had started out as a game, a very objective game, where you won or lost based on whether or not you got the lady in your bed, had turned into an emotional rollercoaster. It scared the crap out of him. What he'd told her minutes ago, outside her bedroom door, was the God's honest truth. She was a fortune. A gold-standard woman. And while she was afraid of falling, he'd already bit the dust.

He was fucking in love!

Jesus, how many times today had he sauntered by where she was working—just to look at her. And she'd kept her head down, stubbornly refused to look at him. She was so busy protecting herself from him, she not only wouldn't go to bed with him, but she wouldn't even look at him—while he'd reached the point he'd consider an afternoon walk in the park with her a home run.

He turned off the shower, shook his head, and combed his hair back with his hands, his shaking hands.

He circled his mental resources around one thought. He still wanted Tracy in his bed, all right, but now he wanted more. He wanted her in his life, damn it! He wanted her to at least consider exploring a relationship with a man who'd spend most of the next three to five years of his life out of the country. He couldn't give up his work, not only did he love it, but he considered bringing American jobs home, instead of exporting them, seriously important work. What he couldn't expect was Tracy to feel the same—after barely a week together—which meant he had a big problem.

He force fed himself some logic.

Goal: He loved Tracy Mae Allson, and he wanted her in his life.

Obstacles: Tracy wanted to set her own goals, plan her own life—not simply buy into his. His schedule was an unyielding bitch, and absence had a way of making the heart grow fonder—for someone else.

He put on gray slacks and a white cotton shirt, brushed his hair, and headed for the door.

It was going to be a hell of a negotiation.

Tracy paced the downstairs hall and waited. She'd done some serious thinking upstairs, but twenty minutes wasn't time enough to make a decision, to decide whether she was being sexually selfish or plain sto-o-pid.

All of which proved how inept she was at making decisions, how important this time in Georgia was.

She heard Colson's door close and pulled in her tummy, knowing it would go all soft and mushy on sight of him.

She hadn't dressed up much, white capris, matching sandals, and her new red tee with the faux rubies around the neck. Now she hoped it was enough. Colson always looked so . . . right, it was a bit unnerving.

He came down the stairs. "This is a first, the lady waiting

for me." He ran a finger along her jaw. "You look spectacular, by the way. I like the tee."

"Thanks." She was pretty sure his finger had left a burn mark, but she resisted the urge to touch it. She tossed him the keys to the rental. "I'm assuming you know where we're going."

He caught the keys, gave her a long look. "I know exactly where we're going, Tracy Mae."

They settled into a booth at the Roadsyde Diner, both smiling at what they termed the "aristocratic" Y. The place hadn't seen a decorator's hand in years, but the booths at the window and the round maple tables in the room's center were mostly full. Soft country music merged with conversation, bursts of laughter, and the clink of cutlery.

They took the last available booth, and a waitress, with the highest boobs and biggest hair Tracy had ever seen, sauntered over and took their orders; Colson's a steak smothered in mushrooms and hers a pasta topped with chicken.

Colson, who'd already ordered them a decent red wine, picked up his glass and settled back into his vinyl padded seat. For a time neither of them spoke, just sat back, people watched, and listened to music. And while she sensed Colson's mind was somewhere else, hers was right here, in the now—as was her heart—struggling to enjoy what time they had left together.

"We have three days before I have to go to Atlanta," he said suddenly. "What do you propose we do with them?"

His question caught her off guard. "I was expecting small talk," she said, instantly wary, "not a planning session."

"I hate small talk, and besides, I have to bring you up to date on my schedule."

"I can't imagine why. And I already know your schedule— or enough to wish I'd invested in an international airline long ago."

"Actually, you don't know enough, and you need to—"

"Colson, if you're going to start—"

"—so you can make an informed decision."

"What are you talking about?"

The waitress came, slid their plates onto the table. "Can I get y'all anything else?" She eyed Colson as if he were a cherry-topped chocolate sundae.

Colson glanced at Tracy; she shook her head. "No, thank you," he said. "We're fine."

"Y'all holler if that changes, now." With that, a wink at Colson, and a smile, she left, boobs, hair and all.

"She wants your body," Tracy said, teasing him, but pleased he'd shown no interest in a pageant-ready blonde with a world-class figure.

"It's taken," he said. "Or will be if a certain stubborn brunette will see things my way." He arched a brow. "And she can have it right now. Cheese and crackers in bed will work for me."

Tracy coughed. She'd asked for that. Damn her for being so girly. She took a drink of water. "This looks good," she mumbled, gesturing at their food. She was sure it was the steam from her pasta that was making her face heat. "Why don't we eat now, talk later."

"Your choice"—he picked up his steak knife, gave her a steely look—"but you'll have to promise to listen hard to what I have to say after we've eaten."

She crossed her heart. "Deal."

When they were done eating—with no conversation other than a brief discussion of paint colors and an acknowledgment of the rain starting to fall outside the diner's windows—Colson said, "You ready?"

"Shoot." She folded her napkin, put it on the table, and got set to deliver on her promise to listen. Not hard, at all, because it gave her the freedom to study the angles and planes of his handsome face, watch his lips compress over certain words, take note of his habit of rubbing his jaw with his thumb when he made a particularly important point.

Colson talked for the next ten minutes, outlining a travel

and meeting schedule that gave her severe jet lag hearing about it. If there was an airport runway on this earth he wasn't landing on or an exotic place he wasn't visiting, she couldn't think where it might be.

". . . all in all, I'll be away maybe eight months out of the next twelve. Two months solid in India early next year, working on bringing home some product branding work along with a marketing strategy project," he finished. "That's it."

"Wow." She picked up her unused spoon, held it between her hands as if it were the linchpin needed to hold her body parts together, keep her erect and looking halfway normal, when she felt like crumbling bones in a sad sack. She wondered why hearing about where Colson would be—which was wherever she wasn't—made her feel lonely. In her heart, her decision to abort this relationship with him before she sank any deeper into it seemed even more right. But right or not, it didn't stop that same heart from aching more than it should. And it didn't make her less angry at fate for bringing her and Colson together on that midnight plane to Georgia, only to put him on a hundred other planes taking him out of her life.

"That's all you've got to say, 'wow'?"

"What do you expect me to say?"

He leaned forward, his gaze intense. "That you'll come with me."

Her jaw slackened, as did the hands still holding the spoon. If he'd asked her to hop aboard a spaceship to Mars, she wouldn't have been more surprised. She must have heard wrong. "Excuse me, could you repeat that?"

"I want you to come with me, Tracy Mae, because . . ." For a moment it looked as if he lost his cool, which Tracy knew must have been a new experience for the logical, brainy, too-sexy-for-his-suit and oh-so-sure-of-himself Colson Jones. "I don't want to end what we started here," he went on. "I want to see where it takes us."

"And to do that, you're proposing it take *me* to India, China, and . . . outer Mongolia or wherever?"

He nodded.

"*C'est fou!*"

He gave her a questioning look.

"Crazy. This is crazy!"

"Crazy to go after what you want? I don't think so. I might have gotten over that sucker punch in the airport—you took my breath away, you know." He smiled at her. "You did know that, didn't you?"

When she didn't answer, he went on, "But after our more intimate time together, I knew there was more going on between us than sexual attraction."

Dear God, so did I, but . . . "Most men would ask the woman to strap on a chastity belt and keep the campfire burning while they went out and conquered the world."

"Then they'd be damned stupid men." He reached across the table and took her hands, massaged the back of them with his thumbs. "And they'd be taking a hell of risk, because with a woman like Tracy Mae Allson, odds are in favor of another wolf"—he smiled—"coming along and taking her away."

"Colson, do I need to remind you, we barely know each other—except in bed—and that was only one night."

"True. And something we need to rectify; both the getting to know each other and that one-night-in-bed count."

"Hah! That's it. You're dangling a life-after-sex scenario in front of my starry eyes so I'll go to bed with you again." She shook her head, gave him a disgusted look.

He leaned back in his seat and for a minute didn't say anything, then, "Do you honestly believe that? That I'd lie, make false promises, to have sex with you?"

Oops! His eyes, hard and cool, attached to her as if she were a thousand-dollar bet on a crooked roulette wheel. And his question felt like a choice between a blue pill and a pink pill; one of them deadly. Fortunately she was saved from answering by the arrival of the pageant-queen waitress.

"Ya'll good here?" She topped their water glasses.

"Fine," Colson said, not looking at her, and through what Tracy was sure were gritted teeth. "The bill, please."

"Sure, honey." She tore the bill from some kind of metal holder thing at her waist and slapped it on the table.

Colson was equally as fast with his cash.

"Thank you, darlin'," she said. "Come back now, hear?" She wriggled off.

"Colson, I'm so—"

"Save it. Let's get out of here."

She didn't move. "You're mad."

He stood over the booth. "Of course I'm mad. You maligned my character."

"So you're saying you *don't* want to take me to bed."

He put his hands on the table, leaned in, and said in a low voice, "Oh, I want to take you to bed, all right, and when I do, you can bet I'm going to make you suffer for that abuse you doled out." He paused. "The thing is, I shouldn't be surprised you're suspicious, considering I've had nothing but sex on my mind since I set eyes on you."

"Me, too," she said.

He rolled his eyes. "Jesus, Tracy, you're making me nuts."

"Good." She held back her smile, slid past him, and got to her feet. "I think we're past our black moment."

He frowned. "Is that a good thing?"

"A very good thing." She touched his face. "You want my answer on your travel idea now . . . or later?" She hoped he'd say later, because she had some plans of her own.

It was his turn to look suspicious, and his frown deepened. "Later, at home, where I can throttle you in private." He took her arm and walked toward the exit.

Outside, the rain—lots of it—came down in big, heavy drops from a warm, dark sky. The car was at the far end of the parking lot, and even though they ran to it, they arrived semi-sodden, moisture clinging to their hair, their faces, and Tracy's ruby red tee.

Colson's cotton shirt plastered itself to his muscles like a gauze bandage. A bandage that needed to be removed, Tracy thought, feeling the tiniest bit smug—and a whole lot happy.

Colson turned the key in the ignition, then looked down at her. "I might have messed up in there, but our conversation isn't over. I meant what I said; I want you to come with me, Tracy. We need to talk about it."

She pushed her wet hair back and met his eyes, her hand still on her forehead. "Drive, Colson. Drive as fast as you can. I've a hankerin' to have my way with you. And—if you can keep me awake after sex—we'll talk then."

His eyes widened, caught the light from a car turning into the diner's parking lot. Dark crystals, she thought, with magic in them. Magic enough to grow wishes and dreams. Magic enough to set her on fire. Magic enough . . . maybe, to make her embark on the biggest journey of her life, and one that had nothing to do with airplanes.

He leaned over and kissed her, soft, slow, and without putting a hand on her. "You know I'm taking this sudden need for my body as a yes, don't you?"

"Not so fast, wolf. I have some conditions of my own."

He eased out of the parking spot, and smiled down at her. "And I can't wait to negotiate them."

Hot slick bodies.

Rain pounding the roof, dripping from eaves, running over window glass. Wind lashing at shutters.

Black night heavy with summer storm and new promise.

Three o'clock in the morning.

Three candles sputtering to their end on the bedside table.

On the worn carpet, two pillows. Tossed and abandoned.

On the bed, rumpled twisted sheets. Movement.

Two cooling, slick bodies . . .

Colson pulled the sheet over Tracy's bare breasts, but she stretched, a long stretch that bared them again. Which was fine by him.

He kissed the nearest nipple and ran his hand down her stomach and over her outer thigh to her knee. Coming back, he stroked the warm, firm skin of her inner thigh, en route to where he planned to spend a lot of his time—for a very long time to come. He tested her crease, then cupped her.

She moaned. "I can't believe it."

He kissed her tummy, felt it contract. "Can't believe what?" He kissed between her breasts, kept his hand steady around the warmth of her sex.

"That I actually want to do—what we've done twice already—again." Her voice held a trace of awe. "I've never—"

"—me either." And it was the truth, because with Tracy Mae the wanting never stopped.

He took her nipple in his mouth, drew on it. "I'm ready to hear your conditions." He drew a finger through her folds, and she arched to his touch.

She grabbed his hand, stopped it. "Not while you have the home advantage, bad boy." She put her other hand on his head, played with his hair. "But we do need to straighten a couple of things out."

She tensed under him, and he heard her take a deep breath. *This is it.* He shifted to her side, propped his head on one hand, and rested the other across her middle. "I'm listening."

"I'm not going with you."

His damn heart stopped. He'd been sure—

"At least not right now," she added quickly.

"Go on."

"I came to Georgia with a plan—not just to help Tommy. Back in Seattle, it seemed everyone had a life—except me. Everyone had a plan—except me. I came here because I needed to think, figure out my life, what I was going to do next. Then . . . well, you came along, and things got crazy. I thought I'd be thinking about career change, where I'd live, what I'd do about my art—if anything. Instead, pretty much all I've thought about is you."

Colson didn't see that as a bad thing. "And?"

"What I need to do is finish what I started here. Stay the three months, or whatever I have. And I want you to come and stay whenever you can between trips." She touched his face. "We need more time together—in bed and out of it—to see if what we have—is enough for me to start drowning in airline tickets." She hesitated but met his eyes, her own wide as if in wonder. "I think I love you, Colson, but it's all so fast, I'm the tiniest bit scared."

"I *know* I love you, Tracy Mae. And I'm not scared at all." He pushed himself up, over her, kissed her long and hard. "But if your staying here for a time is what you want, that's how it will be." He kissed her again, softer this time, and smoothed some curls off her forehead. "But I think I'll work on you to take the India trip with me."

She smiled, stroked his cheek. "Good, I like it when you work on me."

"And to that end, you can count on me landing on Eden's doorstep every chance I get. That's a promise." A promise he intended to keep by having the overworked Melissa scour the next six months of his itinerary for every opening she could find.

She kissed him. "And I promise I'll be here—with the campfire burning."

"What about the chastity belt?" he said, smiling.

"I'm strapping it on as we speak."

"Not so fast, Tracy Mae. I'm not gone yet."

FALL FROM GRACE

Jill Shalvis

One

Janie Mills had done a lot of things in her life, not all of which she was proud of, but killing a guy . . .

Yeah, that was a new one, even for her.

She stood holding the murder weapon in the darkened library where she worked, listening to the sizzling summer storm rage outside, her breath hitching, trying to talk herself out of a panic attack.

Not so easy to do with her heart in her throat, blocking the air passage.

Lightning burst, and for one brief instant, her world lit up in the blue flash, followed by a CRACK of thunder that nearly had her jumping right out of her skin.

Just breathe, she told herself, digging her damp palms into the *Concise Oxford English* dictionary she held. The thing weighed a bazillion pounds, and had swung with ease—

Right against Clayton's head, killing him.

Or so she assumed given the terribly still way he lay at her feet.

Just breathe . . .

But no calming technique was going to help her at the moment, not a single one.

Someone was breathing ridiculously hard. Oh, wait. That was her. Great, now she was hyperventilating. And sweating.

Damn it.

She dropped the dictionary to the floor. It hit with a heavy thunk that echoed into the darkness, reminding her of how it'd sounded against Clayton's skull.

Oh, God. She doubted she'd ever be able to forget the sound of his brain cells clacking together, or forget the sickening thud he'd made as he'd hit the floor like a wrecking ball unchecked.

Good job, Janie. Now she could add murder to the long list of things she shouldn't have done in her lifetime.

Sorry, Mom . . .

If only she'd closed the library on time. If only she hadn't let Clayton Wyatt, town banker, all-around hottie and first-class heel inside when he'd asked. If only the wicked storm hadn't wiped out the electricity.

If only, if only, if only . . . She had a bunch of those, didn't she?

It was called *karma*, coming around to bite her on the ass. But she'd mistakenly assumed that by changing her name, her livelihood, and moving two thousand miles across the country to the small southern town of Grace, Georgia, things would have to improve.

Ding, ding, ding—*wrong*.

When would she learn? There was no hope, not even in this quaint beach town twenty miles out of Savannah, and she needed to remember that. No matter how far she ran, no matter how good she was, bad things happened.

It'd started half an hour ago. She'd been just about to close up when Clayton had pounded on the glass door of the gorgeous old plantation-house-turned-library she ran with such surprising pleasure.

Clayton's melting chocolate eyes had blinked the rain away as he'd begged her to let him in. He came into the library at least once a week for something or another, but never after hours. Tonight he had an emergency meeting with the mayor, Peter Bennett, and needed to bring some Georgia landscape book for a presentation of some kind.

That was just unusual enough—library and emergency in the same sentence?—to let him in. It'd been a ten-hour day already, and Janie did not get paid by the hour, but he'd looked so desperate.

Plus there'd been the guilt factor. He'd asked her out a multitude of times, and she'd continuously turned him down. Gently, but rejection was rejection, and a man like that, an all-American guy with a smile that could both charm and melt, had probably never been told no in his life.

Honestly, did the women in Grace, population 2,568, have no pride? Just because a male had a job and a set of eyes, and okay, also a lean, fit body that he most likely knew how to use, did not mean the female race should just drop their panties and go for it.

Her two fellow coworkers, Leah and Sandy, both claimed they'd drop their panties for him in a heartbeat, which never failed to make Janie shake her head, mystified.

She supposed she'd just never been bitten by the same lust bug as they had.

As for Clayton, she'd been extremely careful not to lead him on in any way, but he never seemed to give up hope.

And yet tonight . . . oddly enough, tonight he'd shown no interest in her at all. He'd simply moved in the direction she'd pointed to get his book, and she'd gone about her closing-up routine. When she'd ended up behind him with an armful of books to put away, it'd been the strangest, most terrifying thing. He'd stiffened, and gone berserk. That was the only explanation for what had happened next.

He'd lunged at her with a scary intent in his eyes.

She knew the look. Also knew better than to hang around and ask questions. So she'd spun on her heel and run like hell, reliving her past in the worst possible way.

That's when the electricity had gone out.

In the dark, all alone, she'd sucked in air, skin damp with sweat and the July humidity, hugging the one book she hadn't dropped while running.

That's when she'd felt a hand close over her arm, spin her around. Reacting without thinking, she'd swung out with the dictionary.

And killed the Golden Boy of Grace. Yeah, Janie, way to fit in. Way to keep a low profile.

Way to ruin your life.

Again.

She stood over the body, breathing like crazy, wondering what the hell to do when suddenly the lights flickered back to life.

Good.

Except . . . Oh, God.

The body crumpled at her feet wasn't Clayton at all, but someone taller, bigger, and far more dangerous for the simple unknown factor.

She had no idea who he was.

What is happening? She'd been running from Clayton . . . she'd hoisted the dictionary in self-defense, and—

And clearly there'd been someone else in the library with them when the lights had gone out.

She stared down at the guy, confused and all the more terrified. In fact, fear clawed at her throat now, and she once again whirled to run—

When the dead guy reached up, his fingers wrapping around her ankle—

And tugged hard.

Down she went like a ton of bricks, right over the dead guy. Only he wasn't dead now, was he? Nope, he had a hold on her but good, yanking her close.

She fought, scrambling for purchase like a woman possessed. And she *was* possessed, with terror! She bashed her forehead on something—his chin?—and heard a low, masculine grunt as she continued to struggle to crawl free.

She almost did it, too, making it a few feet across the smooth wood floor, grabbing a hold of one of the legs of her desk—

"Oh, no you don't," he grated out, rolling, tucking her beneath him, pinning her to the ground with an unwelcome amount of bulk.

He was a big guy, one solid muscle that effectively held her utterly immobile. He could have squashed her like a grape if he'd wanted, but instead he braced one hand next to her head to keep some of his weight off her chest.

A considerate rapist?

A kind murderer?

What the hell?

His face was pasty white as he lifted his head, his movement smashing their lower halves together. Glaring at her from icy blue eyes that promised retribution for the already darkening bruise at his temple, he growled in a low, masculine voice of the south, "You gave me a helluva headache."

The first lesson of self-defense: either incapacitate him, or don't fight; otherwise you'll just piss him off.

Good going, Janie, you pissed him off. "W—what do you want?"

Above them, the lights flickered and threatened to go out again, holding on by a weak thread as she blinked up into his face. "I don't have any money."

"What? I don't want your money!"

"I have my period—"

"Hey, whoa—I'm not going to—*You're* the one who attacked *me!*"

Trapped mercilessly beneath him, she wriggled, desperate to get free. Damn it, she should have swung even harder with that dictionary, or better yet, grabbed for her old-fashioned steel letter opener.

Yeah, now *that* would have made a much more effective weapon. Too bad the terror had slowed her down so much—

"What the hell is going on?" he demanded.

But she couldn't talk; she was too busy kicking her own ass and being squished into the hardwood floor by his even harder body. The guy either had something in his pocket, or his girlfriend had to be an extremely happy woman . . .

"Now see, this is where you talk," he growled, his face a fraction of an inch from hers, his mouth tight, his jaw covered in at least a day's growth. He had long, black lashes—beautiful, and completely wasted on a man, a bad guy to boot.

He wasn't nearly as pretty-boy handsome as Clayton, she thought inanely. Instead, his dark hair, on the wrong side of his last haircut, fell over his temple and into his eyes. His face, square and strong-featured, was clenched with pain. *Good*, because she was going to be covered in bruises from this. He wasn't exactly lightweight.

Thinking it made the panic tighten in her belly, and she renewed her efforts to free herself, sweating in the hot, a/c-less night. So he'd told her he didn't want her money; he'd never said anything about not wanting to kill her.

In their tussle, her sweater had slipped off one arm, but she didn't stop to worry about it, instead trying desperately to knee him in the nads, scratch his eyes out, bite him, whatever it took to make sure she wasn't a statistic on this dark, stormy night from hell.

The man could hold his own, unfortunately, injured or otherwise. She thought she had him for a moment and briefly slipped free. But grunting with effort, he merely tightened his grip on her wrists, then tugged her hands up over her head, straddling her with his long, and as it turned out, powerful legs.

Damn it!

Her heart kicked so hard it was a miracle her ribs didn't crack. "Get off me!"

"Are you kidding? And let you hit me again?" He held on tight, but without further hurting her. "Now, why did you attack me?"

The man had a certain intensity about him, a level of

awareness, a quality of trained alertness that seemed odd in a thug. Still, she clenched her jaw shut and refused to speak.

"Goddamnit," he muttered, and dropped his forehead to hers, a startlingly intimate gesture, as now the entire lengths of their bodies lined up perfectly, from chest, to belly, to thighs . . .

And in between.

She would have screamed, but the library had been built in 1920, renovated in the 70s, and while gorgeous, with a southern hospitality and charming personality in every corner, it was large, cavernous, and all by itself on the street.

She could scream until she was hoarse and no one would ever hear her.

"If you keep squirming," he promised in that slow southern drawl she might have found sexy under very different circumstances, "I'm going to be sick all over you. Now, just be still a second and let me catch my breath."

No. No, she wouldn't just be still, and she upped her efforts to buck him off.

With a sharp oath, he held her pinned.

She fought like mad, and yet he still managed to evade every attempt to make him a eunuch. Finally, exhausted, frustrated, she gave up.

"Thank Jesus," he muttered, and sagged all his weight against her. "Don't. Move."

She didn't see that she had a damn choice, but she was nearly hyperventilating again because she felt quite certain her clothing had slipped in the struggle. Not that she'd care once he killed her, but today, as she'd learned to do every day in the southern heat that was unlike any other heat on earth, she'd dressed for both the hot and steamy weather outside and the icy air-conditioned air inside in a loosely knitted, deep v-necked sweater. It had come completely off one arm now, revealing much of her pale peach tank top beneath.

From the fight, the fear, the sheer adrenaline pumping through her system, she knew her nipples were hard and poking at the insubstantial material of her tank. Plus she had a feeling that her skirt, a floral print in a filmy two-layered gauze, had risen so high on her thighs that if he looked, he'd get quite the peep show.

Again—not going to matter when she was dead.

Unable to do anything else, she lay there steaming with resentment and pent-up frustration, until finally he sighed and again lifted his head as if it caused him great effort. "My head. Is. Going to fall *off.*"

"Good," she spit out, hating being pinned like a butterfly, helpless beneath him, spread for his close perusal. He narrowed his eyes as he did just that, still effortlessly holding her down, clearly waiting for round three as he looked her over with slow deliberation.

She glared at him, passive for now, having decided to save her energy for when she actually had a chance to free herself.

"Tell me," he said in a very soft voice that chased a chill up her spine.

"Tell you what?"

"What the hell is going on, or I'll return the favor with the dictionary."

"You're going to clunk me on the head?"

"That's right. So start talking."

She tightened her lips, but then he actually called her bluff and, pressing her hard into the floor, reached for the fallen dictionary.

TWO

Ryan Patrick tried to move real slow. Not out of deference to the crazy librarian, but because her blow to his poor head had nailed him right on the temple. He supposed he should be grateful the ill-placed hit hadn't killed him, just left him weak and fighting the urge to throw up.

Praying he wouldn't do just that, he eyed the woman pinned spread-eagle beneath him as he reached for the dictionary.

She was soft and warm and delightfully curvy, and he'd been without a woman just long enough that the position made him think things he had no business thinking.

She, on the other hand, was thinking no such things.

Nope, she was spitting daggers at him, remaining mutinous and silent.

And wriggling.

Damn, the woman could wriggle, and that was not helping his already shaky thought process at all.

"Let. Me. Go." She ground this out, still out of breath from the tussle.

"Yeah, can't do that."

"*Why not?*"

"Because the next time you might kill me." He wasn't here

as a citizen, but as a private investigator, following the tracks of his client, who'd vanished earlier in the day and missed a meeting—extremely unlike him.

He didn't know how he knew something was terribly wrong, but instincts were instincts, and they'd saved his sorry ass more than once. So here he was, unable to shake the gut certainty something fishy had gone down, and that this woman was in the middle of it. "You clobbered me over the head and nearly killed me. I just want to know why."

Still struggling, she blew another strand of hair from her eyes. "Nearly doesn't count." She still had a wild riot of blond hair in her face *and* his. Again she blew it away from her mouth, glaring at him from jade eyes still spitting fury.

"So you were trying to kill me?"

"*Get off of me.*" She didn't wriggle again, but he could tell she wanted to.

If he hadn't still felt nauseous and dizzy, he wouldn't have minded the squirming in the least. But his mind was crowded with other things, such as why her name and number had been the last entry on his client's Sidekick, the client who was now missing.

Complicating matters, tonight Ryan had discovered something a little disconcerting about his client. The man was being blackmailed, and yet he hadn't seen fit to mention it to Ryan.

Curious all in itself, because who spent money on a private investigator and then didn't tell that private investigator everything, effectively compromising his own case?

Either way, Ryan wasn't leaving here without answers. Apparently he wasn't leaving without a raging headache either. Damn, he was tired of fighting this petite yet sexy as hell woman he couldn't even really see clearly thanks to his new-found double vision.

Her sweater had nearly come off, and while he should feel bad about that, he didn't, not when all she had on beneath was a flimsy little tank with lace at the breasts, which kept slipping with her every movement. It was a shirt designed to make a man feel things, and in spite of himself, he was definitely feeling them.

Her nipples were hard, peeking out from the insubstantial material of her skimpy tank and the silky strands of her hair, rubbing against his chest.

Damned distracting.

Not to mention, her skirt had risen, revealing toned legs and nearly a hint of panties, making him wonder what color they were—

Catching him looking, she began to struggle anew, and he knew he should feel like a first-class perv, but he didn't. The woman had tried to kill him, and he was justified in restraining her until he knew why.

"Get off," she grated out, arching up, nearly catching him in the balls with her knee, and then his bad leg. Jesus, wasn't she tired yet? He sure as hell was. Plus he was trying not to notice that now he really could see her panties, and they were most definitely a match to her peach tank. "If you'd just stop trying to hurt me—"

"No way—"

"Okay, then how about an answer to—Damn it—" She'd nearly head butted him again. The woman had some serious staying power. "Start talking."

That got him silence from Ms. Wriggler.

"Oh, so *now* you're quiet?" This was crazy. *She* was crazy. After finding her name on his client's Sidekick, he'd looked her up. Beyond her year here in Grace, he could find no info on Janie Mills, quite a feat.

And yet she'd been well received in Grace. Unusual for someone who hadn't been born and bred here, who couldn't count backward at least five generations, but Janie had done it. She'd charmed the local population.

But she wasn't even trying to charm him, not too surprising given the hold he had on her. "Why did you hit me?"

"Because I thought—"

He leaned in to catch the rest of that statement, but she clamped her mouth shut.

"Oh, don't stop there," he murmured, putting a little more pressure on her wrists. "It was just about to get interesting."

She merely fisted her hands and remained stubbornly mute.

Just as well because a wave of nausea hit him hard, making his own hands go clammy. His heart began to thud in his ear, and suddenly he had far too much saliva. Forced to let up on her in order to catch more air, he sat back on his heels. Of course, Janie picked up on his weakness, rolling to her belly beneath him to crawl away.

Goddamnit. Concentrating on not throwing up, he clamped a hand down on her butt to hold her still and simultaneously gulped air. Unfortunately that really set her off, and she kicked out and caught him right on the chin, hard enough to make him see stars to go along with his spots. "Jesus! You are one serious menace to society!"

"Me?" Steam practically came out of her ears. "*I'm* a menace to society? Oh, you have some nerve, you—you dickwad!"

Good one. "Look, why don't we just call the police—"

He hadn't even gotten the word "police" out before she was fighting him again, in earnest now.

She was afraid; he could practically smell it on her.

Afraid of the police?

Flat on her belly, she didn't have much leverage, though she was giving it her all as she tried to reach the leg of her desk, and from there, probably something sharp in one of her drawers to skewer him with. Nice. With every ounce of willpower he had, he hauled her back toward him. Now as she fought, the only thing she was really accomplishing was grinding her very fine ass into his crotch, and in spite of himself, he got a little hot and a lot hard.

Beneath him, she went still.

Yeah, he thought grimly, *that's exactly what you think it is . . .*

With a growl, she jerked back, clipping him right on the chin with her head and then, before he could recover from that blow, slammed an elbow into his ribs.

Goddamnit. He'd been a cop in Savannah before getting shot in the leg on a routine traffic stop. Now, as a PI, he mostly sat behind the wheel of his truck doing surveillance for rich wives looking for their cheating husbands. He'd gone a lot softer than he'd thought if he'd been coldcocked by a woman. Vision fading to gray, he grated his teeth as he flipped her over to her back. "Just relax a minute."

"Like hell." Rearing up, she bit him on the shoulder, hard.

"*Fuck!* Okay, that's it." Telling himself he had no choice, he reached into his pocket for his cuffs. For both their sakes, he thought.

"Oh, don't you dare!" she spit out, and scrambled to get free in earnest.

"I didn't want to have to do this, but—"

"No! I'll . . . I'll be good."

Uh huh. And he was Santa Claus. But still, he hesitated.

And got a knee in the nuts.

More stars exploded in his head, and furious with her, with himself, he slapped the cuffs around one of her wrists, then around one of his. Brawling with him every step of the way, her body glided to his, making him see stars all over again, but this time for a different reason. Breathing way too hard, he sat up, straddling her. And since he hurt like hell from a variety of injuries, all inflicted by this woman, he cared even less about her modesty, which was now even more severely compromised by the latest struggle. Her skirt had twisted itself around her upper thighs, her sweater still off one shoulder, the tank beneath barely, just barely, covering her nipples. *God.*

It drove her crazy, he could tell, and he opened his mouth to apologize, but she tried to knee him again. Luckily he saw it coming, saw it in her eyes, and deflected the blow by turning— and caught the knee in his thigh. Right where he'd been shot. "Damn it. *Stop.*"

"No!"

No longer caring one bit how damn heavy he was, he stretched her cuffed hand high above her head. Huffing like a locomotive, he caught her free hand and held it to her cuffed one. Then, to protect the family jewels, he thrust a thigh between hers. "Look," he managed. "I'm tired." *Hurting.* "All I need are a few answers. You give them to me, and I'll leave."

She blew her hair from her face. "And what about *my* answers?"

"Now see, you have to actually ask a question to get an answer." He was sweating, in serious pain, and somehow, still hard as a rock. Not a proud moment. "Normally this would be a ladies first situation, but I'm in danger of throwing up on you. Tell me why you hit me."

She tightened her mouth. "I thought you were someone else."

"Yeah? Who do you greet with a blow to the head?"

"It's complicated."

He was ready to beg for mercy, not that he could tell her that. "Try me."

But the lights chose that moment to flicker and then go out again. The air conditioner, barely back on since the last outage, stopped humming, as did the computers.

Complete silence, complete darkness.

The woman beneath him gasped, and he tensed in sympathy. He wasn't overly fond of the dark either.

Then, from somewhere behind them in the depths of the library, came a rustling, as if someone were wriggling out of a hiding spot.

Crazy Librarian gripped his shirt in a death vise. "Who—"

"Shh." He set a finger over her lips, straining to hear more over the pounding of his head.

Was that footsteps, running away? He surged to his feet, belatedly remembering he'd cuffed her to him, so she was jerked upright, too.

At the loud jangling of the cuffs, not to mention her second shocked gasp, the footsteps sped up.

And then there came a sort of crashing sound, a grunt, and a thud.

"Ohmigod. You hear that, right?" she whispered, suddenly straining to be closer instead of being free.

Another thud, and then she was in his arms. He opened his mouth, but she wrapped herself around him, cutting off his air, and he couldn't speak. Suffocating, head threatening to fall right off, he reached up to unravel her from him, but thanks to the head blow, he wasn't operating on all cylinders. "Gack," he thought he managed to say, and would have torn free except for one thing.

Her entire body was trembling. She was terrified.

Damn it.

"I can't," she whispered. "I can't—I just can't do this again—"

"Wait. *What?*" In the interest of breathing, he kept trying to pry her loose, but she had the grip of a bulldog. He realized this was not a normal fear, but something else, something triggered and too deep for him to soothe right here, right now, with someone else in the library with them, someone trying to stay hidden. He put his mouth to her ear. "Flashlight?"

She hesitated, then nodded. She loosened her death grip on him and strained toward her desk.

He heard a drawer open, and then a small penlight-sized flashlight was thrust into his free hand. He couldn't see much more than her outline, and nothing of her expression.

"Did we imagine it?" she whispered.

"No." That much he was certain.

And as if to prove it, the front door of the library slammed shut, leaving in its wake a complete and utter silence.

Three

Janie found herself pressed back against her desk, trapped there by the hard body of the stranger who'd attacked her in her own library.

Was it possible to swallow one's own tongue? Because hers felt lodged in her throat, blocking her air passage, pounding, pounding, pounding, pounding in tune with the blood pumping through her veins, swishing in her ears.

She could no longer hear herself think.

He wants to call the cops.

She hugged herself, or tried to, but came up against the restraint of the handcuffs. Oh, God, she was still tied up to this man! Her captor shifted his weight, and she knew he was trying to see behind them. "They left," she said, hoping that was true.

He said nothing, just used the flashlight to survey their immediate surroundings, the narrow beam of light barely cutting into the darkness.

"We heard the door shut," she said. "I assume we scared them off. Don't you?"

"I assume nothing."

The silence felt eerie, too, almost deafening, all-consuming, and so . . . full, it seemed obvious to her that they were alone now. "Seriously. There's no one here—"

"Will you please shut up?"

Oh, no, he did not, but before she could protest, he insisted on searching the place, forcing her up and down the aisles with him, jaw tight, eyes sharp. She noticed he favored his left leg—a weakness she hoped she got a chance to exploit as he searched for God knew what before he finally brought her back to her own desk.

"Who was here?" he demanded.

"I—"

"Oh, why the hell am I asking you," he snapped. "You're not going to tell me. Let's go."

Okay, now he was going to take her to a dark corner and do her in.

No, said a calm voice of reason. If he'd wanted to do that, he'd have done so by now.

Wouldn't he?

Yes. Because if she was being honest, he'd done everything in his power *not* to hurt her. Still, old habits were hard to break, especially a lifelong suspicion of absolutely everyone and everything. "Go where?" she asked warily.

"To have a look around."

"But I don't want to—"

Apparently he didn't care. She dragged her feet, but that meant he had to put his hands all over her to practically carry her, and the feel of those big, warm hands draped so intimately around her waist and ribs, his fingers nearly brushing her breasts, was too much, so she gave up and walked of her own accord.

He seemed relieved, and she had enough self-awareness to be annoyed. Then she had to laugh at herself. Now she was mad he wasn't touching her? That settled it, she'd lost her marbles.

Even more odd, as he pulled her along, he made sure she remained behind him in an oddly protective gesture that was absolutely not going to reach her. Nope, not going to reach her one little bit.

She bashed her shin into a stool and would have fallen if he hadn't caught her. "You all right?" he asked.

"If I say no, will you unhandcuff me?"

"Are you kidding? And let you have a chance at my hide again?"

Without the air-conditioning, it'd continued to get hotter and stickier inside. Or maybe that was just her sheer terror making her sweat. "Your hide is too thick for me to hurt."

"It's my head I'm worried about."

"Your head is too thick, too." It was madness to irritate him, but damn, she hated not having control. Together—she didn't have much choice, now, did she?—he got her to unlock the storage closets and searched those, too.

No sign of Clayton.

Where had he gone?

She was chewing over that when she tripped again, over her own two feet this time, and went down hard on her knees.

"Shit—" Her captor came down right over the top of her, trapping her between the hardwood floor and his even harder body.

She couldn't breathe, she really couldn't. Gaping like a fish out of water, she tried to kick back at him, but she was facedown, flattened by his body weight. "*Hey.*"

Nothing.

"*Hey!*"

He groaned something about his head and his own stupidity, but no matter that he was temporarily incapacitated, she knew how little a threat she really posed. He was tall, built without an ounce of fat, though he did have muscle and lots of it, with or without the bum leg and possible concussion.

And with him pressed so tightly against her, combined with no lights, no sound, it all lent an air of intimacy that she didn't want to face.

She wasn't an intimate sort of woman. She deeply resented

226 / Jill Shalvis

his manhandling of her, so much so that she was calmly planning out how she was going to hurt him as soon as she broke free. Since his head was so damn hard, a kick to the groin might be extremely satisfying—

"Don't even think about it." He drawled this in her ear, his mouth skimming over the sensitive skin just beneath the lobe, reminding her just how vulnerable she was in this position.

She struggled anew because she couldn't help herself, but all it got her was a tough, sinewy forearm wrapped around her middle to hold her immobile, a movement which brought him in even closer to her, her butt to his crotch.

She could feel every inch of him, and as she'd already noticed, there appeared to be a lot of inches. In spite of herself, something deep within her tightened, including her nipples and an odd tingling between her thighs.

That settled it, she had to be sick. "Who are you?"

"Ryan Patrick," he said through what sounded like clenched teeth. "I'm a private investigator."

She went still. A PI? She'd have almost rather him be an escaped felon on the run. Why was a private investigator here? She struggled some more, and he responded by swearing, then pulling their cuffed hands out in front of her, spreading his legs open on either side of hers—a move that effectively held her down as she was sure he'd intended, but also dipped his hips just enough so that there was no mistaking exactly what her squirming had done to him.

"Talk to me, Janie," he grated out. "Who was here tonight?"

"Wait." She put their position—and how unintentionally erotic that position was—out of her head for a minute. "How do you know me?"

"You're the town librarian. It's not a secret. Now, what the hell is going on?"

"Nothing."

"Then why are you hitting perfect strangers over the head?"

"Yeah, hate to break it to you, but you're not so perfect. *Move.*"

"My head is killing me." But though he didn't let her go, he did ease up on one elbow. "I came here tonight, following a lead."

Huh?

He sat back, and she came up on her knees, blinking through the dark at him. She wanted to stand up, gain some distance, but knew better than to show any sign of discomfort and give him the upper hand. "A lead on who?"

"My client."

"And who's that?"

"Privileged information."

"Where is this client?"

"Yeah, that's part of the problem."

"Meaning what?" she asked. "He's missing?"

"A little bit."

"Why would you think he'd be here?"

"Oh, no." Now that she'd sat up, his mouth was close to her ear again, his breath disturbing the hair from her temple. He was warm, big. And oddly, inexplicably, disturbingly sexy.

"You now," he said. "Who did you think I was when you hit me?"

"Besides a murderer?"

He laughed. "In Grace?"

"I'm not from around here. I'm . . . cautious."

"What, you thought I was some big-town bad guy coming after you? In the library?"

Yeah, it sounded crazy. Unless one understood and knew her past, and what she'd been through.

But he didn't.

No one did.

Maybe she could just say she was sorry, and then he'd go far, far away. But pride was a funny thing. She kept choking on hers. "So you want me to believe you're the good guy?"

"Yes!"

She rattled the handcuffs. "Doesn't feel like it."

"You hit me over the damn head!"

"With a *book*, tough guy. And anyway, what kind of private investigator can't take care of himself? I'm like what, five-two tops. You're like seven feet tall."

"Six-four," he muttered. "And that was a fucking heavy book."

Oh, wasn't that just like a man, trying to twist the situation so that the fault, the blame, the every-damn-thing ended up on her shoulders. "You have no reason to hold me, no reason to question me. I've done nothing wrong."

"Try assault."

"It's called self-defense."

He blew out a breath, but didn't let her go.

"I'm going to call the cops," she said.

"Really." His eyes cut to hers, and held. Something seemed to zing through the air. Tension, certainly. Fear, *hers*.

But something else, too, an undeniable awareness that she didn't want to face.

From the both of them.

"You're going to call the cops," he said, heaving with disbelief.

"Yes." A complete bluff, of course. She'd had a serious mistrust going with any law enforcement for most of her childhood, but never more than a year ago.

It'd been hot that night, too, not the sticky heat of the south, but the smog-filled, oppressive dry heat that the Santa Ana winds often brought to Los Angeles.

She could still see Billy, her brother, standing over her cousin David, gun still smoking, and David . . . well, let's just say he'd never again walk the streets looking for trouble.

The smell of that night haunted her; the dirty sidewalks, the blood in her mouth from where she'd bitten through her own cheek to keep from screaming and alerting Billy to her presence.

But he'd known anyway, somehow he'd known.

She'd done her best to remain utterly silent, holding her shaking hands over her mouth to keep the scream in, trembling in her shoes, wanting to be sick because her brother had killed someone in cold blood.

And not just any someone, but her cousin. He'd looked right into David's eyes and pulled the trigger.

And then he'd lifted his head, the moonlight glinting on his wet hair. He'd picked her out of the shadows, his gaze ice with hatred as he lifted his gun toward her.

With the scream backing up in her throat, she'd turned tail and run, and had never looked back.

Never.

Janie's Witness Protection Program—ghetto style.

It'd been a year. A year, damn it, and she still jumped at shadows, constantly looked over her shoulder.

Hit perfect strangers with dictionaries.

Oh, God. She'd hit a perfect stranger with a dictionary. For a moment her strength wavered, and she felt ill. But that passed because he pulled her up and over to her desk.

And the telephone there.

"Um . . . ," she said brilliantly. "Let's not be hasty here."

"You have an aversion to cops for any reason in particular?"

"Of course not."

"How about men. You have an aversion to men? Or is it just me?"

Her breath hitched oddly in her throat, and she wrestled against backing away from him. Not from fear now, but because he felt too close, too masculine, too . . . intoxicating. "Definitely just you."

He didn't smile, though his lips quirked slightly, and she found herself fascinated by the stingy yet somehow beautiful movement.

"I told you, I'm not a bad guy," he said.

She sniffed. "I'm reserving judgment, thanks."

His steely eyes were suddenly not so steely. "Maybe you'd rather take your chances with whoever we heard out there . . ."

She shifted slightly closer to him. "No. No, thank you."

"See, you're getting to like me already."

Somehow she managed a tough-girl laugh, even tilted up her chin to go with it, spewing bad attitude. "Don't flatter yourself. You're the lesser of two evils, that's all."

"You realize," he said, "if I was a rapist, murderer, or kidnapper, I'd have already done to you whatever it was I'd planned on doing, right?"

"It's crossed my mind," she admitted, and turned away from him as much as she could because whew . . .

She needed a cool fan blowing on her face just to look at the guy for more than a few seconds, a realization she would most definitely be keeping to herself.

He merely used the cuffs against her, turning her back, and calling her bluff for the second time that night, he handed her the telephone with which to call the cops.

Four

Ryan watched Janie's pride war with temper. It was a fascinating struggle.

"Okay, fine," she finally said, and snatched the receiver from his hand. "I'll call. Happy?"

"Ecstatic."

She ground her teeth together and stared down at the phone as if it were a poisonous snake.

"You have to actually dial to get connected."

She swallowed hard. "Right."

Seemed his sweet little librarian with the not-so-sweet temper was full of secrets, which tweaked his curiosity. "It's 9–1–1," he offered helpfully.

She made a sound of annoyance and blew a strand of wayward hair away from those drown-in-me eyes. Then she pulled herself up to her full five-two height. "Look, I'll make you a deal."

He could only imagine. A lead pipe to the skull? "Not interested."

"You haven't even heard it yet," she said in surprise. "How can you turn down a deal you haven't heard?"

He shrugged. "Easy."

She bit her lip and stared at him. "If we leave the police out of this, I'll stop fighting you."

"Ah, and just when I got to enjoying the fighting, too."

"Okay, something else, then."

"What, like take out a library book after hours?" He pretended to consider. "No, thanks."

"Not a library book."

"Then what?"

She paused. "What if I said you could choose."

Choose? An entirely inappropriate vision of her naked and stretched out for his own pleasure came to him. Yeah, now that might make him forget about the head injury, and what a pain in the ass she was. "You want me to choose."

"But you have to remove the handcuffs."

"Right. So you can beat the shit out of me again."

"I'll talk. I'll tell you whatever you want to know."

He looked at her for a beat, decided she was just desperate enough to actually mean it, and pulled the key out of his pocket. He stuck the flashlight between his teeth, aimed it at their joined hands, and unlocked the handcuffs.

"You did that in an awful hurry," she said, rubbing her wrist. "So . . . what do you choose?"

His body leapt. *Bad* body. "What makes you think I want to choose anything?"

"Because all men want something."

"Are we talking about sex? Are you offering me sex if I don't call the police?"

"No! God!"

"Well then." Kidding, he reached for the cuffs again.

"A kiss," she said quickly. "You can have a kiss."

Jesus. He hadn't expected that. He was still half braced for violence from her, and now she was offering a kiss. His poor brain didn't know what to do. *Say no,* he told himself. *Just say no.* "Okay," the very bad man inside of him said.

"Okay." She nodded, then unbelievably, closed her eyes and puckered up.

He stared at her. Was she kidding?

When he didn't make a move, she opened her eyes. "What?"

"Oh, no," he said, shaking his head, standing very still because suddenly, shockingly, he was turned on all over again. "*You* have to kiss *me.*"

She frowned. "That's silly."

He reached for the phone.

"*Fine.*" Huffing out a breath of irritation, she sauntered closer to him as if it was no big deal.

But if it was no big deal, then why were they both already breathing as though they'd each run to Savannah and back, uphill each way.

In the snow.

He tried to control his own breathing, but the more he tried, the more ragged it sounded, loud and uneven in the quiet library.

Her eyes held his as she took that last step, closing the gap between them.

God, she was something to look at, her eyes huge, lips parted, pulse beating as wild as a hummingbird . . . He couldn't look away to save his own life.

Then her lips brushed across his, so quickly that if he'd so much as blinked, he'd have missed it.

"There." Looking quite proud of herself, she took a giant step back, clasped her hands in front of her, and smiled.

And though his world felt oddly rocked, he slowly shook his head. "That wasn't a kiss."

"Was, too."

"Not even close."

"My lips touched yours," she pointed out.

"True. But if you think that's a real kiss, your education has been sorely lacking . . ."

She stared at him for a moment, then fisted her hands in his shirt as if to haul him up. Only problem, she was about a foot shorter than he was, so instead she tugged him down.

Still not quite level, and with a growl that made him want to smile, she yanked harder. "I'm lacking in nothing," she growled, nose to nose with him.

Then, while he was still smiling, she planted her mouth on his, and that was the last coherent thought he had because the kiss was—

Out.

Of.

This.

World.

He figured he was alone in this thought, but she slipped her arms around his neck at the same moment he caught her up. Having her soft, giving body in full contact to his bigger, harder one was a relief he hadn't expected, and he staggered back, again coming up against a shelving unit.

"Your head," she murmured.

"I'm fine." Yeah, if fine was crazy.

"But—"

"Shh." Palming her head, he ignored the already fading pain—amazing how adaptable the human body was—and deepened the kiss, dancing his tongue with hers. She let out an erotic little sigh filled with pleasure and excitement and, if he wasn't mistaken, relief as well. God, that turned him on, knowing she needed this, wanted it as much as he. Not that it made any sense to him, none of it.

He blamed the night, so thoroughly dark and disturbing with the violent storm raging both outside and inside. He blamed his own frustration with his case. He blamed the vulnerable sheen in Janie's eyes because he was a sucker for vulnerable.

But mostly he blamed her curvy, hot little bod, the low hum of approval in her throat, the musical lilt in her voice, the sheer determination and fierce independent pride he saw in her every movement.

God, she was sweet.

She tasted like forgotten hopes and dreams—his, hers, he

didn't know, it'd been so long since he'd thought of his own hopes and dreams.

When had been the last time he'd felt like this, so vibrantly, shockingly alive? Since before he'd been shot, he knew that much. Before working the streets of Savannah. No, even before that.

Years.

Maybe never.

Thinking it, marveling, he turned so that he held her against the shelving unit with his body, which freed up his hands nicely. He stroked them up her sides, and she let out a soft murmur, an acceptance sweeter than anything he could remember. Then she arched against him, her body pliant and giving, her mouth hot and hungry for his.

Cupping her breast in his hand, he dragged a thumb over her nipple, groaning at the feel of it pebbling tight in his hand. Oh, yeah, she was amazing, so damned amazing—

An unexpected *pop* sounded from somewhere in the depths of the room, startling them both. Ryan broke off the kiss as the sound echoed in his bemused brain.

What had that been?

Janie also drew an unsteady breath and, propped up against the shelves, stared up at him, mouth wet, her breath coming out unsteadily, looking gorgeously rumpled and quite mystified.

He knew the feeling. He couldn't decide if he'd really heard anything, but his gut was telling him that something was wrong, very wrong. "Did you hear that?"

She put her hands to her head and shook it, a little dazed. "Hear what?"

"That . . . pop."

"I can't hear anything over the sound of the blood rushing through my veins," she admitted.

"Stay here." It took him a second to get his legs to work, but he took the flashlight and went around the corner of the aisle, searching. For what, he wasn't exactly sure, but sud-

236 / *Jill Shalvis*

denly out of the sheer black of the yawning open library came Janie's scream.

And as his head instantly cleared, he realized what that popping noise had been.

A gunshot, muffled by a silencer.

Five

Janie had gone back to her desk for a second flashlight, turned it on, and then gotten the most unpleasant, horror-filled shock of her life.

Hence the scream, which had escaped her before she could help it.

Now she stood there feeling a bit like a deer in the headlights, frozen, her scream still echoing around her.

"Janie!"

She heard Ryan call out for her, but ignored him because she was busy.

Busy staring down at the body at her feet.

She couldn't see much, just the crumpled figure of a man, but somehow she just knew.

This one was really dead.

Ryan came running back to her side, big and oddly comforting in his familiarness, given her evening so far. "Ah, hell," he said very quietly, aiming his light over the body.

"I think he's—"

"Shh." He tugged her away and around a corner, pressing her back against the shelving unit, holding her there while she gulped for air, feeling the hysteria hit her hard.

"Ryan—"

He put his hand over her mouth, his body pressed to hers, holding her immobile. "I know." Keeping her upright, he cocked his head, listening.

For what, she had no idea.

Then from somewhere far, far across the large room came the sound of a door closing.

"Yeah," he said grimly. "Thought so."

She pulled his hand from her mouth, her heart in her throat. "They didn't leave last time."

"They didn't leave last time," he agreed. "Listen to me." He cupped her face in his hands and tilted it up to his. "Are you listening, Janie?"

She nodded.

"Good. I need you to stay here."

"But—"

"Stay." He held her gaze captive. "Promise me."

"Yes. Okay."

"I mean it, Janie. Don't move. Don't even breathe. Don't make a sound."

Fear skittered up her spine. "I won't."

He stroked her jaw once and then was gone.

All alone, reaction set in. Her teeth began to chatter, and hugging herself, she slid down until she was sitting on the floor.

In the dark.

With a body on the floor of her library.

Oh, God.

What had that person been doing in the library, and why hadn't he made himself known?

And who had run out into the night?

Every answer she came up with only posed more terrifying questions, so she stopped thinking. Or tried to anyway.

It might have been an hour, or only a minute later, when Ryan appeared out of the dark. "We're alone," he said.

Yes, but she'd thought they'd been alone all along. Knowing they hadn't been was freaking her out.

As was the guy on the floor.

Ryan tugged her up. "Come on."

They approached the body, which was facedown, arms and legs sprawled out as if he'd fallen while running at top speed.

Why hadn't they heard that?

Oh, that's right—because she'd been pressed up against the shelves, with Ryan's tongue conducting its own search . . .

Ryan hunkered down and checked the body for a pulse, then shook his head at her.

She covered her mouth with her hand and felt herself shudder. "He's really dead."

"Yeah." He flicked his light over the middle of the man's back. There was a hole in his shirt. "What—"

"Hold on." Ryan pulled some keys out of his pocket and, using the tip of one, nudged the material of the shirt away from the body.

Two more shocks hit her like a one-two punch.

The man had been *shot*. With a gun. In her library.

How was that even possible?

How could this happen? Here in Grace, the police reports were filled with things like mischievous teenagers and the occasional drunk.

Not random shootings!

Good God, she'd let her guard down, she'd actually thought she was safe here, but she couldn't have been more dead wrong.

Then that second surprise sank in. The man had pink silk peeking out from beneath his shirt.

A bra? He'd been wearing a bra?

Stranger and stranger . . . "There's no blood," she whispered.

"Died right away."

"I didn't hear the gun go off—"

"Silencer."

"But . . . how could we not have heard any of this?"

Ryan's jaw was tight. "Because they were trying to be quiet."

"They?"

"Well, there were at least two." He locked gazes with her. "And they were watching something. Or someone."

"Who?"

He just looked at her, and the knowledge sank in with a gasp. "Me?" she squeaked. "There's a dead body in my library because of me?"

"I don't know."

Just when she thought things couldn't get worse, they did. Ryan flicked the light over the body, up to the face.

And she went utterly still with the shock of recognition.

Clayton.

Ryan's expression was intense and unfathomable. "You know who this is?"

Oh, God. She shuddered again. No one should ever have to see someone in death and know that person was never again going to open their eyes, never going to laugh or smile or eat an ice cream.

Never going to love.

Much less see it twice in a lifetime. "Yes," she managed to choke out. "I know him."

Ryan waited for more information, which she couldn't give because of the bone-deep cold that had overtaken her.

"Janie." Ryan took her arms in his big, warm hands. "Breathe."

"Right." She gasped for air, pulling it into her deflated lungs. "Breathing."

"You okay?"

She started to nod, but ended up slowly shaking her head instead.

Ryan sighed and pulled her in for a hug, which she was desperate enough to take, and for a moment she allowed herself to cling.

"You know we have to call the police now," he said into her hair.

She took a moment to soak in his strength, his heat. "I know."

He pulled out a cell phone and hit 9–1–1, speaking to dispatch while continuing to hold her close, which was over and above the call of duty but greatly appreciated. When he was done, he slipped the phone back in his pocket. "Funny how a dead body moves you right up to the front of the line."

"So they'll be here fast?"

"Oh, yeah." He looked down at Clayton's body. "Janie? Why is my client dead in your library?"

She gaped. "Clayton is your client?"

"Was." He looked at her. Quiet. Assessing. "Did you see him here?"

She went very still inside. Yep, she'd seen him here. How about she'd seen him only moments before his death, which made her very likely the last person—before the murderer, that was—to see him alive.

Oh, God.

"Janie?"

She broke eye contact. This wasn't going to look good. Clayton being dead was terribly tragic and sad, but beyond that, it was going to bring questions, an investigation, and she was going to be right in the middle of it.

Ryan kept looking at her. There was something about his eyes, about the way he held himself, that told her he knew what to do in this situation, in *any* situation. Getting a job done meant something to him, no matter how messy, how difficult, how terrifying.

He could help her, but it meant trusting him. Too bad she didn't do trust.

"Janie?"

She knew now was the time to tell him. She could open her mouth and tell him everything, because she'd done nothing wrong. He would listen. He would know what to do, and he'd tell her in that dry, deliberately calm voice, and she would be able to breathe again.

But years and years of always being on the defensive, of surviving the things she'd survived, had taught her to be overly cautious.

Not to mention that whole can't-trust thing.

Tell him, said a small voice deep inside. *Trust him.*

He was waiting for her to do just that, watching her with a definite hint of something restless and hungry behind that deceptively calm gaze.

You can trust him . . .

Probably.

Maybe.

Oh, just do it! Drawing a deep breath, she opened her mouth, but karma intervened as a siren whooped. A cornucopia of red, white, and blue lights burst through the windows of the library as the cops pulled into the parking lot. "They're here," she whispered.

"That they are."

She got the uncomfortable impression he could see right through her, deep into her soul even, which was silly. Ridiculous. No one saw into the real Janie Mills.

But then the police were inside with their flashlights and authority, and any opportunity she had to open up to Ryan was over.

It was two hours before she was free to leave, but even then the police sergeant who'd been questioning her advised her not to leave the county.

She knew it was protocol, and that if she was a suspect, it would be only temporary because she had done nothing wrong, but it didn't help with the fear factor.

Each question they'd asked her had filled her with more and more dread, starting with her name.

What if they dug deeper and found she had a different last name than she'd admitted to? What if they leaked that name to the press?

Anyone in the world could find her then, including her

brother, who most likely would be extremely happy to have his last loose thread found.

And killed.

Oh, God.

She stood just outside the library now, staring into the still stormy night, desensitized by all she'd seen and done in the past few hours. One sleepy southern town, a dead body, and now . . . secrets rising. It all equaled an unbelievable nightmare. Hell, the place might never be the same after this shake-up.

A bolt of lightning flashed, followed by a long silence, then a distant boom.

The storm was beginning to move on.

Rain lightly hit the asphalt, dampening her skin. The salty air brushed her face, a scent she'd grown to love. She'd chosen here, far enough from the closest big city—Savannah—but close enough to people; kind, good people who cared about one another.

The sense of a warm community drew her and had kept her here. She'd thought maybe she'd always be here. Now all that security and stability had been compromised.

The raindrops came fewer and fewer now. She'd once thought she'd hate the humid weather here, but she didn't. In fact, she thrived on it, it fed her soul, it made her want to do things for herself that she'd never done.

Like follow her dreams.

Those dreams involved settling down, making a home, maybe take up writing seriously instead of just dabbling with journals . . . possibly landing herself in a relationship for once.

How could she ever get there if she had to keep running?

She stepped off the sidewalk and into the parking lot, which was still filled with vehicles; the coroner's, the police, and more police . . . everyone's car but Clayton's red Jeep, which was noticeably missing.

Was the murderer driving it even now?

She headed toward her car on the far edge of the parking

lot. She always parked as far away as she could because she liked the walk in the mornings, but now that walk seemed extraordinarily far.

As she moved, everything faded away, the lights, the murmured talking, leaving nothing but the night, eerily silent except for the light rain.

Still off balance, she stood by her car and began searching through her purse for her keys. A feeble burst of lightning helped. She found a pen, a lip gloss, her wallet, Mace that she always kept with her . . . oh, and a condom that had been in there for far too long. Maybe if she'd found *only* a perfect stranger tonight, and not a dead body, she'd have pulled this baby out.

But maybes were like her hopes and dreams . . .

Not in the cards.

Ryan had been a maybe. She could admit that, just as she could admit she wouldn't soon forget the look on his face when he'd listened to her being questioned by the police, when he'd realized she'd not only known Clayton, but that she'd seen him tonight and hadn't mentioned it, even when he'd asked her outright.

She could have explained that she didn't do trust, but she decided that wouldn't have helped. He couldn't have understood, who could? She wondered where he was now; she'd lost him in the crowd, but told herself it didn't matter.

She finally located her keys and got out of the rain. Driving home, she felt very alone. And since she was, she could admit the truth. *It did matter . . .*

She'd let him kiss her. *Really* kiss her. She'd let him touch her, and if she was being honest, she'd have let him do even more . . .

Would she see him again, the man with the low, rough, gorgeously southern drawl, not to mention those knowing eyes, which seemed to suggest he knew all manners of pleasurable things to do with a woman?

God, she hoped so.

Pulling into the covered carport of her apartment complex, she got out of the car and began walking up the path toward her door, telling herself it didn't matter if she ever saw him again. Sexy as hell or not, great voice or not, hot bod or not, it just didn't matter, because at the moment she was still blessedly numb.

Numb, she couldn't be afraid. Numb, she'd be able to have a chance at sleeping tonight. Numb, she'd—

Oh, God.

Someone had come out of the shadows and was standing right behind her.

Six

Someone. Right. Behind. Her.

Janie went into survival mode. She was equal distance between her car and the front door of her apartment building. Her car would take precious seconds to unlock. The building door would be locked, too, but that was an electronic code, a four-digit number she could punch in quickly, and despite the late hour, there were a few lights on. Someone was awake. She could start screaming, and someone would hear her.

Or so she hoped.

After all, she'd been here before. Not *here*, but in a bad situation, with only her wits about her to count on. Her fingers tightened on her keys, which she could use to poke someone's eyes out. Her other hand snaked back into her purse for the Mace.

Neither would have worked on her brother that night, of course. Nope, he'd have been far too fast for her, and she knew if he ever caught up to her, he'd prove it.

And she'd be as dead as her cousin.

As Clayton.

But she wasn't going down without a fight. *Bring it on*, she thought, and whipped around.

Nothing but night.

Okay, she was losing it here. Shaking her head at herself, she turned back toward her building.

And again heard footsteps.

"Who's there?" she called out with determination into the night, proud that her voice didn't shake. Much.

Another footstep, and she whirled in the direction from which it'd come, off to her side, and saw a tall, leanly muscled shadow there. She gasped before she could stop herself, and then the shadow moved beneath the one light in the parking structure, and the sigh backed up in her throat because the shadow limped, and she knew that limp. "You."

"Me," Ryan agreed, and with his eyes on the keys and the Mace she held, he carefully took another slow step toward her.

"What are you doing here?"

"You going to Mace me, Janie?"

"I'm thinking about it. Answer my question."

"Ah, you want an answer to your question. Funny that. Because so do I."

He was irritated, and as she knew, with good reason. She'd held out on him. Now he wanted to know what she had to do with his client's death. Well, she wanted to know things, too, damn it! She tightened her grip on the Mace.

"You'd better be quick if you're going to do it," he warned softly.

Oh, she was tempted, so damned tempted. But in the end she dropped the Mace back in her purse, then surprised and shocked them both when her eyes filled. "Shit," she said angrily, and swiped at a tear. *Shit!*

"Hey." He put his hands on her arms and forced her to look at him. "Hey, it's okay—"

"Okay? You call finding a dead guy at my work okay? It's not okay! It's the farthest thing from okay ever!"

"Janie."

She sniffed and promised herself not another single tear. "I am not going to do this, I'm not—"

"Let's go inside; you're cold and—"

"It won't change anything." Clayton would still be dead. She'd still be jumping at shadows, wondering when she would get to live without fear.

But he was steering her toward her building, and she was letting him. Odd, because she never let anyone steer her anywhere, and she never did anything she didn't want to do.

She wanted him to come inside.

She wanted him to keep holding her.

And she wanted more, too. She wanted to forget the fear, the constant edginess. If she could have her dream—a normal life!—then she also wanted oblivion, even if only for a few hours.

She unlocked the building, and together they climbed the stairs. Hers was on the second floor, with three other apartments. At her door, Ryan stopped her from putting in her key. "Wait."

She looked up at him in surprise, then felt more surprise at look on his face. It was the same look he'd gotten when he'd seen the very dead Clayton—intense concentration, and a grimness that made her stomach sink.

Then she saw why.

Her door was ajar.

Someone had been inside.

Ryan swore and pushed Janie behind him. She fought him, of course, so he put a finger to his lips, pointing to just outside the door, waiting until she nodded. He knew that meant she understood he wanted her to wait and be quiet. The question was, would she actually do it?

But she surprised him by backing up and doing as he asked.

Miracle.

Turning his attention back to her apartment, he scanned the living room in one glance. Hardwood floors, high ceiling fans, throw rugs, and antiques, all adding a warm and homey touch . . . except for the fact that the couch was turned over, cushions on the floor, bookshelves emptied, contents scattered.

There was a TV in the corner, and he could see a small stereo across the room on a stand. Both untouched.

Not a robbery.

He moved into the kitchen. Here more of the warm hominess, but the drawers were opened and things scattered everywhere.

And yet in the bedroom, the bed was neatly made, the dresser drawers all neatly closed, and everything tidy and appearing in its place.

Same with the bathroom.

Which meant that whoever had been here, they'd found what they were looking for in the living room and possibly the kitchen, and then hadn't even bothered in this room.

So what had they found?

He moved back to the front door and found Janie just as he'd left her. At his approach, she glanced at him, pale. "I'd like to start this day all over," she whispered.

"Yeah, I hear that." He pulled her inside and slipped an arm around her shoulders as she took in the condition of her apartment with a grim nod.

"What's missing?" he asked.

She shook her head, walking past her upturned couch to a small desk in the corner. She bent and inspected the empty drawers, not saying a word but going even more pale.

"What?"

"My laptop is gone." She looked up. "Why would they take just the laptop, not the TV or the stereo, or my—" Breaking off, she ran into the kitchen, and by the time he followed her, she was looking into yet another empty drawer.

She stared up at him bleakly.

"What else?" he demanded.

"My PDA."

He looked at her for a long moment. "What's on your laptop and PDA that someone would risk a B&E charge for, Janie?"

"I don't know."

"Janie."

"I don't know!"

She looked frazzled and terrified enough to have him believing it, and when she turned in a slow circle beneath the harsh fluorescent light of the kitchen, looking wan and pale and devastated, he sighed and went to her.

"I don't," she said to his chest as he pulled her in. "I really don't."

When he cupped her head and hugged her, she sighed and whispered it one last time as she turned her face to his throat and burrowed in. "I don't know."

"We have to call the police—"

Her lips were against his skin when she let out another long-suffering sigh. "Yeah. That I do know."

The police work went slightly faster this time, which relieved Ryan. The lack of a dead body helped, but the situation was no less intense given that they'd each already been involved with the police once tonight.

Turned out there was at least one interesting parallel. One of Janie's neighbors reported seeing a red Jeep on the street outside her building only an hour ago.

Clearly it hadn't been Clayton driving; he'd already been dead on the library floor.

So where was that Jeep now, and who was in it?

Ryan stayed close during Janie's questioning. He could tell himself it was professional curiosity; it was his job to know everything he could about the woman who'd been the last to see his client alive.

But he knew damn well it was far more than that. He just didn't know what the hell it was. There was something about her, certainly. She reached him somehow, drew him, and it'd been a long time since he'd felt like this.

Still, he wasn't stupid. Janie knew more about Clayton and

what had happened tonight than she'd let on, and he listened carefully to the answers she gave the cops.

Yes, she'd locked her front door when she'd left for work. No, she had no idea why someone would have broken into her house for her computer and PDA. Yes, she lived alone, and had since she'd moved here a year ago from . . .

She was quite vague on that, Ryan noticed. She didn't want to talk about herself or her past.

And he wanted to know why.

By the time they were alone again, it was nearly one in the morning. He looked over at her slumped into a chair, staring blindly into a cup of hot tea one of the cops had made for her, and felt his heart catch. Damn it. Hadn't felt that in a long time either. He could have done without feeling it now. "Let's go."

She didn't move. "Where to?"

"My place."

Only her eyes cut to his, but he had no doubt as to what she was thinking, and it started with a *hell* and ended with a *no*.

"I'm not leaving you here," he said. "Not alone, not tonight."

"We're strangers."

Strangers who'd had each other's tongues down their throats, but yeah, basically they were strangers. "You're still coming with me."

"What if I say no?"

"You're not stupid."

She stared at him for a long moment. "I could go to a hotel."

"You could. Where you'd probably stare at shadows on the walls all night long. Get your stuff, Janie."

"Or?"

"Or I'll get out the handcuffs," he said rashly, knowing damn well that was a false threat. He wasn't going to force her to do anything; he wanted her to come of her own accord. He wanted, shockingly enough, for her to *want* to be with him, but he knew that wasn't going to happen. "Please," he said, using a word that felt rusty. "I don't want you here. Alone."

She looked at him for a long moment, her eyes dark and unreadable. Then they warmed, as did his heart when she nodded.

Seven

Janie had no idea what it said about her that the handcuff comment had actually swayed her. Or maybe it was just Ryan himself, all tall, dark and attitude-ridden, and yet somehow compassionate and empathetic enough to melt through her icy reserve.

No one melted her icy reserve . . .

But he had. He'd gotten through that and her fear and her frustration, and that made him dangerous as hell, at least to her mental health. She glanced at him standing in the middle of her living room, eyes sharp, body tense and battle-ready.

For her.

It'd been too long since she'd had someone on her side. It scared her that she thought of him that way because she had grown used to being on her own.

The fact that after only several hours she'd come to want him scared her bone deep.

After all, what did she really know about him, other than he kissed like heaven on earth, and that he had a way of looking at her which made her want to take her clothes off . . .

And oh, yeah, he was a private investigator, which meant he could access things about her that she didn't want people to know.

Right. That put things back into perspective, didn't it?

Tearing her gaze off him, she moved into her bedroom to pack. She loved this bedroom, and her eyes cut directly to the only personal memento in it, the framed picture on her dresser. It was of her mom, smiling into the camera shortly before she'd died so unexpectedly from an aneurism. That had been the beginning of the end for Janie.

She'd been twelve.

It reminded her of the most important thing here.

Survival. She needed to get to it.

Her bedroom was neat and tidy, as she'd left it. The soft muted colors lulled her to sleep every night, along with the salty air and the soothing sounds of the ocean only two blocks away. She'd been lucky to find this place. She'd picked it because it'd seemed safe and protected. Off the beaten path.

And yet trouble had found her anyway. Because that thought made her stomach hurt, she opened a dresser drawer and pulled out a pair of jeans for tomorrow, and a tank top.

Had someone been in here, too, pawing through her things? And why?

That was somehow more terrifying than knowing her brother was most likely still out for her blood. She knew that threat, knew where it came from, and understood it.

It was the unknown that made everything all the more horrifying.

She picked out a pair of socks. Panties and a bra. Holding the baby blue silk, she turned—

And found Ryan standing right behind her.

Again she experienced that odd little lurch deep in her belly.

His gaze fell to the silk in her fingers, and he paused, mouth open as if he'd lost his train of thought before his words could escape.

"I'm still packing," she said.

"I see that."

A shiver ran down her spine at the way his eyes blazed. He cleared his throat, his eyes glued to the silk.

Men. They might each walk different, talk different, even think different, but they were all just slaves to their penises.

So why was she reacting to his reaction, complete with her nipples tightening and more? Big mystery, and she'd had enough of those for today.

She dropped the lingerie into her bag and, with him watching her every movement, headed into the bathroom to grab a few other essentials.

He followed her, his gaze landing on the small box of condoms in an opened drawer. Reaching out, he fingered the top.

Unopened.

She picked up the box along with her make-up and looked at him.

His eyes were so dark, so flaming hot, she had to swallow hard. Not sure what she was doing, she moved close, then closer still. He took the box from her fingers and, still holding her gaze, dropped it into her bag.

Yeah, she had trouble keeping her breathing even after that.

He touched her jaw. "Did you know I think you're the sexiest woman I've ever met?"

It took her a moment to find her voice. In the end, she went with shaking her head. No. She hadn't known. She zipped up her bag and toyed with the strap, incredibly aware of the box of condoms inside.

Ryan's expression was as dark and unpredictable as the weather outside, but he took the duffel bag from her and flung it over his shoulder. "Ready?"

Was she? She looked into his eyes, which had the ability to shut her out, but they weren't shutting her out now. In fact, she nearly staggered back at the flames flashing there. Probably if he touched her, they'd spontaneously combust. Which wouldn't be a bad thing, she decided. It'd definitely release some tension. "Ready."

He steered her out the door, his gaze watchful on their surroundings. Outside, he put her into his truck on the driver's side and had her slide over before following her in. It was the first time she realized how prepared for danger and possibly more violence he was, and how naïve she'd been to think there wouldn't be more. "This isn't over," she said.

"No," he agreed. "Definitely not over."

For the hundredth time, she thought about how little she really knew about him, other than the police had known and trusted him greatly.

Not necessarily a bonus.

But there was something about being with him that inspired a level of comfort despite his aggressiveness, and also a trust, when she hadn't meant to do that at all. "Where do you live?"

"Tybee Island."

Only a few miles away.

"You're quiet," he said with a quick glance at her. "You hanging in?"

"Of course."

His lips quirked slightly. "Are you always so stoic and tough?"

She wished. "You witnessed my meltdown."

"You call a few tears a meltdown?" He laughed softly, a sound she hadn't heard from him but decided she liked very much. "I grew up with four sisters," he said.

"Wow. That's a lot of hormones."

"And a high-strung mother, and an aunt, and a grandmother, all in the same house."

In his voice was a genuine affection, and she looked at him again. Given the lateness of the hour, traffic was light on the highway, only the occasional car. The headlights slashed across his face, briefly highlighting his expression, which mirrored what she'd heard in his voice.

He loved his family. All those women . . . maybe that's where he'd learned so much about dealing with out-of-control females, not to mention the utterly unself-conscious ease he had of moving, talking . . . being.

In contrast, she'd grown up with a missing father, no

mother from age twelve on, and a gangbanger older brother with a mean streak the Godfather would have admired.

Could they have come from two more entirely different worlds?

"High drama was the norm for me," he said into her silence. "Still the norm."

"Are you married?"

"No."

"Because you're tired of women?"

He let out a soft laugh. "No. I like women just fine."

"Then . . . ?"

She felt him glance at her again but kept her vision straight ahead. "I was in the military for eight years, then a cop. Neither was conducive to a good marriage."

"And now that you're a PI?"

He lifted a shoulder. "Haven't met The One yet."

Oh. Oh, that shouldn't make her yearn and burn to be someone's The One . . . *his* The One.

"You're either the calmest female I've ever met," he said into her silence, "or the best actress."

Definitely the latter. "I don't feel so calm," she heard herself admit.

Another long, assessing glance, then he took a hand off the wheel to squeeze hers. "What did they want with your laptop and PDA, Janie?"

"The laptop was for my own personal use only." She'd been thinking about this. "On-line access, my journal—"

"Journal?"

"Yeah." She shrugged at his look of surprise. "It's cheap therapy."

"Did you have a backup of your files?"

"In my PDA."

He shook his head. "Damn."

"What would they want with my own musings?"

"Plenty," he said grimly, eyes on the road. "Especially if they think you saw something and then wrote it down."

"That's a stretch."

"Is it?"

She thought about it. How many times had she seen Clayton in the past month?

There'd been many, actually. She'd imagined him growing more and more uptight, then attributed that to her own up-tightness because she just wanted to be left alone to live her life.

Even if she wasn't living it quite the way she'd hoped.

"Tell me," Ryan said in that soft, coaxing drawl that could probably coax a nun right out of her panties. "Tell me how you know Clayton, and what happened tonight."

Maybe it was time, she told herself. "He's been asking me out."

"He asks a lot of women out."

"But I was saying no. Tonight in the library, I was annoyed when I saw him because I knew he'd ask again, but . . ."

"But?"

"But he didn't." She shook her head. "He was distracted, very distracted. In fact . . . I got the impression he hardly even saw me."

"Shit," Ryan said very softly beneath his breath, his eyes locked on his rearview mirror.

"What?"

"We caught a tail. Hang on."

He took an unexpected right off the highway, then a series of quick turns that had her dizzy and lost within a space of two minutes.

He sped up, executing another bunch of fast moves, and then suddenly they were back on the highway.

"Did you lose—Oh, my God!" She gasped at the odd ping as the back window shattered.

Another ping, and the dash right in front of her cracked.

"Down," Ryan shouted, and added a hand to the back of her head, shoving her head between her legs. "Stay down!"

Yeah, staying down. *God*. They were being shot at.

It was almost incomprehensible. It was *all* so incomprehensible . . . had she really woken up in a normal world this morning? Eaten a banana nut muffin and opened the library, as she did every morning without a clue as to the terrifying adventure ahead?

Hard to believe.

Ryan drove like a man possessed, each sharp turn slamming her up against the door, or alternately, the stick shift, but those bruises would be nothing next to a bullet in the flesh, and she knew it.

Everything within her wanted to scream, but she bit down hard on her tongue to hold her cries in, not wanting to distract the man keeping her from certain death.

In the slashing lights of an oncoming car, his mouth was grim, and a track of sweat ran down one temple.

"Stay down," he snapped out as if he could feel her eyes on him.

Another bullet tore into the console, inches from her thigh.

Right, she'd just stay down . . .

Eight

Ryan kept driving for long, tense moments during which time Janie concentrated on the fact that she was alive, with no holes in her body.

No bullet holes were good.

In fact, the bullets had stopped flying altogether.

But Ryan still kept driving, turning every minute or so, and just as she was sure she was going to lose her mind, he slowed the car, then stopped altogether.

Then turned to her and hauled her up. "Are you hit?"

"No."

"God." He ran his hands up and down her limbs. "*God.* Are you sure?"

"I'm fine," she said, thinking "fine" was a relative term, but he kept touching her, his concern deep and real. "Ryan." She took his hands in hers. "I'm not hit."

With an exhale of breath, he kept his eyes glued on hers as if he couldn't tear them away. "Jesus."

"Where are we?"

"Tybee Island. On the beach."

She looked up. The night was black, but she could see the ocean directly in front of them, hear it pounding the shore. In the light of day, it would be gorgeous, five miles of beaches backed by sea-oat-covered sand dunes perfect for sunbathing, people watching, and frolicking in the surf, but now it just seemed dark and unknown.

Shock began to make itself known, and she began to shake.

With a low sound of regret, Ryan pulled her closer still, running his hands up and down her back in a comforting, soothing gesture she gladly absorbed.

"It's okay now," he murmured. "They're gone, they can't find us here."

Which meant she could let go of the death grip she had on him. Yeah. Any second now, she'd do just that.

Instead she wound her arms up and around his neck tight and didn't move, didn't want to. There in his arms, she found something she didn't even realize she'd wanted, the feeling that she could let go because he was in charge at the moment, and protective, and humiliating as it was to admit, she needed to know that he had her. She was safe.

No matter how temporary.

It was crazy, she knew, because she didn't do trust, and yet here she sat—her life in his very capable hands.

He tightened his grip on her, apparently in no more of a rush to let go than she was. "You were pretty cool under fire, Janie."

"Yeah."

"You've been that close to flying bullets before."

A long moment passed, a moment that he kept holding her, touching her, and somehow, there in the stormy night air, she found the courage to say things she'd never said before, to anyone. "Yes, I have. I . . . grew up in a tough neighborhood in California."

"Los Angeles?"

She considered making up some other location, but she didn't want to lie, not to him. "South Central, actually. The pit of hell for the most part."

She felt his surprise. "You were raised there?"

"So to speak." Her fingers played with his hair, and she

kept her face buried against his throat. "My older brother . . . raised me."

His arms tightened again. "No parents?"

"My mother died young. My brother promised her he'd keep me, and he did. It's just that . . . he wasn't really equipped to deal with a kid. He was gang, and all the stuff that goes with that."

"Tell me about the bullets."

She tensed; she couldn't help it. "Let's just say I saw things I shouldn't have. Like my brother killing my cousin in cold blood over drug money. I, um, had to leave quickly after that."

"I bet. How long ago was this?"

"A year."

"Should I fill in the blanks?" At her silence, he went on. "You changed your name, right? Got good and far, and hid yourself. Grace, Georgia, appealed because of the distance from LA, and also because it's different from what you'd ever known before."

She closed her eyes and pressed in closer.

"How am I doing?"

Too damn good.

"Tonight probably scared the hell out of you. Which is why you clobbered me first, reacted second."

Yeah. Way too damn good. She tried to pull away then, embarrassed at how easily he read her, only he held on, gently but firmly. "Guess I did good." His voice softened. "I'm sorry, Janie."

"I don't need your pity." Tough words belied by the fact she kept holding on to him.

"How about just some company, then?" he asked, stroking a hand up her spine.

She shrugged, but the truth was she'd warmed from the inside out. He had no idea how much it meant that she could tell him anything, how much *he* already meant to her in such a shockingly short time . . .

He kept hugging her, for long moments, and gradually she

realized she was no longer shaking, and that Ryan's hands no longer offered comfort and warmth so much as . . . awareness.

Yeah, the embrace definitely changed, and with a low murmur, she pressed her face to his throat and just breathed him in.

"I was shot on duty a few years back," he said.

"Left leg?" she guessed.

"Yeah. The pain—there's nothing like it. If you'd been hit—" He sank his fingers into the thick strands of her hair. "God. I've never been so terrified in all my life as I was tonight, with bullets flying—"

Putting her finger to his lips, she shook her head. "But I didn't get hurt. I didn't, because of you, Ryan."

Holding her gaze, he pulled her hand from his mouth and, with his eyes open and on hers, slowly leaned in. He paused a breath away, giving her the time to pull back if she wanted, and when she didn't, his eyes heated. Closing the gap, he kissed her.

She'd never kissed with her eyes open before, had never wanted to. There was no place to hide, no place to get lost in the sheer lust . . . which meant it became more.

With a rough sound, he cupped her face, tilting her head for a deeper angle, pulling her in closer to his body, which was warm and safe against her. He was big and strong, and she felt just weak enough to need everything he could give her.

Pulling back to stare at her mouth, he tangled his fingers in her hair. "I can't seem to get enough of you," he murmured, and stroked his thumb over her lip. "Can't."

Thinking the same thing, she licked her lips, and he groaned from deep in his throat, coming at her again for another soul-deep kiss. "Never enough," he murmured again, sliding his hands down her body, fingers spread wide as if needing to touch as much of her as humanly possible.

"Here?" she managed when he toyed with the buttons on her sweater, the backs of his fingers brushing her already hard nipples.

He hummed his hopeful approval, and while a distant part of her registered that this wasn't the time or the place, the majority of her brain cells were going with "oh, please here, oh, please now."

Her seat belt was in the way, and he released it, turning her to straddle him right there in the driver's seat, a maneuver which seriously adjusted her skirt hemline.

Head bent, Ryan took in the view of her legs, bared now to near indecent heights, and groaned, the sound scraping at her belly. The steering wheel was poking into her back, the gear shaft jabbing her calf, and she didn't care. She needed this, needed him.

"Janie—"

She could hear the tightness in his voice as his palms glided with purpose up her thighs, the hem of her skirt going with them.

In the dark, he couldn't have seen much, but the sound that escaped him assured her that what he did see pleased him.

Her arms slid around his neck, her breasts inches from his mouth. Beneath her bottom she could feel the heat from his body, and how very hard he was.

Their gazes locked, their heavy breathing fogging the windows. "I want you," he said, giving her the time to change her mind.

But she wasn't going to protest, and neither was the night. A quiet wind gently rattled against the windows, hypnotic and soothing. Pressing her face to his throat, she breathed him in, taking in his strength, the scent of his skin. He surrounded her now, with his broad shoulders, his arms, pulling her in closer, tighter, and she went willingly, because with him, the emptiness, the fear, it all dissipated into the background, into something less terrifying, less real.

He was concrete, tangible; she could reach out and touch and rely on him.

And in the moment, he was everything.

That was why when he kissed her, she deepened the connection. And when he slid her sweater down her arms, trapping them at her sides, then did the same to her tank, she only shivered with anticipation. He released her bra, and she sighed in pleasure, her head falling back, her hair tumbling over her shoulders.

Dipping his head, Ryan took a breast into his mouth, teasing first one nipple and then the other, coaxing a sound from her that was shocking in its dark neediness. His mouth knew what to do, so did his fingers, quiet and demanding in the way of the man himself, urging responses from her she hadn't known she had to give him. *"Ryan."*

"Right here." Rearing up, he kissed her mouth again, long and deep, and there in the dark of the night, with her body more alive than it'd ever been, she knew the truth. This was different. He was different. Doing this, now, here, was a turning point in her life, when she hadn't even realized she'd needed one.

He kissed her jaw, the spot beneath her ear. "Still with me?"

She looked in his eyes, blazing with heat and hunger. For her. "Yeah. It just appears I'm more with you than I thought."

He stared at her for a beat, then ran the pad of his thumb over her swollen lower lip. "Is that supposed to scare me away?"

Her heart caught. "Could it?"

"I don't scare easily."

She should have been running, screaming into the night, but instead an intense relief filled her, and she nodded.

At that, he smiled, then leaned in and sank his teeth gently into her lower lip, tugging just enough to have her hissing out a breath, brought right back into the heat, the rush of desire so strong it would have stolen her legs if she'd been standing.

But she wasn't standing. She was in his lap, a perfect place to be, and needing still more, she tugged open his jeans.

And then it became his turn to hiss out a breath when she slipped her hands inside, humming with pleasure at what she found, which was a whole lot of aroused man.

Ryan kept busy himself, gliding hot, wet, opened-mouthed

kisses over her throat, her collarbone, her breast, driving her right to the very edge with nothing more than his mouth. His hands got into the action as well, sliding beneath her skirt . . .

When he found her panties, the sound he made melted her. There was something inherently sexual about the sight of his tough, sinewy forearms coming out from beneath the filmy material, which was draped over his tanned skin, his hands not visible.

But she could feel them, dancing on her skin, *everywhere*. Again her head fell back on her shoulders; her fingers dug into his biceps. *"Ryan."*

"Still here." His thumbs grazed over her inner thighs, then higher, and she sucked in a breath.

Lifting his head, he looked into her eyes as his callused fingers glided over her bare flesh. "Stop me now if you're going to." His voice was low, hoarse, and thrillingly rough. His eyes, glittering with fire, seared through the night, holding hers. Waiting . . .

Slowly she shook her head.

"Is that no we're stopping, or no don't stop."

She swallowed hard. "Don't stop."

"Thank God." And then his busy, industrious fingers curled around the hem of her skirt and shoved it all the way up to her waist.

Nine

With her sweater opened and her skirt up, Janie couldn't breathe, but it was a good kind of couldn't breathe. Sort of like being on a roller coaster, going 150 MPH upside down and backward.

In the dark . . .

Ryan held up her skirt with the hands she desperately wanted all over her, but he couldn't be rushed and took a long moment to enjoy what he'd revealed. Then, with slow precision, he scraped her panties to one side so that he could see her, all of her, spread open for his perusal, and took another long moment to do just that.

"God," he breathed, and stroked a thumb over her, moaning when it came away wet from her excitement. "*God.*" He shifted his hands then, gliding them around the back of her and beneath her panties now so that he held a bare cheek in each hand. With a tug, he yanked her hips closer still, so that the hottest, wettest spot on her nudged the hottest, hard spot on him, cradling his sex in her wet heat. He groaned, long and raw. "You are so . . ."

"Annoying?" she whispered. "Irritating? Frustrating?"

"*Sexy.*" He ran his hands down her legs, cupping the backs

of her thighs, urging her to wrap them around him. "Amazing. *Hot.*"

She moaned low in her throat, a sound he swallowed when he caught her mouth with his once again, just as he slid a finger into her. Crying out, she arched, writhed, but she couldn't stay still, not with his tongue in her mouth, his fingers taking her to heaven, and then there was his deliciously hard sex pressing insistently against her. "Don't stop. Please don't stop."

"Never." His hips moved against her in slow, insistent circles, small, maddening oscillations that stole her breath, melted her resolve, and shrank her world to this, only this.

Him.

Ripping his mouth from hers, his own breathing rang harsh and ragged in the night as he kissed his way up her jaw. "You feel good," he rumbled out, and sucked a patch of her skin into his mouth, sending yummy shivers down her spine.

Her shirt had slipped to the floor, her skirt was still perched up around her ears, her panties shoved to one side, exposing her for his gaze, his fingers, the erection she'd freed from his pants. And as unbelievable as it seemed, she was already a fraction from coming all over him.

His thumb kept grazing over her. Again and again . . . Within a few minutes she was a quivering mass of sensation. In another, she'd flung herself off the edge and into the abyss of a blissful orgasm that had her shuddering and gasping.

When she could hear and see again, she was lying back against the steering wheel, damp and still quivering, her legs wrapped tightly around him, her fingers in his hair with a death grip, breathing like a lunatic. "Um. Wow."

He laughed softly, and she managed to lift her head. "Did you by any chance get a good look at whatever just hit me?"

"Yeah." He smiled. "And here it comes again, so watch out." Leaning in, he kissed her, and she could feel his tension, not to mention the proof of his wanting still nudging up against her. Crazy as it seemed, she dove right back in, already on her way to another screaming orgasm. "Ryan. God."

"I know." Still kissing her, he reached into the glove box and then dropped something into her palm.

A condom.

She closed her fingers around it and felt herself get even wetter.

"In case you want—"

"Oh, I want," she breathed. *So much.*

The men in her life had mostly been alpha, domineering assholes. Ryan, while definitely an alpha, chose instead to give her the power.

The thrill of that!

She unwrapped the condom, then tried to roll it down the hot, silky length of him, but she couldn't get it to fit, and when she growled in mindless frustration, he took over. Then he put his hands back on her, poised at her opening. "Let me in, Janie," he whispered hoarsely, then groaned when she did just that, wrapping her fingers around his thick length, guiding him home.

He sank in deep, and for a beat they both went utterly still, savoring the feel of him filling her to bursting. He slid his fingers into her hair, lightly tugging, feasting his mouth on her exposed throat, then over to a waiting, eager nipple.

Finally, he began to move.

As he did, she lost herself again, just as she always did in his arms. With each thrust, it felt as if he was reaching for her heart, and when he put his mouth to her ear, whispering, "Come again, I want to watch you," she couldn't have stopped to save her life.

Just as her eyes flittered closed, she caught the flare of savage satisfaction in his gaze as she went over, and then she could see nothing, but from somewhere far, far away she heard his low, guttural moan and knew she wasn't alone as she came. And came . . .

It took a while, but finally their breathing steadied, and he lifted his head. Nuzzled at her jaw. "Now we've both been hit."

"Are we going to recover?"

He smiled against her breast and gently kissed the huge curve. "I'm not."

What did that mean? she wondered as he guided her back into her seat, helped her right her clothing, pulling her seat belt back into place.

He started the car and cranked the defroster, waiting for the windows to unfog. "Your place?" she asked.

He shook his head. "If they got my license plate number and ran it, then . . ."

"Then they have your address." Her stomach sank as reality slammed into her once more. For a few blissful moments she'd actually forgotten why she was here, what they still faced ahead. She fell silent, waiting for the despair to rain over her again, but oddly enough, it didn't happen. She glanced at Ryan and knew why.

He'd stand at her side, no matter what. She was no longer alone.

"What?" he asked softly, stroking her jaw. "What did you think just now that made you look so pleasantly surprised."

"That you're not so bad, Ryan Patrick."

In the wake of a smile that took her breath, he said, "Does that mean that you're not going to dump me at the curb like yesterday's trash when this is all over?"

"Why would I do that?"

"Isn't that what you do? Keep your distance?"

Shockingly, she felt her eyes sting. Her entire life had been about not making ties, but God she was so over that. And yet she didn't know anything else, she thought in despair, looking out the window into the night as dark as her heart.

He turned her back toward him. "So we grew up different," he said quietly. "So we've led very different lives. It doesn't mean we wouldn't be good together."

"We don't know each other well enough to even think about 'together.' " She hesitated. "Do we?"

His eyes answered for him, and she licked her suddenly dry

lips. "There's a lot of responsibility that comes with a relationship—"

Apparently unconcerned, he shrugged. "I'm a responsible
sort. You are, too."

"I've never even shared a drawer with someone, much
less—"

"Whoa. Don't panic on me now. I'm not asking you for a
drawer." His beautiful mouth curved. "How about we start
with a date. Can you handle a date?"

"Um—"

"Come on, Janie. After being stalked, finding a dead guy,
discovering your place ransacked, and then being shot at? I'd
think going on a date would be pretty tame in comparison."

"Yeah." She had to laugh at herself. "Yeah, I could probably do a date."

"And then another," he said, still holding her with his
hands, his voice, his eyes . . . "And another."

She couldn't tear her gaze away. "You just want me naked
again."

He laughed. "Oh, yeah, I want you naked again. But I want
all of you, Janie, clothed or not, warts and all. Does that scare
you?"

"I don't have warts."

"It scares you," he said with terrifying gentleness.

"Yeah. Maybe." She dropped her head to his chest. "Okay,
yes, it's the scariest thing I've ever faced, and we both know
that's saying something. I didn't exactly come from a warm,
fuzzy place, Ryan."

"Should that bother me? You had no control over how you
grew up."

She stared at him as those words sank in. She'd had no control for so much of her life. It didn't take a shrink to figure out
that's why she craved control now, over every single little aspect, including not giving herself to anyone emotionally because that would be giving up some of that precious control.

But by holding back, wasn't she letting fate, and by association her brother, win? "I don't know what I have to give you," she said carefully.

"Why don't we find out?"

"Ryan . . . it's not that simple."

"It's as simple as you make it," he insisted. "Getting to know each other isn't going to be painful, you know. I can promise you that much."

"But what happens after that?"

He smiled. "After that . . . we take it from there. As for me, I have a feeling I already know where I want it to go."

She looked into his warm eyes and felt that warmth reflect back at her, and something new as well—a small flicker of . . . hope? "I have to think about it," she whispered. She didn't know what she expected his response to be to that.

He simply leaned in and kissed her, pulling back only far enough to look into her eyes. "Janie, the only thing we have to decide tonight is who the hell is after you, and why. Okay?"

She absorbed his steady gaze, his strength, his quiet confidence, and felt more of that hope wash over her. "Okay."

He smiled, and she found herself smiling back. The going was as rough as it could get, and he was still here. She was beginning to see he'd stick no matter what. She'd marvel over that later. "I really don't know who's after me. If I did, I'd tell you."

His eyes warmed all the more. He knew what it'd cost her to trust him. "It'd help to know what they think they got with your laptop."

"I can't imagine."

"Your journal. You write anything in it about Clayton?"

"Maybe just that I didn't get the universally city-wide appeal of him."

"You two ever go out?"

"No. We didn't even speak very often. Tonight he came in for that book—" She stared at him as it hit her like a one-two fist. "Oh, my God. I just remembered."

"What?"

She put a hand to her mouth and shook her head, unable to believe she'd gotten so thoroughly shaken as to forget.

"Tell me."

"I was side-tracked because I wanted to go home," she said. "And to tell you the truth, he was a little weird this time. Like . . . he didn't want to be there either. Thinking that made me forget that while he asked to come in for one thing, he ended up doing something else. I told you he needed a book for a project he was working on with Peter, the mayor."

"Yes."

"And that's what I told the police. He said he was sorry to be an idiot, waiting until the last minute, yadda yadda, but could I please let him in to get that book."

"Which you did."

"Yes. But then I saw him on the computer. On the other side of the library from where the book he needed was kept."

"Doing what?"

"I have no idea. That's not where he . . ." The image of him dead on the floor had her closing her eyes. "He wasn't shot there."

"But we'd heard running just before that. Something chased him off that computer in a hurry."

They stared at each other.

"That computer," he said. "It'll tell us what he was looking at."

"So we're going back."

He thrust the truck into gear. "Oh, yeah, we're going back."

Ten

Police tape surrounded the library, though the place was dark. Ryan drove around the block, parked on a narrow side street, then turned to the woman next to him.

Janie's face was still flushed from what had turned out to be the most erotic, incredibly intimate hour of his life. Shocking, given that it'd happened in his damn truck.

Even more shocking, just a quick glance from her sent something inside him pinging against his ribs. His heart, he realized. In one night, she'd upturned the elusive organ, landing it right in the palm of her hands.

"What now?" she asked softly, giving him a small, trusting smile that warmed him from the inside out. She felt like a miracle, sitting there looking at him. *His* miracle.

"The place looks empty." He looked the building over for a long moment. "No one stayed behind to watch over the scene, thank God. Small-town politics working for us for a change. Let me have your keys for the library, Janie."

"No."

She said it so sweetly it took a moment to register. His eyes cut from the back door of the library to her. Still flushed and dewy, she had an expression he was coming to recognize well.

Pure tenacity.

"Trust time over?" he asked, pained.

"This isn't about trust." She unhooked her seat belt. "I want to go with you."

"You're safer here."

"But you're not."

"Janie—"

"Shh." Fisting his shirt in her hands, she pulled him close. Her scent teased his nostrils, and for a moment, a weak moment, he allowed himself to bend close and inhale her.

"We do this like everything else we've done since this night began," she said, her arms drawing him in.

He didn't want her to let go, didn't want her to ever let go. "And how's that?"

"Together."

"I do like that word."

"Good." She reached for the door. "Then let's go."

But he grabbed her by the back of the shirt. "Are you going to apply that word to anything else? Us, for instance?"

She kissed him, one quick, hard connection, and got out of the truck, making him think she had no intention of answering. But halfway across the street, she looked at him. "Maybe . . . maybe I'm getting used to the idea."

"That's a start," he said, but a revving engine stopped him from saying anything else. A car was heading down the street, and with no time for more answers from her, at least not the kind he was looking for, he grabbed her hand, rushing her unseen from the street to the back of the library.

There she pulled out her keys, but he put his hands over hers. "We're breaking a few rules here," he warned her.

"More than a few, I imagine."

"There could be trouble."

"I've been in far worse."

"Janie." He held her back. "Trying to protect you here."

"Together, remember?" Turning but not letting go of his hand, she pushed open the door.

He leaned in and whispered in her ear, "I really like the sound of that word on your lips."

Inside, there was a stillness to the air. No hum of electricity, nothing. Without it, the computer was going to be useless.

"Damn." Ryan flicked on the flashlight he'd taken from his truck, and Janie led the way past her front desk to the spot where Clayton had lay earlier. She paused, galvanized by the sight, and Ryan set a hand on her shoulder. "Let's look at the book he wanted," he said quietly.

Nodding, she led him to an aisle in the center of the library. Flicking his light over the titles, he saw they were in the nonfiction area, specifically the state of Georgia.

"Here," she said.

The police had already been through this area and had taken pictures. Janie scrolled her finger down one row of books, then bent, a frown in place. "Wait a minute."

"What?"

She grabbed the flashlight and went down on her knees, a nice position anytime, but then she bent low on her hands and knees, looking at the lowest shelf, unintentionally presenting him with an even better view of her sweet ass.

"Huh."

"What?"

"The book he wanted isn't here," she said.

"He probably pulled it."

"It wasn't on his body, and he didn't check it out." She frowned, and then bent even lower. "I wonder if the police noticed that . . ."

Her butt wriggled as she searched, and if they weren't already breaking and entering, not to mention standing in the middle of a crime scene with the time quickly approaching dawn, he'd have been damn tempted to drop to his knees behind her, put his hands on her hips and—

"Aha."

He blinked the erotic image away just in time to watch her rise to her feet and vanish around the corner.

He followed, and found her in the next aisle over, still talking to herself. "It happens all the time," she was saying. "The books get pushed through to the other side." She reached her hand all the way through the shelf. "See? Annoying." She lifted a large, oversized book titled *Georgia Landmarks*.

"That the book?"

"Yes."

Out of it fell a manila envelope.

Ryan squatted next to it. "Yours?"

"No."

There was no writing on the outside. "Do you have tweezers?" he asked.

"In my desk, actually." She vanished, then came back with a pair, which he used to slide the contents out of the envelope.

In the quiet air, Janie gasped.

Nothing much could shock Ryan, but he had to admit, the pictures came close.

They were eight-by-ten color glossies, full-body shots of Clayton very much alive and smiling his ass off, though these weren't publicity shots, or at least not aimed for his general adoring public.

Not even close.

In the first picture, the tall, leanly muscled, admittedly handsome banker was sprawled on a rug in front of a blazing fire, a secret smile on his lips as he stared into the flames.

Wearing a siren red teddy.

The silk exposed a good part of his body, including the fact that he was a well-built guy and had inherited a lot of . . . hair.

"That's not pretty," Janie finally said.

He flipped to the next picture—Clayton frolicking in the waves in a polka-dotted bikini, head thrown back in laughter as the sun beat down on his tanned body.

Janie slapped a hand over her mouth, the shocked laugh still escaping into the night. "Oh, my."

"I take it you didn't know he was a cross-dresser."

She shook her head, her eyes glued to the pictures. "No."

"You notice anything about these shots?"

"He needs a Brazilian?"

Ryan smiled grimly. "He's not looking into the camera."

"No. He's either a natural photogenic actor, or . . ." She met his gaze. "He didn't know the pictures were being taken."

"I'd bet on the latter," Ryan said.

They were quiet a minute.

"And I'd bet, too," Ryan said, "that whoever took these shots was blackmailing him."

Janie looked at him in surprise. "Blackmail?"

"I think that must be why he really hired me. He wanted to know who."

"I'll give you one guess who," said a low, masculine voice from directly behind them.

Janie gasped. Ryan shoved her behind him as they both whirled to face—

Peter Bennett.

"The library is closed, Mayor," Ryan said, but the gun in his face said Peter knew that.

"I'll take those pictures." Peter waggled his fingers impatiently.

"The proof of your motive, you mean?"

Peter's mouth tightened. "No need to take a turn into Negative Town. Just hand them over."

Janie slipped them out of Ryan's hand and held them behind her back. "Why did you take my computer and PDA?"

"Because several times you saw Clayton come in and leave money in exchange for pictures. He e-mailed me about it."

Which was how she'd ended up in Clayton's Sidekick.

Peter shrugged. "I couldn't have the proof out there in your head, your diaries . . ."

Janie paled. "Funny thing. I never put it all together. I was never a threat to you, Peter."

His eyes hardened. "Well, I'm sorry for that, but you still have to die. Give me the pictures."

"You want them? Come get them."

"Give them to me," Peter said, now training the gun on her. "Now."

Ryan knew what it had to be like for Janie to have a gun in her face again, to be facing her nightmare head-on, and his heart nearly stopped.

"I don't think so," she said, looking strong and sure of herself. Backing from both men, she tossed the pictures casually onto the study desk behind her.

With a roar of fury, Peter dove for them, and the gun went off.

Eleven

The bullet ricocheted past Janie's ear and into the shelves behind her, directly into a book, causing tiny shreds of the pages to fly into the air.

She couldn't help it; she screamed and whipped around, grabbing an untouched volume off the shelf, swinging out and connecting with Peter's head.

Peter crumpled like a stack of wood, hitting the floor with a thud.

The gun went skittering.

Ryan grabbed it and stood over Peter. "That book isn't quite as heavy as a dictionary," he said, and in spite of herself, Janie let out a laugh.

Ohmigod, she thought, *falling for him already.* "You would know." She dropped the book to the floor.

Ryan gestured for her to scoot clear of Peter, who groaned and rolled over to his back. "Jesus! You could have killed me!"

"Ditto," Ryan said, the gun pointed in Peter's face as he pulled his cell from his pocket and dialed 9–1–1.

"Ah, hell, man," Peter managed. "You're messing everything up."

"You were the one blackmailing your boyfriend."

Janie blinked. "Clayton was a cross-dresser *and* gay?"

Peter's face darkened. "You have a problem with that?"

"No," she said. "What I have a problem with is the you murdering him part."

"He cheated on me, all the time! With *women!* Do you have any idea how that makes me feel?"

"Bad enough to blackmailed him?"

Peter had the grace to look ashamed of himself. "He didn't know it was me. I sent him the pictures to rein him in, to scare him into being faithful."

"And when that didn't work, you killed him?" Ryan said. "Gee, guess you showed him not to cheat."

Peter's jaw ticked. From flat on his back, his hands fisted. He eyed the gun, which Ryan made sure to hold steady.

"Don't even think about it, *Mayor*. Janie, want to make sure the door is open for the police?"

She ran to check, then came back. Ryan stood over Peter, looking a little worse for wear from the incredibly long night, but he was so strong, so beautiful, so . . . hers, she could have just stared at him forever. "Ryan?"

He didn't take his eyes off Peter. "Yeah?"

"I'm done thinking about it."

A muscle in his jaw tightened, and he still didn't take his eyes off Peter. "Oh. Okay, sure."

He thought she'd decided *not* to give them a chance; she could see it in the tense lines of his body. "No, you don't understand. I want to see where things go, too."

"They're going to hell in a handbasket," Peter said on a groan.

Janie's heart was in her throat again because though Ryan hadn't taken his eyes off Peter, his mouth had softened into an almost smile. "Although to be honest, I already know exactly where I want them to go," she said, mirroring his own words back at him.

"Yeah?" His voice was low, husky. "Where's that?"

Before she could answer, red and blue lights flooded the

main room from the windows, and the police stormed the building for the second time that night.

Upon command, Ryan dropped the gun, and they all raised their hands. With chaos reigning all around them, Janie never took her gaze off Ryan.

So when he looked at her, his eyes warm and full of promise, she felt her heart catch hard. "Wherever you are," she said. "That's where I want to go."

He smiled, slow and sure, joy and hope filling his eyes as he reached out for her hand. "Works for me."

Epilogue

When the dust settled and Peter was in jail, Janie and Ryan were finally free to go.

Together they stepped outside the library. The sun had just made its sleepy rise over the horizon, and gold and pink and lavender light danced across the town of Grace.

"Beautiful," she said, her breath catching at the glory of it. Her heart, for once free of the fist squeezing it, gave a hard, happy kick.

"So beautiful," Ryan murmured at her side, but when she glanced up at him, he was looking down at her. "What's your real name, from before?"

She stared up at him. "Before doesn't matter anymore. Only here matters, and this new life, which is so much more than I ever thought it could be. And here, I'm Janie. She's who I want to be."

"It fits you. It all fits you." He smiled and drew her close. "So . . . about this new path."

"Yes?"

"What do you say we start with breakfast? On the water somewhere, watching the rest of this sunrise?"

Her heart tumbled right then and fell headfirst in love.

"Or we can skip breakfast and go straight to the rest of the day. The rest of our lives."

"I say yes." She smiled and set her head on his shoulder. "Yes to all of it."

Here's a look at Amy J. Fetzer's latest,
HIT HARD.
Available now from Brava!

Viva inched closer to the American, staring down at Half Ear guy. "Is he dead? He really really looks dead," she said, horrified and curious.

Sam pushed her behind him and cocked his rifle with one hand. "Now would be a good time to run, lady."

He fired a warning shot into the air, and she bolted into the jungle. At least she had the cuff, and put it on before jumping over a low stream and splashing up the other side.

Then she heard the heavy thump of footsteps, the thrashing. Oh God. Bad guys. Bad guys. She pushed faster. Her legs burned with the strain, her body weeped sweat. Anything in her path sliced at her legs, her arms; then through the trees, she saw the rise in terrain, and headed toward it.

She hadn't taken ten steps when it hit her, the hard impact to the back of her legs. Strong arms clamped around her knees and she went down. Her chin hit the ground, her teeth clicked. The collision pushed air from her lungs and she collapsed, dizzy, gasping for air and wondering how this day turned so bad so fast. She inhaled dirt, blew it out, then pushed up.

She twisted. Jungle guy. He was breathing hard and had lost his hat somewhere.

"You make it really hard to help you, lady." He backed off her.

"Thank you for your assistance, but did I ask for you to butt in?" God, the sheer idiocy of that hit her and she faced him, her head ringing too much to stand yet.

"You can go back. I'm sure they'll be interested in a little payback."

"I won't dignify that with a response." She sent him a brittle smile as she brushed off leaves. "I'm quite done with adventure for the day, thank you very much."

Sam shifted back on his haunches, then pulled the bandana from his throat and wiped his face. Shapely, red haired, and a nutcase, he decided. Anyone who'd take on Thai mafia without a weapon was two jacks short of a full deck.

Then she eased back like a crab.

Aware of her intentions, Sam grabbed her ankle, yanking her close. "They're still out there, along with tigers, snakes—" *whoever shot that dart.*

"And you."

"I'm not going to hurt you, for crissake." Sam let her go and stood, dusting off his clothes.

"I appreciate your interception, really, but I have to go to Bangkok."

He gave her a tight glance that said, *We'll just see about that.*

She saw right through it. "Who made you king of the jungle? While you look real cool with that rifle and whip, I'm sure you can see the wisdom of a hasty departure. And I'm not about to join your little band." She motioned behind him as another man walked up. Jungle guy didn't take his gaze from her as the other handed over the hat.

"Ma'am, I'm Max Renfield." Max held out his hand to help her up.

She didn't budge, but glanced between the two. "Where were you when all that was going on?"

He patted the gun at his side. "Backup."

"Effective, was it?" Viva brushed her hair back, took a deep cleansing breath, but the tension refused to leave her body. All my fault, she thought, and wondered where her sanity went to play this morning to antagonize all the wrong people. She fingered the gold cuff that hadn't been worn in a few thousand years, and knew it was worth it. She wore history on her wrist, though she hadn't planned to be a part of it today.

"I'm going to look for Phan," Sam said to Max. "Stay with her."

"I don't need a guard."

"No, you need a brain."

Her smile was nothing short of acidic. "Chivalry isn't your strong suit, I see. If it were, you'd at least be seeing to the wounds you made." She modeled her bloody knees.

They were a mess, but considering the bandits wanted to put two bullets in her head, she shouldn't be complaining. "Sorry, lady, no medical supplies."

"I have something to fix that," Max said.

"Figures."

As Sam walked away, Max moved forward, and knelt. "Don't mind him, he's in a rotten mood."

"I couldn't tell, his effervesent personality just blew me away." Max ripped open a packet and started to clean her knees. "Oh, it's not that bad," she said, taking the antiseptic towel.

He frowned.

"Well—" She flushed. "He knocked me down when a 'hey you, wait' would have done the trick. That man is extreme in every sense of the word."

Max sat back, grinning. She had Sam pegged from the get-go. Interesting. She finished cleaning her knees, pulling her leg up to her face like a dancer to blow off the sting. Great legs.

"Thank you, Max."

He frowned, glanced the way the other had gone. "Come on."

"Shouldn't we wait for him?" She really didn't want to trek through the jungle. The dart had to come from somewhere.

"He's been gone too long."

"Well, that can't be good."

He helped her off the ground and she followed him as they moved into the forest. Max hacked their way through the jungle for a considerable distance when he stopped, and called out softly.

Viva peered around him and she saw his partner.

He waved Max on. "You stay there," he said, pointing.

"Anyone ever mention you have control issues?"

Take a peek at
EX, WHY, AND ME
by Susanna Carr.
Available now from Brava!

It was difficult going all the way with a guy when you were required to wear a tiara, but Michelle Nelson managed it. Barely.

She just never thought it would occur in the middle of the night behind the pinsetters at Pins & Pints, Carbon Hill's bowling alley and the only source of entertainment one could have standing up.

Michelle shifted, her knees aching against the hard, cold floor. The alley was closed, the lanes silent, but she was bumping up against ancient, oily machinery. The location hadn't been her first choice for her first time with her first love.

It didn't seem to hold the right ambiance for Ryan Slater, either. "Let's go back to my place," he suggested in a husky tone that made her skin tingle.

She glanced down at him, but the shadows made it difficult to read his expression. Michelle felt exposed as she straddled him, the weak overhead lights almost reaching her. Her evening dress from the JC Penney catalog bunched up against her thighs, the pink polyester rubbing her bare, flushed skin.

"No," she whispered, her heart pounding in her ears. She pressed her hands against his shoulders, pulling at his T-shirt with desperate fingers. "I can't wait that long."

It had to be now. She was leaving for Europe in the morning. Her bags were packed, she'd said goodbye to her friends, but there was this one last thing to do.

It had taken her all summer to get Ryan Slater. She could have pursued another local guy in a lot less time, but she wanted Ryan and no one else would do. It had been that way ever since she could remember, so at least twenty years. Unfortunately, all the prettier, bolder girls wanted him, too.

No matter what she had done in the past, it wasn't enough to compete for Ryan's attention. He'd never seemed to notice her. Not even when she'd worn the tiara and the Miss Horseradish sash for the past year. And God knew those were hard to miss.

He noticed her now. Had stared at her in awe. Or maybe he was staring at her tiara, which had a tendency to catch the light and blind people. That was probably it, but she couldn't do anything about it now. The crown was pinned and shellacked to her updo.

The glittery distraction would serve her well, Michelle decided as she glided the condom onto Ryan. She didn't want him to feel her hands fumble and shake. Rolling the latex down was not as easy as her best friend Vanessa had led her to believe.

The tip of Ryan's cock nudged against Michelle's flesh. The intimate contact made her feel hot. Tight. She grasped him at the base and lowered down.

Michelle jerked, startled, when Ryan clamped his fingers against her bare hips. "We'll take it slow," he said roughly, almost as if he said it through clenched teeth.

Her heart raced as he guided her. White heat crackled just under her skin when he gently filled her.

She closed her eyes, her breath hitching, as she relished every sensation. Michelle had been expecting pain. Nothing major, but something unpleasant. Nothing like the delicious heavy ache that flooded her muscles.

Michelle rocked against him, smiling as the pleasure heated

her blood with a shower of sparks. She flexed her hips. *Ooh . . .* She swayed the other way. *Mmm . . .*

"Michelle, slow down," Ryan said hoarsely, his fingers tightening, sinking into her hips.

She wanted his hands elsewhere. Everywhere. Cupping her breasts. No, squeezing them. Pinching her nipples until she begged him to take them into his mouth.

She wanted him to thrust. Grind. Drive into her.

Maybe that wasn't possible in this position. But she didn't want to change sides. Here she felt alive. Bold. Free. She was wild. Sexy. Powerful.

She moved against Ryan, each move fierce and unchecked. Her world centered where they joined. He bucked against her, his moves shallow and hesitant.

Michelle countered with a deep roll of her hips, but his cock didn't stretch or fill her to the hilt. She frowned and wiggled.

"Not like that," Ryan said, his voice bouncing off the machines. He tensed. "Damn."

He lay motionless underneath her. No thrusting, no rocking. Nothing. *This is it?* Michelle thought. *You have got to be kidding me!*

She felt his cock softening, drooping—

Michelle froze. *Oh, no . . .*

—as it slipped out.

I killed it.

And coming soon from Brava,
here is Sylvia Day's
ASK FOR IT.

George looked easily over Elizabeth's head to scrutinize the scene. "I say. It appears Lord Westfield is heading this way."

"Are you quite certain, Mr. Stanton?"

"Yes, my lady. Westfield is staring directly at me as we speak."

Tension coiled in the pit of her stomach. Marcus had literally frozen in place when their eyes had first met, and the second glance had been even more disturbing. He was coming for her and she had no time to prepare. George looked down at her as she resumed fanning herself furiously.

Damn Marcus for coming tonight! Her first social event after three years of mourning and he unerringly sought her out within hours of her reemergence, as if he'd been impatiently waiting these last years for exactly this moment. She was well aware that had not been the case at all. While she had been crepe-clad and sequestered in mourning, Marcus had been firmly establishing his scandalous reputation in many a lady's bedroom.

After the callous way he'd broken her heart, Elizabeth would have discounted him regardless of the circumstances but tonight especially. Enjoyment of the festivities was not her aim. She had a man she was waiting for, a man she had arranged covertly to meet. Tonight she would dedicate herself to the memory of her husband. She would find justice for Hawthorne and see it served.

The crowd parted reluctantly before Marcus and then regrouped in his wake, the movements heralding his progress toward her. And then Westfield was there, directly before her. He smiled and her pulse raced. The temptation to retreat, to flee, was great, but the moment when she could reasonably have done so passed far too swiftly.

Squaring her shoulders, Elizabeth took a deep breath. The glass in her hand began to tremble and she quickly swallowed the entirety of its contents to avoid spilling it on her dress. She passed the empty vessel to George without looking. Marcus caught her hand before she could retrieve it.

Bowing low with a charming smile, his gaze never broke contact with hers. "Lady Hawthorne. Ravishing, as ever." His voice was rich and warm, reminding her of crushed velvet. "Would it be folly to hope you still have a dance available, and that you would be willing to dance it with me?"

Elizabeth's mind scrambled, attempting to discover a way to refuse. His wickedly virile energy, potent even across the room, was overwhelming in close proximity.

"I am not in attendance to dance, Lord Westfield. Ask any of the gentlemen around us."

"I've no wish to dance with them," he said dryly. "So their thoughts on the matter are of no consequence to me."

She began to object when she perceived the challenge in his eyes. He smiled with devilish amusement, visibly daring her to proceed, and Elizabeth paused. She would not give him the satisfaction of thinking she was afraid to dance with him. "You may claim this next set, Lord Westfield, if you insist."

He bowed gracefully, his gaze approving. He offered his arm and led her toward the dance floor. As the musicians plied their instruments and music rose in joyous swell through the room, the beautiful strains of the minuet began.

Marcus turned, held his hand out to her, and she placed her

palm atop the back of his, grateful for the gloves that separated their skin. She appraised him for signs of change. The ballroom was ablaze with candles casting him in golden light and bringing to her attention the strength of his shoulder as it flexed.

He had always been an intensely physical man, engaging in a variety of sports and activities. Impossibly it appeared he had grown stronger, more formidable. Marcus was power personified and she marveled at her past naïveté in believing she could tame him. Thank God, she was no longer so foolish.

His one softness was his luxuriously rich brown hair. It shined like sable and was contained at the nape with a simple black ribbon. Even his emerald gaze was sharp, piercing with a fierce intelligence. He had a clever mind to which deceit was naught but a simple game, as she had learned at great cost to her heart and pride.

She had half expected to find the signs of dissipation so common to indulgent lifestyles and yet his handsome face bore no such witness. Instead he wore the sun-kissed appearance of a man who spent much of his time outdoors. His nose was straight and aquiline over lips that were full and sensuous. At the moment those lips were turned up on one side in a half smile that was at once boyish and alluring. He remained perfectly gorgeous from the top of his head to the soles of his feet. He was watching her studying him, fully aware that she could not help but admire his handsomeness. She lowered her eyes and stared resolutely at his jabot.

The scent that clung to him enveloped her senses. It was a wonderful manly scent of sandalwood, citrus, and Marcus' own unique essence. The flush of her skin seeped into her insides, clawing deliciously around her vitals, mingling with her apprehension.

Reading her thoughts, he tilted his head toward her. His voice, when it came, was low and husky. "Elizabeth. It is a long-awaited pleasure to be in your company again."

"The pleasure, Lord Westfield, is entirely yours."

"You once called me Marcus."

"It would no longer be appropriate for me to address you so informally, my lord."

His mouth tilted into a sinful grin. "I give you leave to be inappropriate with me at any time you choose. In fact, I have always relished your moments of inappropriateness."

"You have had a number of willing women who suited you just as well."

"Never, my love. You have always been separate and apart from every other female."

Elizabeth had met her share of scoundrels and rogues but always their slick confidence and overtly intimate manners left her unmoved. Marcus was so skilled at seducing women he managed the appearance of utter sincerity. She'd once believed every declaration of adoration and devotion that had fallen from his lips. Even now the way he looked at her with such fierce longing seemed so genuine she almost believed it.

He made her want to forget what kind of man he was—a heartless seducer. But her body would not let her forget. She felt feverish and faintly dizzy.